Love in the Time of Climate Change

Love in the Time of Climate Change

BRIAN ADAMS

GREEN WRITERS PRESS   *Brattleboro, Vermont*

Printed in the United States
10 9 8 7 6 5 3 3

Green Writers Press is a Vermont-based publisher whose mission
is to spread a message of hope and renewal through the words and
images we publish. Throughout we will adhere to our commitment
to preserving and protecting the natural resources of the earth. To
that end, a percentage of our proceeds will be donated to the environmental activist group, 350.org. Green Writers Press gratefully
acknowledges support from individual donors, friends, and readers
to help support the environment and our publishing initiative.

Giving Voice to Writers Who Will Make the World a Better Place
Green Writers Press |Brattleboro, Vermont
www.greenwriterspress.com

Visit the author's website for more info and A Call to Action:
https://brianadamsauthor.wordpress.com

ISBN: 978-0996087209

PRINTED ON PAPER WITH PULP THAT COMES FROM FSC-CERTIFIED FORESTS, MANAGED
FORESTS THAT GUARANTEE RESPONSIBLE ENVIRONMENTAL, SOCIAL, AND ECONOMIC
PRACTICES BY LIGHTNING SOURCE ALL WOOD PRODUCT COMPONENTS USED IN BLACK &
WHITE, STANDARD COLOR, OR SELECT COLOR PAPERBACK BOOKS, UTILIZING EITHER CREAM
OR WHITE BOOKBLOCK PAPER, THAT ARE MANUFACTURED IN THE LAVERGNE, TENNESSEE
PRODUCTION CENTER ARE SUSTAINABLE FORESTRY INITIATIVE® (SFI®) CERTIFIED SOURCING

*To all of the climate change activists
working so hard to save the world*

Prologue

THERE IS AN ANCIENT Chinese curse that goes like this: "May you live in interesting times."

Damn those ancient Chinese! They were clearly onto something.

Times are always interesting, but we've certainly managed to ratchet things up a few notches in the last decades.

One issue that virtually all of the world's scientists agree on is that we are in the midst of an alarming, unprecedented, and potentially catastrophic era of climate change. Essentially, we are knee-deep in shit and sinking rapidly. Climatologists may phrase it a little differently, tweak a word here or two, but that's it in a nutshell. No matter what illusions or mind-boggling fantasies some of the right-wing nutcases continue to cling to, there is overwhelming consensus on this one: global warming is real, it is happening, and we are the cause of it.

It is *The* Issue.

A quick primer on how the hell we got into this mess . . .

—

As always in complex situations, there are lots of folks to point fingers at. The blame game can take on astronomical proportions here.

Let's begin by going back in time to the Carboniferous Period, 350 million years ago, when the earth was dominated by dinosaurs and ancient fernlike species of plants. Cool as they were, these things had the sheer audacity not only to survive and to thrive, but also to die in this whacked-out way, crunched and squeezed and pummeled into the earth, their pressurized remains becoming coal, oil, and natural gas.

Curse them and their fossilized remains! It's ashes-to-ashes and dust-to-dust for the rest of us. Why did they have to go and make such a lasting impression? I mean, seriously—what the hell were they thinking?

Fast-forward a few hundred million years to the middle of the eighteenth century and we have a human to blame this time: James Watt, one of Scotland's finest. Tinkering with the steam engine, he helped usher in the modern industrial revolution. No more resting in peace—now we could finally do something with all those ancient dead bodies. Blast, dig, drill, frack, whatever it took to get them out of the ground so we could burn the hell out of them. The world was transformed.

Whoa, you may argue: don't get carried away here. Don't go dumping on poor James. After all, let's give credit where credit is due. Wasn't the Industrial Revolution a good thing? Didn't it substantially improve our quality of life? Didn't it make the world a much better place to live for millions, now billions, of people?

It's useful to recall the terrifying tale of Johann Faust and his legendary pact with Satan. Faust's obsessive quest for knowledge leads to a deal with the devil which, after a few really awesome years for Johann, ultimately does not go down well. The original Faustian bargain ends with splattered brains and gouged-out eyes, and with Faust, not the Prince of Darkness, getting the raw end of the deal.

Who knows? Dig deep enough and there may just be a modern-day moral to that fable.

Of course, we could take the easy way out and blame the nonliving. Lacking a voice to defend itself, carbon dioxide, that son of a bitch, makes for an easy scapegoat. The primary greenhouse (heat-trapping) gas, it just begs for vociferous curses to be hurled its way. But you can't really blame something you can't see or touch or even smell, even though every time we burn oil or coal or natural gas to heat our homes or drive our cars or make our electricity, more and more of the shit goes into the atmosphere. The higher the concentrations of carbon dioxide, the hotter the planet gets.

It's as simple, or complicated, as that.

Of course, without carbon dioxide we'd be completely fucked. The earth needs it to keep us from freezing our asses off. Plants need it to photosynthesize. Without photosynthesis there's no oxygen. Without oxygen there's, well, no us.

But here's the rub: too much of a good thing turns out not to be a good thing. In fact, too much carbon dioxide could end life as we know it.

Which, most of us agree, would really suck.

While it would be so much easier if carbon dioxide weren't such a Dr.-Jekyll-and-Mr.-Hyde kind of molecule, there's simply no way around it: we've got to add CO_2 to the naughty list.

Who else to blame? Hmm . . . so many culprits and so little time. I suppose that, ultimately, and in good conscience, we need to point the finger where it really and truly belongs.

Yup. You guessed it.

Look in the mirror, bro.

The blame sits squarely on your shoulders. Yours and mine.

We're oil junkies. We're coal addicts. We want our natural gas and, damn it, we want it now.

And we're hell-bent on frying the planet and everything on it in order to keep getting our fix—no matter the consequences.

We are the ultimate fossil fools.

Once again—curse those ancient Chinese!

"May you live in interesting times" indeed!!

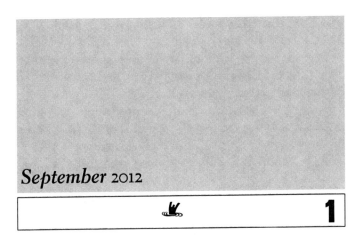

September 2012

1

EVERY SEMESTER, in all of the classes I teach, I start things off the same way:

"Welcome," I begin. "My name is Casey and I have OCD."

Then I wait. I count to five in my head, slowly and silently, as students gawk at me.

One . . . two . . . three . . . four . . . five . . .

It's a long enough pause to be slightly awkward, long enough to get students thinking to themselves, "What is up with this dude? What the hell am I getting myself into?" but not long enough to give them time to beat a hasty retreat towards the door.

"OCD," I repeat.

Then I pause again, not quite as long this time, before hitting them with the punch line.

"Obsessive Climate Disorder."

Most of the students laugh. Most of them get it. Not all of them, but the majority.

I am well aware that I run the risk of offending those

who have that other OCD. God knows, I probably have more folks with acronyms in my class (ADHD, ADD, PTSD) than those without. In no way do I wish to trivialize or belittle anybody's diagnosis; I simply want to be upfront and honest about my own.

I wait every semester for an incensed phone call from my dean advising me that it's best to start things off on a different tack. Surprisingly, no such call has come yet.

As a community college science professor—an awesome teaching gig if there ever was one—I have defined my mission in as succinct a way as possible: Educate my students about the issue of climate change, guide them to the edge of the abyss but not over it and into despair, and inspire them to get off their asses and do something about it.

Not exactly an easy thing to do.

Climate change is a concept so big, so complicated, so fraught with raw emotion and angst that it's easy to be overcome with paralysis. It's the biggest environmental issue of our time, yet the sheer magnitude of its significance tends to overwhelm. Papers should be screaming it daily from their headlines, rather than burying it in the back sections next to celebrity gossip. Politicians, who pontificate about it endlessly, should bring on their legislative A-game. And the general public should turn off their reality TV, if only for one night a week, and confront the real threat that's out there.

The fate of the world is hanging in the balance, yet most folks are perfectly content to go right on fiddling while the earth burns.

For those of us with OCD, this really sucks.

Somehow I've made it to age thirty-two teaching climate change with some shredded remnants of my sanity still marginally intact. I've tied my fate to the mantra: "It's better to be an optimist and a fool than a pessimist and right." I repeat this every day. It's on a sticky note stuck to my bathroom mirror, and I read it over and over while I take a dump.

After all, without optimism what's left? The dark side is way too much of a downer. And I truly do believe there is a way out of the hellhole we're tottering towards. It ain't going to be easy, or pretty, but there definitely *is* a way. I'm not quite sure of the direction, and MapQuest is no damn help, but there is a way.

There has to be.

Anyway, back to the first day of class.

I know it's college, and I know it's science, but I begin the semester reading to my students the best environmental book ever written.

No.

Let me rephrase that.

The best *book* ever written.

The Lorax. By Dr. Seuss.

For a children's book, it lays down a surprisingly dark and destructive tale of environmental devastation caused by greed and short sightedness. Quick recap: Pristine environment destroyed by unfettered capitalism. All that, plus awesome hallucinogenic Dr. Seussian drawings. Who could ask for more?

Best yet, it ends with a wonderful call to environmental action.

I began my reading on this particular opening day by putting on my Cat in the Hat hat, tall and floppy with its signature outlandish red and white stripes. It was a present I had received in middle school and I've cherished it ever since. I figured if I'm going to be weird, why not go all out?

> *"Catch!" calls the Once-ler.*
> *He lets something fall.*
> *"It's a Truffula Seed.*
> *It's the last one of all!*
> *You're in charge of the last of the Truffula Seeds.*

And Truffula Trees are what everyone needs.
Plant a new Truffula. Treat it with care.
Give it clean water. And feed it fresh air.
Grow a forest. Protect it from axes that hack.
Then the Lorax
and all of his friends
may come back."

I have a hard time reading the story and not getting all choked up and teary eyed. But the students love it. Whether you're three or a hundred and three, a good children's book always carries the day.

It sure beats the hell out of introducing the semester by blah, blah, blahing over the damn syllabus and sending students off to Snoozeland.

I feel a twinge of guilt that I've laid it all out for them during the very first class. In fact, I've blown my wad in the first five minutes. The semester might as well be over. I have nothing more relevant to say. But, amazingly, almost all of the students elect to return for the next class.

"But now," says the Once-ler,
"now that you're here,
the word of the Lorax seems perfectly clear.
UNLESS someone like you
cares a whole awful lot,
nothing is going to get better.
It's not."

So that's my goal. That's my mission.

"UNLESS someone like you cares a whole awful lot, nothing is going to get better. It's not," I repeat to them.

Despair is not an option. Once there, it's difficult to turn back.

Hey, I know I'm laying down an awfully heavy burden, but I'm pretty confident they're up to the task.

Better to be an optimist and a fool.

2

ON THE FIRST DAY OF CLASS, I ask students to write down the answers to three introductory questions.

Number One: Why are you in this class?

Number Two: What aspects of climate change are you most interested in?

Number Three: What do you think will be the biggest effect of climate change on your life?

I tell them to be honest. If the only reason they're here is because a Tuesday/Thursday afternoon class fits neatly into their schedule and they desperately need the credits to graduate, then say it.

"There's no party line," I tell them. "Don't tell me what you think I want to hear. I want the honest truth. Spare me the bullshit."

Students laugh and nudge each other. They think it's funny when I use the word *shit*. I stay away from the F word, but *shit* is fair game. Acknowledging my role as part stand-up comic/entertainer, I say it a lot.

Shit, shit, shit.

They laugh every time.

Answers to the questions above are sometimes revealing, sometimes not, but I usually get at least a glimpse of the lay of the class.

This semester's Tuesday/Thursday afternoon section promised to be interesting.

Half the class seemed utterly clueless, a few borderline literate. One student, in a barely legible scrawl, answered "don't no" for each question.

Joy and rapture!

Yet the other half seemed thoughtful and insightful, informed on *The* Issue and chomping at the bit to plow full-speed ahead.

In other words, the usual community-college crowd. Brilliant scholar next to slacker airhead.

The boys in the back with their caps on backwards, tilting back their chairs, no book, no paper, no pen, no nothing, trying to make their texting not too obvious.

The girls up front, textbooks open, hanging on every word I say as if it were the Sermon on the Fucking Mount, with lightbulbs brilliantly, blindingly flashing over their heads.

Not to stereotype, but . . .

I loved it. Both the fore and the aft. I was the captain and this was my ship and damned if we weren't going to run downwind and sail away.

Preaching to the converted was one thing. Getting the word out to the rest of the seething masses, some of whom had already donated their brains to science before they were done with them, was quite another. This was the art of teaching. Keeping those in the crow's nest actively engaged while throwing down the life rafts to save the ones sinking to the bottom.

I like to think I'm good at it. At the very least I think I'm getting better. But every semester I lose students early on and I worry about what I said or didn't say, did or didn't do, that caused them to disappear and drop off the face of the earth. .

It's one of the many things that keep me up at night.

After the first day of each semester I go home and read highlights to Jesse, my roommate. He and I have been best friends since the end of middle school. We went to college together. We've been in each other's lives, for better or for worse, for the last two decades. He's a great friend and, honestly, I'm not sure what I'd do without him.

Jesse is a computer geek. His three great hobbies are surfing the Net, smoking vast quantities of pot, and chasing after nurses. He works in IT at Franklin County Medical Center, the hospital in the same town in western Massachusetts where I teach.

Frankly, Neo-Luddite as I am, I'm not all that interested in what he does. I know it's good work, but computers are just not my thing. I try to be empathetic when he bitches about the latest medical software and systems going down and moronic doctors who can't input data correctly. But it's pretty much in one ear and out the other. Fortunately, my incomprehension doesn't seem to bother him.

He, on the other hand, can't get enough of my classroom drama. He loves the stories I tell and is a wonderful sounding board for ideas and strategies. Given his certifiable insanity and his perpetually scrambled gray matter, particularly after a toke or two, he's hit-or-miss with his suggestions. So while I often take his input with a grain of salt, I can't complain. He's a wonderful roommate.

I put my Cat in the Hat hat back on and read to him the opening-day highlights.

"No way!" he groaned after one particularly unintelligible response bemoaning climate change's potential impact on the major-league baseball schedule. "Some of the doctors at work can write better than this bullshit! How the hell did this fool graduate from high school?"

"Welcome to my world," I sighed. "Here's another one: 'I don't worry about this issue because I know there is a place for me in heaven in the hereafter.'"

"Jesus Christ, are you kidding me? He can't be serious! 'Hereafter' my ass. He must be yanking your chain."

"Don't count on it. There are some pretty scary people out there. But hey, check this one out." I proceeded to read one student's answer to the "how will climate change affect me" question:

> It makes me sad. I am a middle-school science teacher and I am sad for my students. Sad that they are growing up in such uncertain and difficult times. Sad that they hear the truth and are frightened. Sad that they look at every storm with questioning eyes. Sad that I'm 29 years old and my generation is handing over to them a world so fraught with the potential for chaos. Sad that we know what to do, that the future is in our hands, and yet we seem to be plummeting pell-mell toward catastrophe. Sad, sad, sad.

"Jesus," Jesse said, passing me a joint. "That's a buzz-kill. You sure *you* didn't write it?"

"No way!" I said, taking a hit and wondering how the Cat in the Hat, who was able to put a positive spin on everything, would deal with climate change.

> *I know it is wet*
> *And the sun is not sunny.*
> *But we can have*
> *Lots of good fun that is funny!*

I passed the joint back to Jesse. "A teacher," he said. "Just give her an A now and be done with it."

Hands down, her response was my fave. A distant second went to one of the boys in the back who worried that, in a hotter world, he'd sweat too much and scare off the women. At least he was being honest.

Cancelled baseball games, sweaty armpits, tearful children.

Different strokes for different folks. If that's what it takes to get them out of their couches and into the streets, then so be it.

—

The day I began teaching at Pioneer Valley Community College (PVCC) —in fact, before I had even been hired—I was determined to start a student group. Not a discussion group, not a bunch of late-teens/twenty-somethings sitting around twiddling their thumbs and endlessly bitching without *doing* shit, but a group that would actually accomplish things.

An activist group focused on (duh!) *The* Issue.

Three years earlier, during my interview for the job, the dean had posed an interesting question: "Tell us one thing you will accomplish here in your first year." I didn't hesitate for a moment before firing off a definitive answer. "Bring a group of students together to save the world," I replied, somewhat arrogantly. "The Climate Changers."

I hadn't prepared for that question, and the group name just popped into my head. But I thought it was a good answer.

The hiring committee evidently agreed because, shocker though it was, I actually got the job.

To be honest, I hadn't thought I had a chance in hell. Scoring one of these highly coveted, few-and-far-between, tenure-track teaching positions was quite a coup. When I got the call and told Jesse, he thought I was joking.

"No fucking way!" he shouted in disbelief.

"Way!"

"You're serious?"

"I am!"

"No fucking way!" he shouted again, clapping his

hands and jumping up and down like a giddy little kid at the top of the stairs on Christmas morning. He was good—no, *great*—that way, getting all excited whenever something good, really good, happened to me. I did my best to do the same for him—minus, of course, the scary clapping and jumping.

It wasn't as if the hiring committee's decision was coming totally out of left field. I was, in fact, quite qualified for the job. I had worked for Mass Wildlife as a field biologist for four years after grad school, and had done time in the trenches seasonally for them for four previous years. I had been an active member of their Climate Change Advisory Group, developing plans for wildlife corridors and enhanced protected areas and invasive species protocols that might help to mitigate impending catastrophe. Five years ago, I had picked up an on-the-side job as an adjunct professor at a sister community college, and *boom*, it hit me—here was where my passion lay.

I loved the field biology thing, and I was pretty good at it, but it was the teaching I adored. Being around the energy, the enthusiasm, the passion, the naiveté, and the unbelievable weirdness of college students was a total turn-on. I couldn't get enough of it, and as a teacher I wasn't *pretty* good, I was *really* good.

The offer of a full-time professorship blew my mind.

I waited to survive my first semester before venturing forth and forming that student group. There was a process I had to go through—checking with my department chair, the dean, Student Life—nothing too odious. And then getting the word out and actively recruiting students.

Colleagues had given me the yellow light, cautioning me that clubs at community colleges were a tough sell, and most were destined for failure.

"Don't get your hopes up," the natural-history professor warned me.

"Remember who our clientele are. They commute,

they work, sometimes two or even three jobs. Many are parents. Most don't have time to wipe their ass after taking a crap."

But I was thrilled with the response. Fifteen had showed up at our first meeting and we had held at about a dozen students ever since then. Students came and students went (it was, after all, a community college), but semester after semester there were key players, the ones who followed through, the ones who did amazing work. Every year had brought forth a fabulous cadre of bright, dedicated students chomping at the bit to fulfill my interview pledge: Save the World.

I had been an "active" member of a student group in my undergraduate years and, frankly, we didn't do shit. Every other Thursday night, we'd sit around dissing capitalism, trashing the system, ranting and railing against "The Man," and singing the praises of the socialist revolution that we knew for certain was just around the very next corner. Then, after a couple of hours of heated rhetoric and political inaction, we'd all get high and watch *South Park*.

It was great. We didn't do anything but it was still great.

The closest we ever came to actually accomplishing something was when one of our "comrades" (as we liked to call ourselves) got busted for possession of pot. We were outraged, incensed, morally fired up. They had sent down one of our own. We marched on the local police station carrying signs that said "Free Phillip," demanding that he be released and chanting "Hey, Hey, USA! How many kids have you busted today!" Not that any of this worked, but it was the thought that mattered. And at least, for Christ sake, for once we had gotten off our sorry asses and *done* something.

I loved being in that clique. I adored our meetings. Being surrounded by my peeps, secure in the feeling that we were so much wiser and hipper and more politically correct than anyone else on campus. We were the epitome of "right on" and only vaguely aware that we lacked focus, a mission, and a game plan—hell, it was college, what else was new?

I can't say we floundered, but we sure as hell didn't swim.

Once hired at PVCC, I was determined not to let history repeat itself. I had no interest in taking control, and no desire to mold students into (God forbid!) mini-mes, but I was arrogant enough to think that I could do a good job of facilitating activism. I'm reasonably adept at keeping folks on track, I'm proficient at navigating the web of college bureaucracy, I'm a good sounding board, and, for some bizarre reason, students like and trust me.

And so far it's worked. It really has. The Climate Changers have an impressive list of accomplishments under their belt. They've brought the issue of climate change to the forefront of the college campus, they've pressured the administration into school-wide sustainability days, they've planted trees on Earth Day, they've sponsored successful and well-attended lecture and film series, and they've helped raise money for photovoltaic panels—the list goes on and on and on.

Plus, we have fun. Lots of it.

As Mother Jones, the great early-twentieth-century labor activist, so famously said, "If I can't dance I don't want to be part of your revolution."

And dance we do, figuratively and literally. That and laugh. Lots of laughter. Most of it directed inwardly or at me, much of it inappropriate, but all of it joyous.

That's not to say everything is a bed of roses. Far from it. *The* Issue is adept at bringing folks to their knees, to the brink of that dreaded abyss, so there are plenty of tears to go round.

But, thank God, it's balanced by loads of laughter.

The Issue is a tough one to organize around. True change requires a retooling of every aspect of society, from the economic to the political to the personal. It's so easy to be overwhelmed by the sheer magnitude of the tasks at hand that action, any action, can seem futile. One can almost forgive all those folks who've taken the path of least resistance, sticking to a life of intentional ignorance and outright denial rather than tackling such a behemoth of an elephant head-on.

Which is why I was so thrilled to have two of my climate gurus, Hannah and Trevor, my most active activists from last year, back in the saddle again, pumped and ready to lead the pack this semester. Both had full-blown OCD and were as committed to climate change advocacy as I was, only they were younger, less jaded, and brimming over with exuberance and hubris and a take-no-prisoners attitude.

One fascinating characteristic of *The* Issue was its amazing ability to bring people together from all walks of life. Hannah and Trevor were about as unlike as two people could possibly be, and their ability to go at it was legendary, but their passion for activism around climate change had made them willing bedfellows. Strange bedfellows, but bedfellows nonetheless.

Hannah was a business major, impeccably dressed for the 1950s with cardigan button-down sweaters and Catholic schoolgirl skirts. Once I had even seen her in high heels! Can you imagine? High heels at a community college! She listened to classical music and read renaissance poetry. When we ate together as a group, while the rest of us dug in she would fold her hands, close her eyes, and silently mouth a prayer. She was a beautiful young woman, tall and athletic, with long, flowing black hair.

Trevor was all about the 1960s. A throwback to the hippie days, he was perpetually into a five-day beard with his long, scruffy hair wrapped in a bandana or a Che Guevara cap. I had never seen him without ripped jeans and a T-shirt screaming out a political slogan or an image of a pot plant or the face of Bob Marley. His music of choice was "noise," he was a vocal atheist, and never once did he let you forget that he was out to smash the state.

As opposite as they were, Hannah's and Trevor's strengths and weaknesses complemented each other remarkably well, and their work together was stunning. While their interpersonal battles were monumental (fireworks was their modus operandi, much to the delight of their fellow Climate Changers), after their vicious cat-and-dog, tooth-and-nail fights, they would always forgive, forget, and come back to the magnet that held them together: *The* Issue. Push would often came to shove, but they would miraculously, stupendously, pull it all together and make magic happen.

I had never had two students so creative, so intense, so organized, so gung-ho to save the world. Other students had tremendous respect for them and would work hard at whatever task they were assigned, sometimes it seemed, just to please them.

They were every professor's Dream Team.

3

Motor vehicle emissions represent 31 percent of total carbon dioxide, 81 percent of carbon monoxide, and 39 percent of nitrogen oxides released in the U.S.
— The Green Commuter, a publication of the Clean Air Council

A short, four-mile round trip by bicycle keeps about 15 pounds of pollutants out of the air we breathe.
— WorldWatch Institute

It was the Tuesday of Bike-to-School Week at PVCC and tensions were already running high. What had been billed as a wonderful way to promote the greenest of fast transportation had suddenly and with a sick vengeance turned into a bitter struggle for bike master supremacy.

The noblest of ideas, when cast into the raging inferno of competition hell, can sour quickly.

The Climate Changers had worked hard on this event.

They had postered the school for weeks, promoting Bike-to-School Week with creative, catchy slogans stolen from various places:

"The revolution will not be motorized!"

"It's too bad that the people who really know how to run this country are too busy riding their bikes!"

"Friends don't let friends drive!"

"We are not blocking traffic. We *are* traffic!"

"'The theory of relativity. I thought of that while riding my bike.' (Albert Einstein)."

Tabling outside the cafeteria from noon to one every day were Hannah and Trevor, bike fanatics extraordinaire. They were clinically diagnosed with a double whammy, OCD—Obsessive Climate Disorder—and OBD—Obsessive Bike Disorder. Rain, snow, ice, night—it made no difference to them. Hannah in her skirt. Trevor in his tie-dye. They'd cycle through a hurricane without batting an eye. The worse the weather, the greater the bragging rights.

Hannah once claimed to have ridden seven miles in the middle of a winter nor'easter with snow falling so fast that even plows were grounded. Trevor, of course, claimed this was total and complete bullshit. He and Hannah could be tires on glass shards; there was sure to be a blowout every time their biking egos got the best of them.

So far they had managed to check their hubris at the door and were playing nice in the sandbox. At their busy table they were catching the lunch crowd and disseminating bike propaganda, giving out free stickers ("Think globally, bike locally"). They were also promoting Wednesday's "Learn How to Fix Your Bike" workshop (described as "appropriate even for those knuckleheads who think a Phillips-head screwdriver is a mixed drink") and Thursday's demonstration of an electric-assist bike built and ridden by the whacked-out (in a good way) engineering professor.

They had a catchy factoid on the table. If one hundred PVCC students with a ten-mile round-trip commute switched their cars for bikes ten times over the course of the academic year (just ten times!), there would be 300 fewer gallons of gasoline burned and 8,000 fewer pounds of carbon dioxide released into the atmosphere. How's that for a climate-change headline grabber?

Stunning!

Moral of the story? Little actions equal big results.

Hannah and Trev were hard at work signing up students for the "Contest." It seemed simple enough. "Contestants" were to log the miles they rode to and from school during this particular week of September. Whoever logged the most miles won a T-shirt and a water bottle, both with a beautiful design of a bike engulfed in leafy greens.

Set up a contest, make sure there is a prize for the winner and *nada* for the loser, and, sure as shooting, no matter how "politically correct" the event is supposed to be, the shit always seems to hit the fan. Unfortunately, this event proved to be no exception.

It had started innocently enough.

"You ever played one of those cooperative games?" Hannah asked Trevor. "You know, the ones where you work together and everyone wins?"

"Never," said Trevor.

"I suggest you keep it that way," Hannah replied. "They totally suck! I mean, if you can't kick butt, what's the point?"

"Truth. Which is why I'm going to kick your ass."

"What do you mean?"

"It's all about the miles, sweetheart. All about the miles and the smiles!" Trevor dangled his commuting log in Hannah's face.

"Trevor. Don't be a moron. We have the exact same commute."

Hannah and Trevor lived in the same apartment complex in Glenfield, about three miles from campus.

"Yeah, but, how many miles did you put in this morning?" Trevor asked, an evil twinkle in his eye.

"What are you talking about? We've measured the route what, seventeen thousand times?"

"How many miles" Trevor persisted.

"Three, of course," Hannah said.

"Wow. I always knew you were a lightweight, Hannah, but *three*? What'd you do, ride your trike? Or have you made the leap to training wheels?"

Annoyed, Hannah cocked her head. "All right, out with it, what are you up to?"

"Check out my log." Trevor crowed, thrusting it at Hannah.

She looked up in disgust.

"Trevor, I know you're languishing in developmental math for what, the third time, but you seem to have moved the decimal point a tad too far to the right."

"Read it and weep, darling. Thirty miles."

"You rode thirty miles?"

"Yeah."

"Today?"

"Yeah."

"You've gone home and back, what, ten times already?" she asked.

"Nope, just once to school."

"What the heck, Trevor? That is so low. You'd actually cheat on a bike log? What a loser!"

"I didn't cheat, Hannah. I took the long way. The scenic route. A little diversion up the Mohawk Trail, past Apex Orchard, back through town. Sure, I was late to economics. Actually, I missed economics and was late to English, but hey, that's the price you pay for being a winner. Thirty miles."

"You can't do that!" Hannah whined.

"Why not?"

"Because it's cheating!"

"It's not cheating, Hannah. I rode thirty miles to school. There are no rules on the route you have to take. I'm going to ride another fifteen home. Anyway, who made you the two-wheeler police?"

"My god, Trevor! What is this, the Tour de France and you're Lance Armstrong? Better go pee in this cup and I'll test you for doping!"

Day Two and the battle lines were drawn. The Great Bike Week War had begun.

That afternoon Trevor found the air let out of his tires. He had a sneaking suspicion about who did it.

Hannah woke up the next morning to find her bike locked to the rack in front of her apartment, same as it always was. Only it was Trevor's lock.

On Thursday they declared a truce. Let the most miles win.

Hannah missed an exam in history and a meeting with her advisor. She logged seventy-two miles.

Trevor blew off economics and English again. He had cruised sixty-seven miles when he blew a second tire and had to eat crow and call for a ride home.

Both had missed their shifts at the Thursday table and texted me to fill in.

I sensed, somehow, this was in violation of the spirit of the event. Friday morning, I sat the two of them down.

"I don't mean to be condescending or insulting," I began, "but maybe, just maybe, the two of you need to take a step back and think about the bigger picture here." They were glaring at each other in my office, a low, hyena-like growl emanating from Hannah, Trevor grinding his teeth, clenching and unclenching his fists.

"I didn't start it," Hannah said.

"Dude!" Trevor roared. "Air out of tires? Hello!"

I rolled my eyes, wishing the twenty-nine-year-old middle-school science teacher in my Tuesday/Thursday class were here. I could have used her expertise. This seemed much more seventh grade than college.

"Well, it's irrelevant. Unless you are both superhuman, neither of you is in the hunt. This kid Teresa Jones has put in 235 miles. Legitimate miles. And she's got a return trip home to go again today. Pack it up, you two. The game is ovah! T-shirt and bottle? Hers. And for you? Nothing!"

Trevor and Hannah looked incredulous.

"Two hundred and forty-five miles?" they groaned.

"Two hundred and forty-five miles!" I laughed, not bothering to hide my inner glee. "And a bunch more to go!"

I handed them each a Kleenex.

"Something to dry your tears. Don't sweat, there's always next year!"

Bingo. Tension gone. Those two were roadkill.

Teresa had whupped their tushes. Nothing like getting crushed to put you in your place.

And there had been another upside to Bike-to-School Week.

Both Tuesday and Thursday, Samantha, the Twenty-Nine-Year-Old, had ridden her bike to class while dressed in a stunning, tight spandex bottom and a revealing riding top. I tried my best all through my alternative transportation lecture to avoid any visual contact with her. It was all I could do to breathe.

4

I CAN DATE MY FIRST REAL INTEREST in her to the class after bike week.

I had walked into the room after break to find Samantha chatting it up with another student. I fiddled with the computer and pretended to look busy, all the while doing what I do best—eavesdropping.

"I was so upset." she was saying "I could've killed him! Honestly."

"What did he say?" the girl with the pink hair asked.

"'Don't make a mountain out of a molehill. It's not a big deal.' 'It is to me!' I told him. 'Enough molehills make a mountain!' 'Chill' he says. 'You are so overreacting.' God, if there is one thing I can't stand, it's when people tell me I'm 'overreacting.' I absolutely despise that!"

"I'm with you" Pink Hair said. "Last month I was totally freaking out 'cause I was three days late and my boyfriend told me I was overreacting. I kicked him in the you-know-wheres! Jerk."

"Guys! They are so clueless."

Both women rolled their eyes.

I continued to pretend not to hear while inching ever closer for a clearer earful.

Naturally, I assumed they were talking girl stuff. Truth be told, there is nothing—*nothing*—I like to overhear more than intimate details of women's lives.

It never ceases to amaze me how they open up immediately to each other about the most personal of things. I've done introductory exercises where I ask students to briefly interview their seatmate and then share what they learn with the rest of class. In three minutes women will reveal the most astounding of details to each other. How many partners they've had. First orgasm. Favorite position.

Okay. So I'm exaggerating. But with guys you're lucky to get anything more than their favorite friggin' football player.

Samantha continued. "I read somewhere that a hundred acres of forest a day are cut down to make those. A day! If that's not a mountain then I don't know what is!"

The plot thickened. Eavesdropping midway into an interesting conversation can present a delightful puzzle. I had just assumed the conversation had to do with sex. But a hundred acres? For what?

Hmm. . . Latex comes from rubber trees. Were they talking condoms?

"BYOC," Samantha went on.

"What's that mean?" Pink Hair asked.

"Bring Your Own Chopsticks. Otherwise, just say no."

Pink Hair laughed.

I was confused. While women's issues remain a vast conspiratorial convoluted mystery to me, I do try to keep up on the latest. But chopsticks? *Chopsticks?* Was this a new slang word for contraception? Some sort of intravaginal device that picked up sperm one by one and flung them out? I moistened my lips and bought some time by shutting down and restarting the computer.

"Next time I do Chinese I'll remember that," Pink Hair said. "No more disposable chopsticks for me. One hundred acres."

"A day!" Samantha emphasized. "Imagine that! It's a tragedy!"

Whoa, whoa, whoa . . . they weren't talking sex here. They were talking deforestation! They were on task. This had to do with *The* Issue!

I couldn't believe it. Here, I thought I was the only one who had a shit-fit at Panda Garden every time the Roommate insisted on eating the Chinese way. The only one who couldn't leave it alone even when we went out to eat.

Hmm. . . I thought to myself. Chopsticks.

This one could be interesting.

—

It was a Tuesday and Samantha came to class dressed like a pirate. Striped shirt and blue jean bell bottoms. A flowing fake black beard and an eye patch. A cocked hat proudly displaying the skull and crossbones. Hook on one hand, plastic sword in the other. There was even a fake parrot perched on her shoulder.

She made a stunning pirate.

From the very first class, I couldn't help but notice that she was a beautiful woman. I wasn't nearly as distracted by my younger attractive students. I looked at them as . . . students. But beautiful women in my class who were also my age? Arrrrrrr. . .

"Ahoy, me hearties!" she growled, entering class with a swashbuckling flourish.

"And to what do we owe the honor of this, my . . . captain?" I asked smilingly.

"Shiver me timbers!" she exclaimed. "Don't tell me you land-lubbing bilge rats don't know what today is?"

"Dress Like a Lunatic Day?" one student shyly asked.

"Yo ho ho! Though not at all funny. It's September 19!"

"And . . . ?" I asked.

"International Talk Like a Pirate Day."

"Are you serious?" a student asked.

"I'd sooner walk the plank then tell a lie to me crew! 'Tis the tenth anniversary today. Celebrated around the world and, closer to home, at Glenfield Middle School. You're looking at this year's seventh-grade honorary captain!"

The class applauded while giving each other furtive glances. She bowed, theatrically, tipping her hat.

"I was going to change my outfit but then I thought, Hey, why not. For the rest of the class you will kindly address me as Mad Sam Bellamy, Pirate Extraordinaire."

"Aye aye, Captain!" the class called out in unison.

"You do know who Sam Bellamy is?" she asked.

"Umm. . ." I replied. "That would be . . . you?" Her name was Samantha. Samantha Bellamy.

"My goodness. 'Black Sam' Bellamy. His ship, the Whydah, is the only real pirate ship ever recovered. Sunk in 1711, treasure and all. The plunder is in a museum in Provincetown on Cape Cod."

"Who would have thought?" I said.

"And check this out, me beauties!" she *arrrrrr*ed, disengaging the parrot from her shoulder and passing it around.

Placed prominently on the bird's chest was a big button.

"Pirates Against Global Warming," it read, with a smiling picture of Samantha dressed in her pirate garb.

"I want one!" one of the students demanded.

"Me too! Me too!" I clamored, hopping up and down like one of her students. "Where did you get that?"

"Me very own button-making machine, me hearties. No seventh-grade class should be without one. If my kids do particularly well on a project, or stick with a particularly difficult assignment, whatever, they get to make a button. It's a fabulous incentive!"

God, I thought, I could use one of those in my classroom. Grades would skyrocket. Work would come in on time. Papers would exceed the bare minimum and might even be—*gasp*—literate.

Be gone, ye slackers!

After all, college students are only a hop, skip, and jump away from seventh grade. The things we'll do for trinkets!

The button was a big hit. As was the pirate.

"Wow!" I overheard one of my guy students comment as they were walking towards the door at the end of class. "If she's the captain, then sign me up. I'd be the first to drop anchor in her lagoon."

Shiver me timbers! I thought, briefly allowing inappropriate faculty–student interactions to entertain themselves in my head.

Me too. Me too.

5

Consenting romantic and sexual relationships between faculty and student are deemed unprofessional. Because such relationships interfere with or impair required professional responsibilities and relationships, they are looked upon with disfavor and are strongly discouraged. Codes of Ethics for most professional associations forbid professional–client sexual relationships. In this context the professor–student relationship is properly regarded as one of professional and client. The respect and trust accorded to faculty by students, as well as the power exercised by the faculty in giving praise or criticism, grades, recommendations for further study and employment, and other benefits or opportunities diminish the student's actual freedom of choice such that relationships thought to be consensual may, in fact, be the product of implicit coercion. — Policy Against Sexual Harassment and Discriminatory Harassment, Pioneer Valley Community College

COMMUNITY COLLEGE TEACHING is an awesome gig. Unlike in K–12, classroom management consists of keeping students awake, not keeping them from going at it with each other. I can't recall ever yelling at anyone. Discipline is a piece of cake.

Unlike universities, there is no pressure to "publish or perish," no constant scrambling for elusive research dollars. With the focus exclusively on teaching, faculty relationships lack the competitive edge that can be so negative and disruptive. Department meetings, at least ours in the science department, are remarkably devoid of hair pulling and throat lunging and other academia barroom battles.

Of course, truth be told, incredibly dull, boring, and unproductive as those meetings often are, a stab in the back now and then would liven things up.

As long as it wasn't my back.

And then there's the class of company I keep. Surrounded by students who are excited, enthusiastic, eager to learn. Well, most of them anyway. It's nothing short of inspirational. I totally feed off it. I know it sounds like hyperbolic bullshit but it's a privilege, it really is, to be in constant interaction with people who truly want to learn.

I have no tolerance, none, for those colleagues who constantly bitch, bitch, bitch about this or that pain-in-the-ass student. God knows I've had my share of bad apples out there, but, for the most part, they are truly few and far between.

If I ever to get to be that cynical, that heartless, that mean about my students, then somebody, please, shoot me.

Like I said, it's a privilege. Being a catalyst for those "aha!" moments when things really click in student minds is awesome. The onslaught of awareness is like a thunderbolt. One moment they're on their feet, naïve as hell, oblivious to The Issue and then . . . bam! They're flat on their asses.

New mental jigsaw pieces locked forever into place. And once they know, once they really get it—there is no turning back. Ever. The old brain will never be the same again.

Every semester I get students coming to see me during my office hours, reeling from the early stages of OCD.

"Oh my god!" they gasp. "Did you know that temperatures might rise ten degrees by the end of the century?"

"Wow!" I reply.

"Ten degrees! This is not good!" they gasp again.

"It is not good," I agree.

"We have to do something! We have to do something right now!"

Yes! Got 'em!

Of course, what that really means is that they're now doomed for a lifetime of extreme anxiety, possible depression, constant angst, and a whole host of other intellectual trauma, a.k.a. OCD.

But hey, such is the price of education. Right?

If ignorance is bliss then knowledge is . . . chaos?

Not that I don't have occasional bouts of severe misgivings over this. I often think to myself, what the hell am I doing? I mean, who am I to sear these images of global catastrophe deep into my students' consciousness? Who am I to shake the foundations of innocence and naïveté and force them to confront demons and devils?

Better to let sleeping dragons lie, you may argue.

Trouble is, like it or not, dragons do wake up.

My sister Cheryl is obsessed about when to reveal to her kids the curse of the human condition, the reality of life's sorrows and tragedies. The Holocaust. Genocide. Racism. Abject poverty. Death.

The Issue.

When to let the proverbial cat out of the bag?

"You are not to mention climate change when you're around them!" she forever admonishes me. "Do you understand me? Not one single word!"

"Relax." I reply. "The oldest know about it already and

the youngest are four and two, for Christ sake. They don't even know what the word 'climate' means!"

"I'm quite sure you'd figure out a way to explain it. Anyway, Jennifer is very smart."

Jennifer is my four-year-old niece.

"Last time you visited, she had nightmares for weeks about the monster stories you told her. She doesn't need you to feed her new ones. And true ones at that."

"That's why I give her fake ones! Think how wonderful it is to be tormented by things that aren't real! She needs to enjoy it while it lasts!"

"She doesn't know they aren't real."

"Of course she does. You just said how smart she is. Last time I tried to read her *Winnie the Pooh*, she threw the book at me. 'Monsters or nothing!' she demanded. She forced me into it. It's not like I had a choice. I'm trying to be a good uncle. Christ, what am I supposed to do?"

"You're not the one she's climbing into bed with, whimpering, at two in the morning."

"Look, Sis, the real demons are a few years away. Chill. I promise I won't tell her a thing. Just yet. But damned if I'm keeping my mouth shut about that two-headed, oozing-eyed, projectile-vomiting monster lurking, lurking, lurking, under her bed!"

"Humph," humphed my sister. But she knew I had her.

Back to being a professor.

There is a perk to the job that aids considerably in its enjoyment. One that makes all of the inept bureaucracy, the administrative bullshit, the absurd paperwork, the never-ending multitude of gross, petty annoyances so very much more tolerable.

One that truly makes it a joy to teach.

Women.

I am surrounded on a daily basis by the most striking, sparkling, attractive women on the planet.

That first day of class in the fall, when the weather is

warm and beautiful and my female students, fresh and new, come to class dressed the way they dress.

Oh my god.

The wonderful thing about the community college scene is that, not only do I get the gorgeous nineteen- to twenty-two-year-olds, but I get women in their thirties, forties, sometimes even fifties. The diversity is overwhelming.

There are times when I walk into class, take a look at those stunning bodies, and think to myself: And they actually pay me to do this?

"How's this year's crop?" the Roommate eagerly asked, as he's wont to do, after the second day of school.

"Christ, that is so sexist. Leave it to you to objectify women, to treat my students as objects instead of the vibrant, intellectual beings that they are. How dare you degrade and denigrate half my class! What do you think I am? A pervert? Jesus, give me a fucking break!"

"How's this year's crop?" he asks again.

"Oh my god!" I gasp. "Amazing! Every single class I have a few 10s! Seriously. Could be the best semester ever!"

Oh well, so much for holding the moral high ground.

Thank God, what I share with the Roommate stays with the Roommate. I pride myself on keeping my relationships with my female students professional, exemplary, free of any sexual innuendoes or potentially uncomfortable interactions that could lead to any sense of inappropriateness. I do an excellent job confining my saliva to my mouth, keeping my eyes focused on their eyes, not letting my mind wander, when I'm in the classroom, to forbidden places. In the rare (very rare) cases that students flirt with me I am pretty good at shutting it down immediately with a minimal degree of awkwardness.

I know and value my role. I know my place. I am aware of the power dynamics, the position I hold, and the responsibilities it entails. I'd be a fool to screw that up.

Of course, none of that negates the fact that it truly is a joy and a wonder to be a daily witness to such beauty.

And this semester I certainly had the beauties.

Jesse can't get enough of it. Working in the IT department at the Medical Center, most of his day is spent hunched over desks looking at computer screens, dealing with technological fuckups. Make no mistake, he certainly has his share of doctors and nurses to lust after, but he's got nothing like I have.

Every semester he insists on making a "visit" to my classes to check out the particular hotties that I have described in considerable detail to him. He's good about camouflaging his ogling leers and looking just generally goofy as he strolls in at the end of lecture and fades into a corner, slyly surveying the scene.

His presence in the classroom for the above reasons is so wrong. Just plain wrong. No ifs, ands or buts about it. And so politically incorrect. I would never, ever, dream of doing something like this with a colleague. And if the dean found out? Christ!

But the fact is, appropriate or not, having him come in gives me an outlet to talk about the women in class with someone. Otherwise I'd lose it.

"Who's the beauty in the front row?" he asked after his scouting mission to my Introduction to Climate Change class.

"Left or right?"

"Left. Blond pigtails. Freckly. Late twenties. Scarf. Weird hat."

"Yeah," I sighed. "Phewwww . . . oh my. She's a looker. And so totally into The Issue. She's the one who teaches middle-school science in Glenfield. God, so age-appropriate."

"They're all age-appropriate, for Christ sake. Every single one of them. Jesus, I don't know how you can stand it. I'd have to masturbate before every class, otherwise I'd have a continual hard-on. I wouldn't be able to stand up in front of them. I'd have to sit with a jacket on my lap."

"Nice," I said. "Very nice. There's an image I can live without."

"Seriously. How do you do it? How old is she again?"

"Who?"

"The teacher."

"Twenty-nine."

"Twenty-nine? God, that's perfect. The total prime of womanhood. Old enough to be confident, self-assured, experienced. Young enough to still glow. Is she married?"

"Stop it! How am I supposed to know?"

"You know she's twenty-nine, you know she's a teacher, you know she's hot. Wait, she's not even a real student, is she?"

"What do you mean?" I asked.

"She's a teacher. She's got her degree. She's there for some professional development deal or whatever. Right?"

"And your point is?"

"Dude, you can ask her out!"

"What? Are you serious?"

"Totally. I mean, there must be like a special category for people like her. You know, students who aren't really students. Askoutables."

"Oh. Yeah. Right." I slapped myself on the side of the head. "That is such a brilliant suggestion. Why didn't I think of that? You are so smart! I'll do it right now! Hmm . . . should I call her, or text? Wait. Better yet, you could do it for me! Tell her you were the one with the boner drooling in the shadows the other day. Brilliant!"

"All I'm saying is that it's not like she's a real student. She's a teacher. It's a different thing."

"Good to know. Thanks. Now, refresh my memory— how much do you take home a week again?"

"What are you talking about?"

"How much money do you make?" I asked.

"What's that have to do with dating the hottie?"

"I'm totally serious. We need to talk finances right now so when I get FUCKING FIRED you can support the two of us!"

"Don't be so melodramatic, Casey. You wouldn't get fired!"

"Are you nuts? Are you totally whacked out? Christ, I don't care where she's coming from, she's still a student! It's clear as day what the boundaries are. One step over the line and I am out of there. I couldn't even pull that shit off with tenure!"

"Jesus, Casey, don't go ballistic on me. It's just a suggestion. Maybe after the semester's over. Think about it. She teaches the stuff. You said she's in to it. She's cute as hell. God, maybe she'd even say yes!"

"Stop. No more! Enough already! Case closed!"

Ask her out.

My god, the ignorance of people!

Ask her out.

Humphhhhh!

6

I CAME HOME TO FIND JESSE ENGAGED in his favorite after-work pastime: getting stoned while Facebook-stalking his colleagues.

"Christ!" he bitched. "The shit people put out there for all the world to see. As if I give a flying fuck about the ER nurse's indoor miniature golf score. My god, they need to get a life!"

"Wait a minute!" I peered over his shoulder. "Indoor miniature golf? Are you serious? Where?"

"Look, dude. Check it out. The Chicopee Mall. Are we there or what!"

We spent a happily high half hour YouTubing indoor mini-golf sites throughout the country, adding to our bucket list a road trip to the three-story, thirty-six-hole South Carolina range with live alligators, a llama you can ride, and a fifteen-foot dragon that spews real fire.

Awesome or what?

And then back to the business at hand: stalking.

For all its trials and tribulations, Jesse loved working

at the hospital. He was proud of the work he did: he was always rushing into the thick of things to troubleshoot computers on the fritz. He loved hospital drama. And, as jealous as he was of me because of my students, he was continually feeling the fire down below when it came to his doctors and nurses.

"So many beautiful women," he sighed, stalling out on one of the profiles. "And those outfits are so fucking hot!"

"Which ones?" I asked. "The nurses or the mini-golf?"

He ignored me.

"You checked her out yet?"

"Who?"

"Dude. Who do you think?"

"I don't do students."

"Bullshit. What's her name again?"

"I told you. I don't Facebook students."

"Tell me her name? Some pirate thing, right?"

"I'm not going to tell you her name!"

"Dude, come on, I'll make dinner tonight. Tell me her name?" he pleaded.

"I don't Facebook students."

"You don't have to. I will."

"No."

"Come on, Casey!"

"No."

"The next two nights."

"Done."

It was the typical Facebook site for a teacher, little to go on, not much divulged. Nothing for middle-school eyes to gawk at. You couldn't access squat without the coveted friend status.

With one perplexing exception.

"Uh oh!" Jesse gasped. "Could be time to flip fantasies."

"Huh? Where? What are you talking about?" All my attention was focused on that stunning face, those dazzling freckles, those deep, blue, adorable eyes.

I had barely noticed that there was another person in one of the pictures.

"Christ, are they holding hands?" Jesse asked.

I looked again. The image was taken from quite a distance, but the two women looked awful close.

"They're not holding hands."

"Are you sure?"

"They're not holding hands!"

"Hard to tell. You may be barking up the wrong tree," Jesse said.

"I'm not barking."

"*Woof woof.*"

"Shut up! I'm not barking, damn it. Even if I was, it doesn't mean anything."

"Dude. She's holding hands with another woman. It means something."

"For the tenth time, she's not holding hands!"

"Relax. Take another hit. Why are you getting so defensive?"

"I'm not getting defensive," I argued, my voice rising a notch.

"You are. What's up with that? It's not like she's potential. She's a student, remember? Untouchable. Beyond reach. Taboo. Forbidden."

"Believe me, I remember!"

"God, she *is* hot though. So's the woman she's holding hands with."

"Jesus, will you stop already! She's not holding hands. Anyway, it could be her sister."

"Do you hold hands with your sister?"

"A best friend."

"Do you hold hands with me?"

"Women are different. You know that. They're always arm in arm, hugging and shit like that. They're totally into it. It could be her best friend."

"Best friend with benefits," Jesse said.

"Shut up!"

"Why don't you friend her and ask? You could be like, 'Hey darling. It's your sex obsessed, desperate-to-get-in-your-pants, climate-change prof here. Just drooling over your profile and wondering if you were doing the deed with the chick in the pic. Please get back. LOL. As in: Lots of Lust.'"

I punched him in the arm.

"You're a pervert," I groaned. "You really are."

"Whatever," Jesse answered, pulling up another one of his nurses. "Good thing it doesn't matter."

"Yeah," I sighed. "Good thing."

7

MR. CONDOM CAME TO MY CLASS Thursday afternoon.

I had met him at a workshop a number of years earlier at the University of Massachusetts, and we had clicked immediately. He was an Indian gentlemen (Indian as in India), now in his sixties, with deep, dark wrinkles and a British Indian accent to die for.

I would have given anything to talk like him. All of my social awkwardness, my angst, my occasional bouts of low self-esteem would disappear in a heartbeat if only I could speak with that lilting roll. Everything he said, no matter how seemingly trivial or mundane, sounded just right.

He had worked for years in the Indian government on population-control issues, and had retired to this country to be closer to his daughter who had relocated here. This was the third semester in a row I had invited him in as a guest presenter.

"I am extremely happy to be here," he said to my class, smiling as the wrinkles danced on his face. "Beyond happy. Ecstatic! And I want to share something wondrous that happened on my way to your lovely college this afternoon."

He reached into the oversized backpack he had slung across his shoulder and took out a rusty-looking brass lamp.

"On a whim," he said (God, how I loved how he said the word *whim*), "I stopped by that antique store on Olive Street. What do you call it?"

"Treasures and Trash," one of my students called out.

"Correct," Mr. Condom replied. "Treasures and Trash. Perhaps more of the latter than the former but I was not disappointed. Oh no. Far from it! For this, this is what I found."

He paused for dramatic effect, holding the lamp aloft.

I saw one of my students nudge another and exchange a WTF-type of glance.

"I paid for it and then sat in my car, nibbling on a biscuit, wondering why I had done such an impulsive thing. It is not like me. I don't go out and buy brass lamps on a whim! Even a very cheap one such as this!"

There was that word again. *Whim.* And nibbling on a *biscuit.* I made a mental note to see if I could audit a British as a second language class next semester.

"For some unknown reason I took the lamp off the dashboard where I had been staring at it, put my biscuit in the cup holder, and rubbed the lamp three times with my left hand. Just like this." He rubbed the lamp with a slow, counterclockwise motion.

The students were transfixed. They didn't have a clue where the hell this was going.

"Suddenly, *POOF!*" As he yelled the word *poof,* he threw the lamp up in the air, and then caught it.

"Do you know what happened then?" he asked.

It was like story time in the kids' section of the public library. My students were wide-eyed, some with mouths agape. They were hanging onto his every word. It was a rare day when I got anywhere close to receiving this degree of rapt attention.

"At that very moment, just as I finished the last rub, a beautiful genie sprang from the lamp. A genie! She was dressed in a flowing Indian sari of silk and satin comprised of iridescent pink and purple hues. Shapely and buxom with jet black hair and deep-brown skin. Rings on her fingers and bells on her toes. A genie!"

You could have heard a pin drop.

"'Praise be to you, master,' the genie cried. 'You have freed me! I have been trapped in this lantern forever. Praise be to you!'" He bent his knees and lowered his head, bowing down as the genie had done in his story.

"Well," continued Mr. Condom. "You can imagine that I was quite surprised. It is not every day a genie appears out of a brass lantern.

"'Master!' says the genie. 'In appreciation for my freedom I shall grant you one wish!'

"'One wish?' I exclaimed. 'What a rip off! I thought I got three!'"

The students laughed.

"The genie shook her head. 'One wish, and one wish only. And no, it can't be for a hundred other wishes or for a billion dollars. It has to be for something politically correct. I am, after all, that kind of genie!'

"Whoa. Was I lucky or what? Talk about being in the right place at the right time. But one wish. Only one. What was I to wish for? The genie asked for a bite of my biscuit, and I was happy to oblige. Evidently one gets quite hungry trapped in a lantern for eternity. While it happily munched away, I thought and thought.

"One wish. How about, a reversal of climate change? No more melting glaciers, rising sea levels, terrible droughts!" He turned with a flair toward me.

I gave him two thumbs up.

"But wait?" he went on. "How about putting an end to species extinction? Why stop at saving the polar bears? I could keep all of God's creatures alive!" He did a little jig and flapped his arms. A few students applauded.

"But then again there's that whole issue of crushing, oppressive poverty. I must think of my brothers and sisters back home in India. So much pain, so much misery. With my one wish I could end it forever!

"Well, by this time the genie had finished my biscuit and was clearly getting bored with my deliberations.

"'Look' she said, glancing at her watch. 'Time's a-wastin'. I'd love to chat but I've got places to go and things to do. Let me give you a hint, bro. You know those three things you'd love to do? Stop global warming? No more extinctions? End poverty?'

"'Whoa, dude,' I cried. 'You could read my mind?'

"'I'm a genie,' she said. 'I can do all sorts of cool shit.'"

The students laughed again, still transfixed.

"'Believe it or not, I can grant you one wish that will take care of not just those three wishes but a hell of a lot more as well!'

"'Tell me, oh wise one,' I said, attempting to bow my head but hitting it instead on the steering wheel.

"'It's a simple wish,' said the genie. 'A very simple wish. It's cheap. It's easy. And it's totally doable. Just wish for everyone, every time, to simply use one of these!'"

My speaker reached into the brass lamp and, with a dramatic flair, pulled out a Trojan Maxima condom. With one smooth motion he unwrapped it with his teeth, and waved it above his head.

"'Use this every time you humans do the deed, and your problems will be solved! Global warming, extinction, poverty. *Poof!* Gone. Agreed?'

"'Agreed!' I shouted.

"'Thanks again, darling! Good luck saving the world. I gotta run.' The genie kissed me on the cheek and—*poof!*—she was gone.

"End of story."

My students gave him a thunderous round of applause.

Mr. Condom put down the brass lamp and turned serious.

"No environmental problem—not climate change, not species extinction, not poverty—will be solved without addressing the birth mother of them all: the human population explosion."

He then launched into a population PowerPoint—irreverent, funny, hard hitting.

It started off brutal. After all, cataclysmic, exponential growth rates are not an easy pill to swallow. Seven-plus billion of us on the planet. Seventy-plus million new us coming on board each year. Those countries and regions of the world most stressed and least able to handle it were the ones getting hammered with the greatest increases in population. Those people struggling the most, barely getting by, hungry and desperate and already driven to despair, were the ones having the most children.

He led us to the abyss, had us peer into the yawning chasm, and then gently guided us back.

"I am not a two-point-plan man, preaching gloom and doom. Your professor and I share the same mantra: 'Better to be an optimist and a fool, than a pessimist and right.' However, I am quite convinced that I can actually be three of those four.

"I know I'm a fool. I am confident I have done a more than adequate job of convincing you of that today.

"I know I'm an optimist. I wake up every day knowing that things will get better. The world is a beautiful place and I do believe it will stay that way no matter how much we humans attempt to screw it up.

"And I am entirely arrogant enough to honestly, truly, deeply believe that I, like your professor, am right."

I basked in the glory of being singled out by him.

He pointed to dramatic reductions in developing countries' birthrates over the last few decades. He correlated the rise of maternal health programs, reduction of infant mortality, and increased access to education, particularly among girls and women, with profound reductions in population growth. He charted a realistic path toward zero and even negative growth. His optimism was compelling and contagious.

An hour and a quarter had flown by. It was close to the end of class. Mr. Condom exited out of his PowerPoint, then turned and faced my students.

"How many of you plan on having sex tonight?" he asked, dramatically pausing for just a moment to chuckle at the stunned looks. "Don't answer that. Although I encourage you to do so. It is fun, healthy, and much, much better than anything you will ever find on television."

There was a final burst of applause, accompanied by a few hoots and hollers from the boys in the back.

"Not to be overdramatic but, for those of you who do, please, for yourselves, for your future, for the future of life on this precious planet. . ." He reached back into the magic genie lamp and pulled out the condom. "Put this on!"

He bowed, passed around the lamp which just so happened to be loaded with condoms, and thanked us all for our attention.

My students flocked to him, asking questions and pressing for additional details. I couldn't help but notice the Twenty-Nine-Year-Old reaching out and lightly touching his arm, profusely thanking him. Pressed for time and needing to leave, he was still surrounded by students as he made his exit.

I knew I should have been appreciative. He had had the class eating out of the palm of his hand. I knew I should have been thankful. They'd be referencing his presentation for weeks.

But, as ludicrous as it was, I couldn't help but agonize over the situation. Samantha didn't touch *me* on the arm or tell *me* how wonderful I was. How could she fawn all over him like that? He wasn't an inch over five feet. He was old. He had lost a few of his teeth and most of his hair.

Self-centered, narcissistic, delusional ass that I was, I was consumed with jealousy.

I had just placed the opened condom on my finger and was wagging it in the air, making a point to the invisible masses that I was every bit as awesome as the guest lecturer, when Samantha poked her head around the corner.

"Hey," she said.

"Hey," I replied, stopping my finger in mid wag, which sent the condom flying across the room.

"I'm sorry. Am I interrupting something?" she asked.

"No, no, of course not," I stammered, feeling the blush creeping through my face. "I'm just . . . tidying things up here."

"I can see that!"

I made my way across the room, picked up the condom, and dropped it into the trash can.

"Anyway," she continued, "I just came to tell you how fabulous Mister Condom was! Thanks for inviting him. Think I'd get fired if I had him speak to my seventh graders?"

"Job security is overrated," I laughed. "Anyway, 'tis always better to seek forgiveness than to ask for permission."

"Hmm. . ." she pondered. "I better sleep on that one."

She bent down and picked up one of the unopened condoms that had fallen underneath one of the desks.

"Here," she said, handing it to me, smiling. "Somebody must have dropped it. I won't be needing it."

Awkwardly, I took it out of her hand.

"Anyway, have a wonderful weekend," she said, turning to leave.

"You too," I replied.

I sat back down on my desk to catch my breath, waiting for the pounding in my chest to subside.

—

"It can mean a lot of things," Jesse said. He was pondering the words of the Twenty-Nine-Year-Old. As always, I had told him everything. This was, after all, the kind of shit he lived for.

"One: Just like I said. She's a lesbian."

"For the last time, she was not—"

"—Holding hands with that woman. Whatever. Two: She's on the pill and doesn't need them. Which seems extremely likely. She's totally hot, she's employed, how could she not be in a relationship?"

"Whoa!" I cautioned. "Wait just a minute. We're hot. We're employed. We're not in relationships."

Jesse snickered dismissively.

"I'll pretend you didn't just say that. Reason Three: She's a nun and has taken a vow of celibacy and forsaken the pleasures of the flesh for a marriage to Christ."

"Jesus, give me a break."

"I'm simply going through the options. Some may be ones you don't want to hear. But hey, how about this one? Reason Four: she's been waiting, waiting, for what is it, three weeks now, for you to make the move. Her slipping you that condom is about as Freudian as it gets. She was flashing you the green light, dude—go, go, go! She would have taken you right then and there in your classroom if you had just had the balls. I could see her right now, bending over the table, hiking up her skirt. . . ."

I put my hands tightly over my ears.

"*La-la-la-la-la-la-la!* You can stop talking now because I can't hear you! I can't hear you!"

I went to my room, shut the door, and for the fourth time that evening, took the condom she had handed me out of my wallet, closed my eyes, and rubbed it counterclockwise three times.

8

Factoid: Incandescent lightbulbs use four times the electricity of a compact fluorescent and five times that of an LED for comparable light. Switching over to compact fluorescents or LEDs means that you will release 75–80 percent less CO_2 into the atmosphere from lighting.

WE WERE AT THE FARMER'S MARKET, Jesse and I, doing the right thing, buying local. It was the height of harvest and everything was fresh, good-looking, and yum, yum, yummy. We bought all the veggies and fruit for our week: potatoes, summer squash, lettuce, broccoli, apples, pears, onions, tomatoes, carrots, and loads and loads of purple pod beans. All of that plus a chicken, a free-range, happy-as-a-clam-till-its-head-got-lopped-off chicken, born and bred in our very same town, now dead and frozen and ready for our Sunday night fiesta.

The farmer's market was the place to be and be seen. Granted, the ultimate was growing your own, but Jesse and I had had limited success with that one. Try as we might, our backyard plot had turned into a desolate, neglected tangle of weeds and rocks, our beans decimated by Mexican bean beetles, our cucumbers stalks whacked off by leaf-cutter worms, our tomatoes all leaves and no fruit. Even our zucchini, which friends had said that even the green-thumbless could grow, had some sort of fungal infestation that turned them black and stunted and mushy and very, very scary.

So Saturday mornings we did the farmer's market. I went out of my way to look conspicuous, making sure my students, whom I often saw there, saw me. Mostly I liked to chat it up with the garlic lady, an old hippie in her seventies with braided gray hair, a wide brim Mexican sombrero, a flouncy skirt and a button-down hot-pink cardigan.

Back in the day I had assumed that garlic was garlic, that one bulb was the same as any other. Silly me! How could anyone be so wrong! With the help of the garlic lady I had turned into something of a garlic snob, and I could now delightedly talk garlic talk with the best of them, waxing eloquent on the difference between softnecks and hardnecks, Elephant, Porcelain, Rocambole, Silverskin, Creole, Turban and, my hands-down favorite, Purple Stripe.

"You know he's got a thing for you," Jesse said, pointing at me and winking at the garlic lady.

"Most people do," she grinned. "It's the garlic. The sweet breath of life. Even the smell is an aphrodisiac. You can't imagine how many offers I turn down every market. Too bad I'm a one-man woman."

She glanced over at her hubby, offloading a crate of Purple Stripes; a poster child for hippiedom, he wore overalls, big clunky boots, a shirt with "Make cheese not war," and a red bandana tying back his wild gray ponytail. They were clearly two peas in a pod.

Or was it two cloves in a bulb?

"Half dozen of the usual?" she asked.

"You got it," I replied, slipping a sample sliver of an Elephant into my mouth.

"And we'll see you and your class in a few weeks?"

"Looking forward to it," I said.

Shopping done, I was set to head back to the house when I noticed that Jesse had waylaid two young women, not much older than most of my students. He was madly waving the bulbs of garlic around, slinging shit about some classy garlicky hors d'oeuvres I knew he would never get around to making.

"Typical," I sighed, and sat down on an empty apple crate to wait, content to watch the gaggle of happy farmer's marketers parade on by, bags and strollers and dogs in hand.

I had faded into a sensual daydream involving the Twenty-Nine-Year-Old, me, and a lovely field of garlic in full, luscious bloom, when Jesse rudely interrupted and tapped me on the shoulder. I looked up to see him flanked by his two new friends.

"Casey, this is Patty and Rebecca. They're grad students in Renaissance Studies at U Mass. Casey teaches at Pioneer Valley Community College."

"Oh, really?" said Patty or Rebecca.

I couldn't tell which one was which.

"What do you teach?"

"Environmental science, climate change, that kind of stuff."

"Awesome." Rebecca/Patty replied.

"They invited us to head over to their place," Jesse said, giving me a wink and a follow-my-lead-and-we-could-get-lucky look.

"It's just up the street. Maybe roast a little garlic. Smoke a joint. Spend a lovely afternoon with two lovely ladies!"

God, he moved fast. He had known them for what, five minutes, and already he was halfway to first base!

"I don't know," I said. "I've got a lot of grading to do. I should probably head back."

He shot me the evil eye, silently mouthing the do-as-I-say-or-I'm-going-to-kick-your-ass command. I had been down this road with him before. To disobey was not an option.

"Dude, grading can wait. These two can't. Let's go!"

The twins (they weren't, but they could have been) had a spacious second-floor apartment on Federal Street, about a block from the center of town.

We sat on their couch. Jesse, clearly taking to heart the market woman's words of wisdom, proceeded to hold forth with garlic still in hand.

The two women put on the Red Hot Chili Peppers, passed around a quart of fresh apple cider and a killer joint, and gave us the lowdown on the trials and tribulations of Renaissance Studies. Gossip and palace intrigue fit for queens and kings. They went off on the relationships between the natural and the supernatural in sixteenth-century England, and the animated discussion about visions, apparitions, miracles, demonic possession, and mystical ecstasy reached such a crescendo that Jesse disappeared into the bedroom with Patty (or was it Rebecca? The pot had not helped in keeping the two of them straight . . . as it were).

I was enjoying myself. What was not to like? They were animated, smart, witty, and cute as hell. I was high, and so were they. Whichever one was left was clearly interested in me. God knows, I hadn't had it in a long time, and here it was being handed to me on a silver platter. Ripe for the plucking. A feast for a renaissance king.

But just as Rebecca/Patty moved closer next to me and things began to get really interesting—curse and nuisance! blight and bother!—my OCD kicked in. Big time. The goddamn climate-change freight train came roaring down the tracks!

No! I silently screamed to myself. No! Not now!

From the moment I had walked into their apartment door I had done my best to ignore the surroundings and keep my eyes on the prize.

Don't go there! I had told myself, as I breathed deeply in through the nose, out through the mouth, desperate to banish the incoming explosive images from my head.

Just close your eyes! Close your damn eyes. Don't look around. Focus on her beautiful breasts. Screen out the picture of climate chaos that was their apartment.

It didn't work. Try as I might, the combination of pot, an unfamiliar setting, and my general anxiety around women had made my climate radar kick into high gear. I was helplessly falling, flailing, unable to stop myself.

Be gone, ye demons! Out, out, you devils!

None of my manful efforts to silence the shrill voice of OCD had any effect.

Their apartment was a torture chamber, an inquisitor's tool kit of energy no-nos.

Disaster #1: Incandescent lightbulbs. The evil ones. Energy-sucking little bastards. Their apartment was full of them. Not one lamp had a compact fluorescent or LED bulb. *And they were all turned on!* It was the middle of the day and all of the lights were on—*all of them!*

Disaster #2: Everything else was on. And there was a lot of everything else! Three computers, two tablets, two Kindles, six digital clocks, the list went on and on and on. They had every electronic gadget known to human kind. Multiple generations of the same gadget. Their apartment was a virtual museum of electronic gadgetry. *And they were all turned on! All of them!*

Disaster #3: The heat was blasting and it was a beautiful September day. And the windows—the windows, for Christ sake—were *wide open.* I am not making this up. No wonder I was dripping sweat. It was pushing ninety-five in the apartment and *the goddamn heat was on!*

Disaster #3: The straw that broke the camel's back. There they were, lying in plain view for the whole world to see, as God is my witness—recyclables in the trash can. And not just recyclables but returnables. Three beer bottles and a Pepsi. *Returnables in the friggin' trash can!*

I desperately tried to focus on Twin Number One, who was inching, inching ever closer. She had taken off her sweater and I could see her nipples, hard and erect, poinking through her braless top. Her hand was on my thigh and her tongue was in my mouth and I was *losing it!*

I could now hear Jesse and Twin Number Two, giggling and frolicking in the back bedroom, oblivious to the living Climate Hell that was happening here, right here, at this very moment!

What was wrong with me? I breathed in and out, out and in, desperate to make my OCD go away. Make it stop. Don't be so crazy, don't think these crazy thoughts, don't let all of this crazy climate crap get in the way of fondling some absolutely fabulous breasts.

This was pathological. This was insane.

What was wrong with me!

"Are you okay?" Twin Number One asked. I think it was Patty.

"I don't know," I gasped. "I think I might have a clove of garlic stuck in my throat. All of a sudden I feel nauseated. I can't breathe. I need to step outside. I am so sorry. I feel like such a jerk but I have got to get some air!"

I got up, grabbed my bags of food from the farmer's market, and staggered out the door.

—

"What the fuck is wrong with you?" Jesse yelled. He had come back late that evening and found me curled up on the couch eating garlic cloves and watching the cartoon channel.

"You got up and walked because she didn't have the right lightbulbs? You forfeited your first chance in months to get laid because she had recyclables in the trash can?"

"Returnables," I whispered, eyes cast downward.

"What?"

"Returnables. There is a difference."

"Who gives a flying fuck! Jesus, Casey, there could have been the goddamn Hope Diamond in the trash and I wouldn't have given a shit. What the hell is wrong with you? She was twenty-something. She was hot. She wanted it. And you turned her down because she doesn't recycle?"

I couldn't look him in the eye.

"If I'm going to make love to someone, then I want there to be. . . ."

"Make love?" Jesse interrupted, incredulous. "Make love? Earth to Casey. Dude, no one was about to make love. You were going to have sex. Sex! Do you even remember what that is? Sweet Mary and Joseph, how long has it been?"

Once again, downcast eyes. It was not turning into a banner day for my self-esteem.

"God!" Jesse continued, spittle dribbling down his chin. Once he got on a rant like this there was no stopping him. "Please don't tell me it was with that visiting professor from Uzbekistan or Turkmenistan or Fuckistan or wherever the hell she was from—the one who didn't speak any English?"

"She spoke English," I replied.

"I hate to clue you, bro, but 'yes, yes, do me' is not fluent English. And that was, what, almost a year ago?"

It was times like these that I wish I had a woman for a roommate. A woman wouldn't go off on me like this. A woman would be empathetic, kind, adept at getting me to open up and talk about my feelings. She would wrap her arms around me in a roommatey, warm-and-fuzzy kind of way and tell me what a wonderful, sensitive person I was and how everything was going to be all right. She wouldn't launch zingers straight for the jugular.

Jesse banged his fist on the table.

"I know why you're so infatuated with her," Jesse said.

"Who?"

"You know who!"

"I don't know who you're talking about."

"You do too. The pirate. The Twenty-Nine-Year-Old. The teacher in your class."

"I am not infatuated with her."

"Please. Spare me. Do you know why?"

"Do tell."

"She's one of your students. That means she's forbidden, off-limits. You've set her on a pedestal and you can't get close enough to tear her down. She's your perfect woman."

"Once again, I don't have a clue what you're talking about."

"Sure you do," Jesse said. "Look at your dating life. It's a sad series of one-and-done. Do you know why?"

"No, but I'm quite sure you do."

"It's your OCD, dude. No one lives up to this ridiculous ideal you've set. They either drive a car that gets shitty gas mileage, they eat with disposable chopsticks, they don't know the parts per million of carbon dioxide in the goddamn atmosphere—there's always something, something that keeps you distant. Why can't you just take gorgeous breasts and progressive politics and be done with it? You're so over-the-top. I mean seriously, do you actually want them to be as obsessed as you are? That is a total recipe for disaster!"

"She doesn't eat with chopsticks."

"Who?"

"You know who."

"Dude, did you listen to a word I just said?"

"At least we have each other." I offered.

Jesse shook his fists in the air. "You know what else I'm tired of?" he said. "I am sick and tired of wasting all my time at my therapist's talking about how fucked up you are. Seriously. I never get a chance to talk about how fucked up *I* am. I'm too goddamn busy going on and on about you. There is just so much rich material there. Seriously, I can't compete! You know what?" He was practically screaming. I hadn't seen him this wound up since I lost half an ounce of weed at a party. The neighbors had no need to put their ears to the wall for this one.

I sighed.

"What?"

"I want my last three damn co-pays back. Twenty bucks a session. I want it back. All of it. Sixty bucks. Seriously—I'm not kidding. You owe me!" He stormed into his room and slammed the door.

Wallowing in self-pity, I slowly let another garlic clove dissolve in my mouth and turned to watch, my eyes watering, the coyote get blown to smithereens by the roadrunner.

9

I HAVE A LOVE/HATE RELATIONSHIP with really warm weather. The love part is the outfits women wear to class. These skimpy, lacey, borderline-see-through things that sometimes leave little to the imagination. Quite a feast for the eyes. I feel so lucky to be alive when those gorgeous late-teen/twenty-somethings come in struttin' their stuff. Oooh-la-la!

It almost makes global warming seem like a good thing.

The challenging part is keeping my baseball-cap-on-backwards, slumped-in-the-back-row guy crowd focuses off of their classmates' lovely rear ends and on *The* Issue.

Of course, keeping myself on track is not always an easy thing, either.

My students were taking their first quiz and Samantha was sitting in the front row. I was grading papers at the desk facing her.

There is something about women in their late twenties that is enough to make a grown man cry. They're at the absolute pinnacle of their physical peak; it's hard to imagine anything more spectacular.

Even my gay friends say the same thing.

Ralph, a guy I hang out with in the art department, told me once that one of the few times he has ever questioned his sexual orientation was on a sunny fall afternoon, painting outside, surrounded by his barely clothed female students.

"A very pretty picture," he said.

"Tell me about it," I replied.

Anyway, try as I might, I was having incredible difficulty not staring at her. *Gawking* is probably a better word. Cleavage, after all, is like heroin for the eyes. One look and you're hooked.

In my defense, it was important for me to glance up occasionally. Make sure no one was using cell phones to access information. No one was copying off of each other. Give my students at least the illusion that Big Brother was watching.

It was the looking back down that required superhuman effort.

My god, she was beautiful. Golden hair, a face full of freckles, breasts to die for, and a swimmer's body. It was hard to imagine anything more perfect.

Later that evening, I was folding laundry when the Roommate walked in. After his cascade of complaints about the usual suspects (incompetent boss, slacker colleagues, bullshit bureaucracy, no toilet paper in the men's room), he actually asked me about my day.

"I gave a quiz, and of course meanwhile I had a shitload of grading to do, but it was all I could do not to stare. Curse her for sitting in the front row! Curse her! I could hear every breath, every in and out. Every time she crossed and uncrossed her legs. Each time she nibbled on her pen. It was driving me nuts. I didn't get a damn thing done."

"Let me guess. The Twenty-Nine-Year-Old? The one you're not infatuated with?"

"Duh! Who do you think?" I sighed. "Oh my god, she has, like, the baby bear of breasts."

"The what?"

"You know, Goldilocks and the Three Bears."

"Dude, you're going weird on me again," Jesse said.

"The children's story. It was the baby bear's porridge, his chair, his bed. That's what Goldilocks chose. Not too big, not to small. Not too hard, not too soft. Everything was just right. That's her. That's Samantha. The baby bear."

"Hold on. Did I miss something here?" Jesse asked. "How do you know how hard or soft they are?"

"Hypothetically speaking. I'm telling you. She's beautiful. Goldilocks would have gone nuts!"

"Goldilocks was a lesbian, too?" Jesse asked.

"Asshole!" I threw a pair of underwear at him.

—

As previously noted, one of my favorite pastimes is eavesdropping on student conversations. I consider myself quite an expert on this subtle art. I'm a master at the casual tipping back of the chair, the looking engaged with something else when I'm not, the ear cocked sideways in a not overtly obvious way. It's how I gather some of my best information. While obviously partial to juicy tidbits about sexual indiscretions, vicious family feuds, inappropriate drug and alcohol use, and other fascinating glimpses into the dark side of student lives, I am, on occasion, willing to accept on-topic academic droppings.

I was at the cafeteria, attempting to be productive and grade papers, when a conversation struck me as worth tuning in to.

"No way!" Student #1 gasped.

"Way," reiterated Student #2.

"They actually shit on their legs?"

I tipped my chair back even further to get a clearer earful from the table behind me.

"Shit and piss. Evaporation works, dude. Cools those blood vessels on their feet right down. Urohidrosis. God, I even remember the name for it. Science word of the day in the lunatic's class."

The lunatic was my natural-history colleague. Walking past his classroom was always a treat. More than once I've heard him bellowing out obscure, bizarre nature vocabulary words.

"Know this, my minions!" he'd shriek. "It is, after all, the *Science Word of the Day!*"

Evidently *urohidrosis* was today's.

"Awesome bird!" applauded #2. "Eats road kill. Throws up. Shits on their legs. My kind of party animal!"

They went on to have a reasonably intelligent conversation about these particular party animals—turkey vultures, a marvelously adapted raptor. Evidently it was all fact. The mix of urine and feces on the bird's feet was an effective mechanism for cooling blood vessels.

"Dude," continued #1, "they're the poster child for evolution. I mean, it got me thinking."

Wow! Students thinking! It was every professor's dream come true. Here they were excitedly talking about a lecture while wolfing down burgers and fries. What could be better?

"I wonder if we're next?"

"What do you mean?" #2 asked.

"You know, with all this climate change shit going down, I wonder what we'll look like in a thousand years. Ears the size of elephants? Hairless? Wicked big eyes for seeing in the dark because you can't venture out during the day?"

"Dude, I dated someone who looked just like that," #2

laughed. "She kept telling me she was ahead of her time. I just never believed her."

"Look on the bright side," #1 said. "No more trips to the bathroom during keggers. Just let it go. Piss on your own feet."

"Dude! You do that now anyway!"

"That's because I'm so fucking evolved!"

Just then my chair, which had been tilting precipitously, got the best of me and I went sprawling to the floor. Students 1 and 2 leapt up to help me to my feet. The whole cafeteria stared in amusement.

I thanked them and slunk out the door, trying to avoid eye contact, once more painfully reminded that if life truly is the survival of the fittest, then I was completely screwed.

—

"Interesting. Very interesting."

The Roommate was in his weekend position, prone on the couch, laptop in lap, music blasting, pot smoke circling lazily overhead.

I had just come back from working out at the Glenfield Y, trying to stick with my new forty-minutes-on-the-elliptical-four-times-a-week routine.

"Hey," I said.

"Hey." He looked up. "My, you're looking buffer and buffer. She's going to have a hard time keeping her hands off of you."

"Who?"

"You know who. Captain Mad Sam or whatever you said her pirate name was."

"What are you talking about?"

"Check it out!" He turned the computer towards me.

"Christ! Now you're stalking her?" I took a hit off the joint and sat down next to him.

"Got to keep you in the loop, dude. There's news to be had."

I looked at the screen. There she was, a new picture of her up on her Facebook page, this time in proud pirate profile. It was the same outfit she had worn during Talk Like a Pirate Day. She had a huge smile on her face and she was kissing the stuffed parrot.

"I'd love to fire my cannon through her porthole!" Jesse murmured.

"Shut up. You're worse than my students."

"She'd find out why me Roger is so Jolly. I'd ask her to scrape the barnacles off of me rudder in an instant."

"God, that is so wrong. Will you please get off that page!"

"She is so hot! How do you hide your hard-on in front of the class?"

"Stop!" I tried to grab the laptop from him.

"Not so fast. Not so fast. Notice anything different?"

"No. What. Tell me."

"Look carefully."

Even though I could have stared all day, there wasn't a whole lot of material to work with. Just a few images.

"I'm not seeing it," I said. "What?"

"No more lezbo shot."

"Jesus, will you stop already with that. You are so . . ."

"Seriously, dude. The woman she was holding hands with—gone."

"You know, if it wasn't funny the first time then you can pretty much guarantee it's not going to be funny the tenth."

"Gone. Disappeared. This is good news, dude. I'd even call it great news. From lesbian to pirate. You must be working your magic. It's quite a switch! Unless, of course, she's a lesbian pirate, and in that case. . . ."

"Shut up!"

I got up, stormed out, stomped into my room and loudly slammed the door behind me. Christ, it was middle school all over again.

I lay on my bed, buried my face in my pillow and cursed my eternal adolescence, cursed my lame, thirteen-year-old brain trapped in a thirty-two-year-old body, cursed the squeaking goddamn hamster wheel that was my life, endlessly cycling through the fucking seventh grade. After all these years, I would have thought the bearings would have rusted, the wheel torn asunder, the metal chewed apart . . . but no, *squeak, squeak, squeak*, on and on it went, around and around and around, until all that was left were twenty-nine-year-old pirates glaring, snarling, laughing at what a loser I was.

Seriously, it was enough to make one piss on one's own two feet.

10

IT WAS A WEDNESDAY NIGHT and the Roommate had done it again. In all of my thirty-two years, I had never known anyone who could clog a toilet the way that he could.

"Christ!" I groaned. "I've heard of wanting to be regular but enough already. What is this, the third time this month?"

"Fifth," he said. "If you count the ones at work."

"Work? For God's sake, don't tell me you did it in one of those mega-industrial flushers?"

"Twice in one day, thank you very much."

"You're like a freak of nature," I told him. "How do you keep doing this?"

"Oh, so you've never clogged a toilet before?"

"Actually, no, I can't remember the last time I did such a thing."

"That's because you're always full of shit."

"Very funny," I said, trying not to smile.

"Anyway, we have a problem."

"No, you have a problem."

"Actually, we do. I broke the plunger."

"You what?" I asked.

"You heard me."

"How can you break a toilet plunger?"

"No clue. It snapped right in half."

"You've got to be kidding me. Jesus, you're amazing. Is there like a Guinness Book of World Record for this kind of shit? If so, you're there bro. Your claim to fame—number one on number two!"

"Thanks for the vote."

I groaned again.

"So, do you mind?"

"Mind what?"

"Going out and getting one?" Jesse asked.

"No, no, no, no, no. He who breaks it, gets it."

"Come on, you know I hate to drive at night. And my stomach is still a little on the queasy side from these three burritos I had for lunch."

"Jesus, no wonder you clogged the damn toilet! You ever heard of self-control?"

"You know my motto. Everything in moderation, including moderation."

"I'm not going."

"Please?" he begged.

"No way. I'm not going out at eleven at night and getting you a toilet plunger."

"Getting *us* a plunger. Remember, dude, there's only one toilet and you don't want to go anywhere near there. I can *see* the smell."

"Go across the street and borrow one from Scary Man," I said, doing my best to suppress the gag reflex.

Jesse genuflected.

Scary Man, in the house adjacent to ours, was always glaring at us. Three "Romney for President" signs dotted his lawn. His gas-guzzling car, which he'd let idle for what seemed like hours every morning before he left for work, had a bumper sticker with Obama and a slash through it. He incessantly, constantly, obsessively mowed his lawn.

He thought we were a gay couple. Just to annoy him we held hands and one time even kissed while he watched.

We hated him.

"Are you kidding me?" Jesse groaned again. "I can't even look in that direction without getting the heebie-jeebies. Come on, I'll fix dinner the next two nights."

"Four."

"Three."

"Done."

I grabbed my jacket and headed for the car.

I realized immediately that there was one significant problem. One huge obstacle standing in the way of a successful plunger retrieval mission.

The only store open at eleven at night was Walmart.

Walmart! God, I hated that store. I loathed it. I despised it. It creeped me out even more than Scary Man. It was the mistress of the big-box bitches. It epitomized all that was wrong with capitalism run amuck. Out to make a dime, they couldn't give a damn who or what they had to run over to get it—their workers, employee health and safety, small-town downtowns, the environment. If corporations were people, like our enlightened Supreme Court has so fascistically ruled, then Walmart should be tarred and feathered, water-boarded, and then lynched. Not necessarily in that order.

Ugh! Walmart! But the glaring reality was that we had a toilet to unclog. Desperate times called for desperate measures.

Cursing the Roommate and his prolific bowel movements, I headed out to the devil's store.

Depressingly enough, I could barely find a place to park. Almost midnight on a Wednesday and the store was absolutely packed. And, of course, finding any sort of live person inside who could help you was an absolute impossibility.

Attention shoppers: Best of luck finding anything!

Emergency supplies? Housewares? Toiletries? Where the hell would they put plungers?

After about ten minutes of fruitless wandering, I began to get paranoid.

One: What if I didn't find one? God knows, the house had been intolerable enough when I left. Coming home empty-handed was clearly not an option.

Two: Even more of a concern, what if a student saw me here? How would I explain myself? For all my vocal "shop local" and anti-corporate rhetoric, for all my litany of environmental atrocities that Walmart has spewed, getting busted here could significantly damage my reputation.

Three: Worse-case scenario, what if *She* were here. I couldn't imagine a scenario like that possibly unfolding, unless maybe she had experienced a similar clogging emergency.

I couldn't go there.

I began to sneak a peek down each aisle before venturing forth, furtively spying on shoppers for faces I knew, slinking from toys to women's clothing, and then, damn it, somehow back to toys again. I grabbed a pack of compact fluorescent lightbulbs as a cover, a pathetic attempt to mitigate the grossness of my shopping transgression should I get spotted.

I could plead an energy-efficient-lightbulb emergency; after all, I had to see in order to grade papers. Feeble excuse, but it was the best I could think of.

After what seemed like eternity, and on the verge of abandoning all hope, I stumbled around the corner of Kleenex and paper towels and, hallelujah, praise the Lord, there they were—toilet plungers! A rack to themselves, marked down to half price, three types to choose from. Victory was within my grasp!

I took what looked to be the sturdiest design, then went back and grabbed a second as a backup, and plotted my escape.

I was a shadow, flitting from section to section, unseen by shoppers' eyes, the Invisible Man. The checkout was within sight, the finish line in plain view.

"Hey Mr. C! What's up?"

I jumped. It was Charlie from the Climate Changers. Sometimes they called me Mr. C. It was a nondescript nickname that had stuck.

Curses for my bad luck!

"I wouldn't have thought I'd see you here," he said, smiling in what I took to be an evil kind of way.

"Hi, Mr. C!" said the checkout woman, a student in one of my classes.

Double curses!

I waved the two toilet plungers over my head and babbled some incoherent gibberish concerning roommates and bowel issues and mitigating circumstances.

The two laughed at my obvious discomfort.

Trying my best to hide my growing embarrassment, I checked out and started to leave the store. Suddenly, a man stepped between me and the exit, blocking my way.

"Excuse me, sir. What is that in your pocket?"

"What is what?" I replied.

He opened up his jacket and showed his badge.

"Walmart Security," it read.

He pointed to my pants.

I looked down and there, sticking out like a giant erection, were the light bulbs. In my anxiety over being discovered, I had somehow, inadvertently and stupidly, thrust them into my pocket. I had meant to hide the plungers, but where would I have put them?

"Shit!" I cried. "Seriously, I had no idea. I mean, I am not a shoplifter. Especially from this store!"

"Excuse me?" the guard said, raising his eyebrows.

"No, no. That's not what I meant. Seriously!" I was totally flustered. "I grabbed these as a cover. You know in case I got caught."

"Caught?"

"No, no, not that kind of caught. I would never do something like this. Shit!" I cried again.

After a brief interrogation, fortunately lacking tar, feathers, water-boards, and rope, plus outstanding character references from both giggling students, I was somehow allowed to go free. Minus, of course, the lightbulbs.

"I hope you had a nice shopping experience," the Walmart greeter said as I made my escape.

I managed to self-edit and, wanly, smiled back.

Reputation? What reputation!

—

What keeps me going and glowing, as a teacher, are those truly spectacular gems of moments when what goes down in my classroom is nothing short of brilliant. I'm on, the students are on. There's animated discussion, witty asides, articulate back and forth. So many lightbulbs (compact fluorescent of course!) flashing above student heads that it sears the ceiling. No one antsy or disengaged, no squirming or fiddling with backpacks.

Class ends and students seem reluctant to leave. Some don't. They remain, immersed in passionate discourse, still hammering away at saving the world. Enough "aha!" moments in an hour and a quarter to fill a pirate's treasure chest.

When the room empties, I sit on my desk, pat myself on the back, and think, Wow, damn good class. Socrates, you got nothing on me, bro.

It certainly makes work worth getting up in the morning for.

All right, so that's only happened a few times in the last

five years. Well, maybe twice. But when it *has* happened: Somebody stop me! Absolutely awesome.

Then there are those times, unfortunately quite a bit more frequent, when things don't go as well as one would hope. Classes that, frankly, suck.

Really suck.

Like yesterday.

I was droning on and on and on about the difference between direct causality and structural causality. How you couldn't blame this last single extreme weather event on climate change (there was no direct cause and effect; A was not directly responsible for B) but there was a structural systemic basis for causation. I know, I know, you probably just fell asleep reading that last sentence. But I thought it was interesting. Important. Something I thought that we all need to know.

The problem was no one else did.

Even the best and the brightest were doodling, drooling, outright snoozing. Those still awake stared wistfully at the clock, counting seconds imperceptibly limping by in slow-mo.

Even the Twenty-Nine-Year-Old, my go-to talker, contributor numero uno, was off in La-la Land, utterly immersed in nibbling on her cuticles.

Something was screwy with one of the overhead lights. It flickered on and off and on. Mesmerizing. A monotonous annoying buzz came from down the hall, one of the electricians drilling away, oblivious to the fact that I HAVE A CLASS TO TEACH!

Occasionally when I'm teaching I have a surreal out-of-body experience where I seem to float ever so gently up to the ceiling and observe my class from a perch high above. Maybe it was the residual pot still in my system, maybe it was actually happening, but there I was, hanging with the blinking light, witness to the pedagogic disaster unfolding below.

I could see myself, plain as day, dialing up the dull-as-dishwater blah-blah-blah with no end in sight. No interaction with the students. No eye contact. Other than cuticle munching, the blinking overhead light, an annoying snore from one of the boys-in-the-back, and the increasingly agonizing buzz from the hallway, there was nothing. Absolutely nothing.

I asked the class a question.

"Anyone? Anyone? Anyone?"

No response. My lips were moving but their brain cells were clearly not receiving. The entire class was lost in a vast intellectual wasteland.

But hey, I thought to myself, I'm powering through it, right? Every day can't be Einstein and Ecstasy. At least no one was. . . .

NOOOOOO!!! The girl with the pink hair and multiple piercings! The silent one in the back corner! There was no mistaking it. I could see the twitching fingers and the poorly hidden flashing screen.

"Cynthia!" I shouted, desperate to make my voice menacing.

Students stirred. Eyes opened.

"You dare to text in my class?"

"Sorry," she said, visibly embarrassed. "It was important."

Like all teachers, I tragically suffer from another acronym: TIM—Texting Induced Madness, a.k.a. Text Rage. There is nothing—*nothing*—I hate more. Prominently displayed in big bold letters on my syllabus, as the first of my Classroom Ten Commandments, is the pronouncement:

THOU SHALT NOT TEXT IN CLASS!

"Important?" I yelled, my body plunging from the ceiling with a large thump. Finally I had the class's attention. I banged my fist on the table. "*Important?* Do tell, please enlighten me—what is so much more important than the fate of the earth?"

Cynthia squirmed. I knew I was pushing it. I knew

I should end it right then and there but I was in a pissy mood and it was a shitty class and I just had to take it out on someone. I shot her my most vicious evil eye.

"Well," Cynthia stammered. "My boyfriend's at the market and doesn't know what kind of frozen burritos to get for dinner."

BOOM! It was as though lightning had struck the room. Like a bomb had dropped. The class, comatose a moment ago, sprang miraculously to life.

"Where is he?" someone shouted.

"Stop and Shop," Cynthia replied.

"What the hell's he doing at Stop and Drop? He should get his tush down to Vera Cruzana. You can't get a burrito worth crap at Stop and Shop!"

"I beg to differ, hombre!" piped up one of the boys-in-the-back with the backward baseball caps, his first words of the entire semester. "To the left of the pizzas. Morey's Burritos. They rock!"

"Morey's?" yelled his neighbor, leaping out of his seat, shaking his head incredulously. "Morey's? Are you clinically insane? You want her to be glued to the shitter all night?"

These had been brain-dead folks snoozing through a dull class and now voices were rising, tempers flaring, accusations flying. Fingers were pointing at each other in a threatening way. Even Samantha had gotten in on the action and had abandoned her cuticles to loudly debate the fineries of burritos with one of her classmates.

Poor Cynthia, still frantically texting away, seemed on the verge of tears.

I was speechless. The class had erupted into total, complete chaos over burritos! Burritos! Not the environmental case against overly packaged, additive-infested supermarket burritos. Not the environmental merits of slow food and lovingly cooking your own. That I could have handled. That I could have dealt with. But the fur was flying around which fucking brand of frozen burritos to buy!

Climate change had been totally trumped by a rising tide of burrito bedlam.

Certainly not my finest hour.

As the threat of violence escalated with punches soon to be thrown I was saved by the light. There was a *zap* and a *pop* and all of the classroom lights sputtered out, plunging the room into darkness—a fitting metaphor for the afternoon lecture. I could hear a string of curses from the electrician down the hall.

I gave up. Total defeat.

"Chapter 3!" I hollered hopelessly as students, still locking horns in the battle of the burrito, fled from the darkened room. "Thursday! Chapter 3!"

Grasping at straws, I took solace from the fact that even Socrates must have had bad days, losing it with disciples who surreptitiously passed stone tablets to each other under the table, or whatever the hell else went down back in the day.

As the wise man himself said: "Education is the kindling of a flame, not the filling of a vessel." The trick seems to lie in fanning the fire and keeping it burning in at least the general direction you want, rather than have it roar off into raging BIM: Burrito Induced Madness.

After class, feeling fatigued and unmotivated, I left school early. In somewhat of a trance I drove to Stop and Shop, where I found myself dazed and confused and frozen in place at the fast-food freezer, paralyzed with indecision about which damn burrito to bring home for dinner.

11

"WHAT'S WRONG?" Jesse asked.

Usually when I came home from meditation class I was the personification of peace on earth—relaxed, calm, one with the universe, comfortable in myself, once again ready to face life's curveballs.

Not so this time.

"I'm fucked," I groaned. "I can't go back. I'm cast out. Done. Finished. Kaput!"

"What are you talking about?"

"Sometimes I amaze even myself!" I flopped down on the couch, scrunched a pillow over my head, and groaned again.

I could hear Jesse shut down his laptop, lean back in his beat up La-Z- Boy, stretch out his legs, and roll a joint.

"So you amaze even yourself," he repeated, but in a Sigmund Freud accent.

Silly accent aside, he was a good listener. Often his advice sucked, but at least he listened.

I had been going, on and off, to a meditation center for over a year. "Practicing" as they say. It was a mindfulness-based stress-reduction program, the focus of which was to calm the mind.

Which, needless to say, I was in desperate need of.

I lived with a constant CNN ticker tape scrolling horrific factoids down the bottom of my brain screen. Other than a few, often restless hours for sleep, it ran pretty much 23/7.

"2012: *Worst drought since the '50s!*" it would scream.

"*Fires blaze through Texas!*"

"*Temperatures expected to rise eight degrees!*"

Endlessly cycling on and on and on.

For years I had tried the "whack a mole" strategy. Every time an evil factoid reared its ugly head: *BAM!* The hammer came down. Hard!

Glaciers melting?

BAM!

Polar bears dying?

BAM!

Republicans obstructing?

BAM! BAM! BAM!

The problem was, it didn't work. The factoids were like the heads of the mythical Hydra: chop one off and two grew in its place. I was aware that somehow Hercules had sealed the deal and figured out how to end the madness, but, truth be told, I was not him.

Mindfulness-based stress-reduction seemed a much kinder, gentler approach.

As the monsters emerged, I would gently acknowledge them, observe them, and allow them to pass on through while I got back to the breath.

Back to the breath.

Always back to the breath.

I removed the pillow from my head just enough so I could take a hit. Fortunately, when meditation failed, there was always pot to take the edge off.

"So," Freud continued. "Tell ze doctor vhat happened."

"You know the woman who runs the show?"

"The guru."

"Christ, you sound like my mother. She's not a guru. She's a meditation leader. There is a big difference."

"Whatever. Go on."

"You know how I've, um, had issues around her."

"Yes. Difficult to focus on the breath when you're focusing on the breasts."

The doctor spoke the truth. The woman who led the meditation group was absolutely gorgeous. In the prime of her fifties, she was the living refutation of the bald-faced lie that women in the second half of their century couldn't continue to stun. When she would direct us to close our eyes and enter that zone of tranquility, that place of peace, I was constantly cheating and sneaking a peak at those fabulous breasts of hers.

As I noted previously, second only to climate change on my list of compulsive obsessions were women's breasts. After all, what can be more perfect? Shape, texture, feel, look, smell. The single, or rather double, package has it all. Everything about breasts spells beauty.

On that issue I pity heterosexual women and gay men. I really do. I mean, look at a guy's chest. Man-boobs seem ridiculous, out of place, the nipples just some comical, vestigial remnant. I mean, hello, why are they even there? What is the point?

Women's, on the other hand—wow!

There is simply no comparison.

I'd try and match my breath to the rise and fall of her breasts. I knew our meditative exercises were meant to clear the mind, but it could be difficult to keep those gorgeosities out of my head. In any event, they were certainly a much more pleasant image than dying polar bears.

A number of months earlier Jesse had suggested I join another group, practice with some old, decrepit guy who would not lead my mind astray.

Yeah, right. As if that was going to happen.

I took another hit and continued.

"So, she was leading us through a guided meditation: 'We are a lake. While the winds may whip whitecaps and the surface froth and churn, deep in the interior we are unruffled and serene. No matter how rough the weather, inside all is calm. . . .'

"It was a lying-down meditation. I was stretched out on my mat, feeling her voice, being the lake. . . ."

"Salivating over her breasts," Jesse said.

"No. Not at all. For whatever reason I was all about the water. Or so I thought. Anyway, her voice was so soft, so soothing, I went totally under."

"That's it?" Jesse asked. "That's all you've got for me? I've never been to a meditation session where I didn't fall asleep."

"Let me finish. I'm totally out. Zonked. Probably snoring and screwing it up for everyone else. Next thing I know she's gently shaking my shoulder. The exercise is over. Everyone else is sitting up. And I'm still lying there, all eyes on me, with an enormous hard-on."

"Visible?"

"God yes! I've got these tight yoga pants on and my damn thing is sticking straight up like the Washington Monument."

"Come on now, bro. Don't kid yourself. No making mountains out of molehills."

"Thanks. That's helpful. It really is. I mean, I couldn't even sit up."

"Were people gawking? Laughing? Pointing?" he asked.

"How am I supposed to know? I was drowning. Drowning in the damn lake! With a boner the size of Superior."

Jesse laughed. "But hey, your mind was free from OCD."

"Only to be held hostage by EF."

"EF?"

"Erectile Function."

"Wow. Out of the frying pan into the fire."

"God. Why do I always feel like I'm in middle school?"

"Aha! Now ve are finally getting somevere," Jesse said, laying on thick the Freudian accent.

"What are you talking about?" I asked.

"The source of the fantasy is revealed. 'Tis not the guru you desire, but someone else."

"Start making sense or I want my money back."

"Think about it. Middle school. Fantasy woman. Doesn't take Freud to get to this one."

"Oh god. Get a life!" I said, annoyed. "What am I going to do? I can never go back there."

"To seventh grade? Count your blessings!"

"No! To the meditation class, moron."

"Watch your name calling. Freud has feelings too you know!"

"My apologies. But seriously, I like that class. It's helpful. It keeps me marginally sane. And now I can't go back."

"*You* can't go back?" Jesse said, grimacing. "What about me? I'm stuck forever with this god-awful image seared forever in my brain of you lying in a lake of yogis, your boat's paddle sticking straight up, front and center, for the whole world to see. Once again, thanks to you, I'm scarred for life. More fodder, and money, for my therapist."

I took another hit and closed my eyes, forbidding The Issue or meditation leaders or even middle-school science teachers from interfering with the breath. And desperately, desperately willing myself to stop paddling against the goddamn wind, to stop drowning or sinking or even treading water and just be one with the breath and the lake.

Only this time without the hard-on.

October

12

I HAD REPLIED TO AN E-MAIL from Nurture Earth, a retreat center in one of the Berkshire towns that offers a variety of programs on pressing environmental and social justice topics. They were promoting an evening of "climate action through spiritual awareness." While generally not one to jump on the New Age bandwagon (I usually run the other way, screaming) I was intrigued. The facilitator looked interesting, the price was right, a scrumptious vegetarian buffet was promised prepared by "The Mistress of Berkshire Vegan Chefs," and, once again, I was dateless on a Saturday night.

After considerable bribery (cleaning the toilet—*yuck*—for the next three weeks), I got Jesse on board. He was, as he put it, "in between" women and had nothing better to do. Not exactly a ringing endorsement—but, hey, I didn't want to go it alone.

A drive through the Berkshires on an early October afternoon is absolutely stunning. We puttered along on Route 9 through the center of Williamsburg, up the big winding hill through Goshen and into the cute-as-a-button town of Cummington. One can see why all those damn leaf peepers trek hours from Boston and New York City, in fact from all over the world, to witness Western Massachusetts in all its autumnal glory.

Once, a few years ago, a Cadillac with New Jersey license plates stopped beside me in downtown Glenfield.

"Where are the leaves?" the driver barked, her accent unmistakable, from her open car window. Two cameras dangled from her neck; she had a video cam in one hand, a cigarette and the steering wheel in the other while the big car idled away.

"Excuse me?" I asked

"Where do I go for the leaves?" she squawked.

She was parked under perhaps the most beautiful red maple tree in the Connecticut River Valley. It was at its absolute height of brilliant fall foliage. Reminiscent of a Thomas Cole or Albert Bierstadt painting from the Hudson River School of landscape artists, the sun streamed in and detailed each lobed leaf in perfect redness. At that very moment it was hard to picture any tree, anywhere, more spectacular than that one red maple.

I picked up one of the fallen leaves and solemnly handed it to her.

"Ma'am," I said, choking back fake tears. "You have just run over the very last one!" Then I silently walked away.

Kabam! Take that, New Joisy!

We drove to Nurture Earth on just such a day. Blue, blue sky, glorious leaves, ideal temperature. It just didn't get any better.

When we turned down the long, winding road into the conference center, Jesse perked up.

Women. Beautiful women. Long, flowing, flowery dresses and skirts, red maple leaves tucked in their black and auburn and golden hair. It was a spectacular sight.

"This could work!" Jesse said as he checked his nose

for creepy crawlies in the rearview mirror. We parked and followed the throngs to the building's entrance.

"Hi!" I said to the women at the door. "We registered for the program."

They looked back at us awkwardly, exchanging perplexed glances with each other.

"Hmm . . . there seems to be some confusion. You are . . . ?"

"Casey," I said, "And friend."

"And you're here for . . . ?"

"Climate action through spiritual awareness. The workshop this evening."

"Well, ahh . . ." There was a long pause. "There seems to be a bit of a mix up. You see, tonight's event is . . ."

She was interrupted by a burst of bustle and I was practically tackled from behind.

"Casey! What the hell are you doing here?"

It was an old friend from a sister community college. A wonderfully quirky colleague who taught social action and environmental studies. She was a whirlwind of energy and hope and faith and good work. A great role model for me.

And a very out lesbian.

Smothered in her embrace I managed to catch my breath enough to reply.

"Becca, how are you?"

"Fabulous!"

"Here for the program?"

"Of course. Wouldn't miss it for the world. And you?"

"As well," I said, and introduced Jesse.

Rebecca laughed out loud, an open mouthed hurrah of a laugh that turned heads and brought smiles.

I was confused. She was always an ode to joy but, even for her, this was a little over the top.

"Well, well, well," she snorted. "Just like you. Don't move. Let me see what I can do."

She turned and sashayed away, leaving Jesse and me, somewhat perplexed.

The greeters at the door were dealing with other women and left us standing to the side.

As I watched folks enter and get settled, it dawned on me—they were all women. We were the only guys there. Just us two. This was clearly a dude-free gathering.

"Fabulous," Jesse whispered. "These women are friggin' gorgeous. And no competition!"

"Christ," I groaned, scrunching my shoulders and massaging my temples, waiting for Becca's return.

She bounced back with a twinkle in her eye.

"Didn't read the fine print, now did we?" she said, grinning that marvelous grin.

"Excuse me? Fine print?"

She held out the flyer. Prominently displayed on the bottom, in big, bold font, clearly not to be missed, was "THIS IS A WOMAN-CENTERED EVENT."

"Whoops," I replied sheepishly.

"Androgynous names will get you anywhere, you sneak! Look," Becca said. "This program is seriously underenrolled. I can vouch for you. These are my people. Hang out in the car and let me see what I can do."

We slunk back to the vehicle. Jesse reached into the glove compartment.

"Put the fucking joint away!" I admonished him. "It's bizarre enough as it is without you getting high."

He took a hit and passed it to me.

"Only one," I said, drawing the smoke in deeply.

Twenty minutes later, happily stoned, we were dreamily watching leaves flutter in the wind. The Roommate was on a roll, contemplating why it was that all the nice women were lesbians. Becca tapped at our window.

"Sorry it took so long," she said. "But good news—the sense of the group is wonderfully inclusive. If you're still into it, you're welcome with open arms."

She took a sniff in the air. "Shit. You two are a trip!"

An apt remark, given that the rest of the evening was just that.

Activity #1: Introductions and a loud "Hurrah!" from the group as we stumbled in.

"Our token men!" one shouted.

"Oh my god! How did they know?" Jesse whispered.

"Token, not tokin'," I whispered back.

Activity #2: The best buffet ever. Scrumpdillyumptious feast of local food and vegan fare fit for queens and two interloping kings. Straight out of gourmet heaven. With our marijuana-fueled cases of the munchies reaching a resounding crescendo, our complete inability to even moderately restrain ourselves was ridiculously apparent. Some of the women looked on in obvious horror, some gasped in delight, but all but the most oblivious must have felt a wave of awe watching two human bodies consume such a vast quantity of food in so short a period of time.

There was not a crumb, not a single morsel, that was not, by far, THE MOST DELICIOUS FOOD EVER EATEN BY A HUMAN BEING!

While scheduled as a time for introductions and sharing, the few words coming out of my mouth consisted mostly of "mmmppphhhh" and a barely audible "Excuse me while I get *even more!*" Jesse left twice to go the bathroom so he could create additional room for the feeding frenzy.

Much to his relief, and mine, the toilet remained, miraculously, unclogged.

Activity #3: Drumming and venting. In a tight-knit circle we beat and pounded away on drums; congas, bongos, an African drum known as a *djembe*, a Native American hoop drum. My hands and fingers were beings unto themselves, alive and powerful. We wailed, chanted, groaned, and cried out against the injustice of a world burning up, against corporations that put profits over people and the rest of creation, against the apathy and ignorance that paralyze so many of our sisters and brothers.

At one point Becca leapt up, spun into the center of the circle and twirled and whirled her way round and round as drums cried and mantras called forth kindred spirits to help put an end to the madness.

Activity #3: Lecture and discussion facilitated by a speaker vibrant and compelling. Much of her talk centered on an eco-feminist philosophical paradigm arguing that ecosystem abuse and exploitation was deeply rooted in misogynistic practices and androcentricity.

She passionately argued that men viewed nature the way men viewed women—as inferior, as lacking intrinsic worth, as ripe for the plucking. Rape was rape, whether of women or of the world's resources. The need to bring equality to the sexes was as important as bringing equality to the rest of creation. Perhaps the second could not be done without the first.

As we were the only guys, this could have been insanely awkward and visibly uncomfortable for us. Thankfully, it wasn't. In a large part thanks to Becca, the group had embraced us as kindred spirits.

"Nature is not a foe to be conquered but a lover to be revered!" the speaker thundered.

"Yes!" we cried.

"Mother Earth is not a demon to be exorcised but our home to be nurtured."

"Yes!"

"Change the relationships between men and women. Change the relationships between humans and the earth!"

"Yes!"

I was transfixed. Mesmerized. Never had I felt my estrogen levels so high. The woman in me was bursting forth. My penis felt oddly out of place. I reached down and massaged my breasts, surprised that they hadn't become engorged and enlarged.

Jesse was on the verge of tears. I reached out and held his hand.

Activity #5: Action steps. In small groups we sat around and brainstormed ways to save the world. Marches, letters to the editor, civil disobedience, boycotts, divestment, education, education, education—the list went on and on. Fabulous, tangible must-do lists.

Activity #6: More drumming! More venting! Dancing, chanting, singing! Raging against the machine!

Activity #7: Dessert! Yes!

And then it was over. Goodbyes and goddess bless and thank yous. We walked to the car, alive and thoughtful. I felt higher than I had when we had walked in the second time.

"How'd you two stoners do?" Becca asked as we were getting ready to pull out.

Mildly embarrassed, I stopped the car, opened the door, and gave her a huge hug.

"It was a wonderful evening." I gushed. "Absolutely wonderful!"

Jesse nodded.

"Thank you so much for making it happen."

"Hey, no worries. Next time there's a guy only event, count me in," she said, smiling. .

"Don't hold your breath," sighed Jesse. "Guys don't do shit like this. We're too . . ."

"Fucked up!" I finished.

"That's the spirit!" said Becca, slapping me on the back. "Keep that attitude up and we really will fry in hell on earth!"

"No, no, no!" Jesse sputtered. "That's not what we meant. It's just that, you know, guys are, well . . ."

"Fucked up," Becca finished.

"Exactly."

"Well, you guys are working on it. Be the change you want to see. And do yourselves a favor, will you?"

"Anything." I replied.

"Next time, read the fine print!"

"Are you kidding me? And miss something like this?"

Becca laughed once more, that raucous, life-affirming, celebratory laugh, and pounded the back of the car as we drove away delightfully soothed and comforted by the fact that we were not alone.

13

OFF WE WENT ON A BEAUTIFUL SATURDAY MORNING in October to Quonquont Farm in Whately to pick apples. It had become an annual fall ritual, eagerly anticipated. When the leaves reached their pinnacle of peak—mapley reds and birchy golds and oaky browns—it was apple-picking time.

I went with Jesse and his new lust, Sarah, one of the nurses from the hospital. He'd been chatting her up for weeks and had finally convinced her to go apple picking. Why exactly I was along was a bit of a mystery, but evidently this was not a "date" but an "outing." The Roommate, for all his bluster and bravado, was a lot like me: socially awkward and generally scared to death of women.

I was happy for him. He'd been wanting to get involved with someone for a long time. The one-night (or afternoon, as was the case with the Farmer's Market escapade) stand was not his thing, nor, obviously, mine.

The "outing" had certainly started out awkward enough. The whole drive up, Jesse was talking out of his ass about apples, making a somewhat feeble attempt to impress his non-date.

"I must admit," he said. "I'm somewhat of an apple snob. But there is something so endearing about Cortlands. They have a crisp, robust flavor, an excellent accompaniment to seriously sharp cheddar."

I coughed into my hand, stifling the gag reflex but managing to keep my mouth shut. Just before we had left home, Jesse had furiously surfed the net memorizing apropos apple lines. I don't know if these were supposed to be a turn-on or what, but clearly they were not doing the trick.

Sarah stared out the window, visibly bored. I could read the bubble words forming over her head: "I wasted an entire afternoon for this? Why?"

"I've never been one to ogle over Red Delicious." Jesse continued.

'Ogle over Red Delicious'? Jesus, enough already. He was sounding like a fruitcake. Even I, spaz that I was, wouldn't come out with a line like that.

"I mean, they have their place, I suppose, but give me a good Cortland any day."

"What's not to like?" Sarah said, grimacing. "That crisp, robust flavor."

Oh god, she was on to his bullshit.

Jesse blushed, clearly floundering. He glanced in my direction with a deer-in-the-headlights look. "Help!" He flashed. "Help!"

I had to do something, fast, or this would be yet another one-and-done.

"You know," I jumped in, "for all of his apple-y good deeds and his preaching of the apple gospel, evidently Johnny Appleseed was one seriously weird dude. I guess he ran off with some thirteen-year-old girl, whose father found out and then went after him. It was all very warped."

"That's bizarre," Sarah replied, perking up. "You mean there really was a Johnny Appleseed?"

"You better believe it," Jesse chimed in, shooting me a gracious "thank you" look.

"John Chapman, a.k.a. Johnny Appleseed, born and bred a few towns over in Leominster. Quite the character. Barefooted, vegetarian, clothed in a coffee sack, orchard planter, proselytizer of apples and the holy gospel from Massachusetts to Ohio."

The Roommate had done his research on the god of apples as well.

"You like animals, right?" he continued.

Sarah nodded.

"I guess he was quite the animal-rights dude. Story is that he once quenched his campfire because mosquitoes were flying into the blaze and getting burned. 'God forbid that I should build a fire for my comfort, that should be the means of destroying any of his creatures,' he said. Or something like that." Jesse used his best Appleseedy voice on that one, weird but effective, eliciting the first real smile from Sarah.

"Another time he slept out in the snow rather than disturb a mother bear and her cubs from the hollow log he was hoping to crash in."

"A man ahead of his time," Sarah replied. She was getting into it.

"And apples. Damn if he wasn't the one that made them America's fruit. He'd be like one step ahead of pioneer settlements, planting an orchard and waiting for folks to catch up. As soon as they did he'd offload the real estate, move west, and plant another orchard. Quite the guy."

"Sounds like it." she said.

"Did you know apples weren't eaten until like the 1900s or something?" Jesse continued.

"What do you mean weren't eaten?"

"Nobody ate them."

"Then what'd they do with them?" she asked.

"They drank them. A lot of the water in early America

was unfit to drink, so they'd take apples and make hard cider and drink that. The alcohol content zapped the bad shit. Christ, it was the drink of choice even for kids. Everybody had a buzz on!"

"Seriously?" Sarah asked.

"Seriously!" Jesse said.

I breathed a sigh of relief. Sarah had stopped looking out the window and was looking at Jesse. Things had clearly picked up.

"But did he like Cortlands?" Sarah said smiling, visibly impressed with the wealth of apple knowledge spewing forth.

"Worshipped them. Adored them. I'm convinced they were his hands-down favorite."

"Along with thirteen-year-olds."

"Yuck!"

After more idle, apple-y chitchat, we finally pulled off of Whatley Street and onto the dirt farm road leading to Quonquont. It was a winding lane leading up a hill, and dust kicked up behind us and a big sky opened up in front. A Jacob's Ladder moment when the rays of sunlight streamed through the gaps in the gorgeous clouds, looking like a stairway to heaven.

We pulled the car over and gazed in wonder.

A woman, looking somewhat bedraggled and harried, came out from the apple barn.

"Look at the sky!" we gawked. "Absolutely beautiful."

"It is," she agreed. "It really is. I wish I could say the same about the orchard."

"The orchard? What's wrong with the orchard?"

"No apples," the woman sighed.

"What?" I said. "You're all picked out already? But it's so early!"

"No. I mean no apples. We got no apples this year. None."

We looked down the hill and onto the beautiful, green

apple trees below. Row after row as far as the eye could see. Healthy, vibrant trees, each one appleless. Not a single piece of fruit on any tree. Not a one.

"Oh my god!" Sarah gasped. "Why?"

"March," frowned the orchardist. "Remember those ten days of summer this last March? Ten days with temperatures over 80 degrees? Fooled the trees into blooming. And then, *bam!* A few freezing nights in April and the entire crop was gone. Nothing. Healthy trees. No apples."

Sarah looked like she was going to cry. Jesse put his hand lightly on her arm.

"Bummer," he said.

"Yeah," the orchard woman replied, her voice tired and sad. "Big time. No apples. We can only hope for a good crop next year, but with all the weird weather, I don't know. I just don't know. We can only hope."

No apples? *No apples?*

What kind of fucked-up metaphor was this? What a slap to the face to the Apple God himself. Jesus! If Johnny Appleseed were here right now he'd be crapping his pants!

I looked out over the orchard and saw his ghost rising over the barren fruit trees, forlorn and foreboding. I could see him giving us the finger as he ascended Jacob's Ladder. I could hear his voice booming out over the valley, startling squirrels and spooking crows and knocking the leaves off of fruitless trees: "Look around, man. Look what you've done! Do you get it now? Do you? NO FUCKING APPLES!"

I pounded the steering wheel in frustration, accidentally honking the horn.

"Don't go off!" Jesse turned to me. "Please, I don't want to hear it. Seriously dude, think it, don't say it! I don't want this trip to turn into one depressing drag!"

"Say what?" Sarah asked.

Jesse whispered in her ear.

"Just what I was thinking," she said. "You guys don't like to talk about it?"

"It's all we talk about," Jesse groaned. "I was hoping for a little bit of a respite. Check the OCD at the door, at least for the afternoon."

I sighed, visualizing my breath, acknowledging the negative, pushing it right on through to the other side.

Or at least trying to.

But no apples!

Jesus! Had it really come to this?

"How about miniature golf?" Jesse offered. "Not that either of you would stand a chance. I am somewhat of a master at the sport. Similar to what I am in so many sports."

"Crisp and robust?" Sarah said, giggling.

"More like full of shit!" I said, rolling my eyes and, relegating the climate demons to the trunk of the Prius.

We waved to the orchard woman. I turned the car around, and we drove out of the appleless apple orchard.

Next year there would be apples.

There had to be. There just had to be.

14

IT WAS THE MIDDLE OF OCTOBER. Another beautiful New England fall day with the sky blue, blue, blue and the leaves kissing the season goodbye (or was it hello?) with a symphony of color.

The college had gotten its act together and, however long overdue, finally entered the solar age by finishing construction on a 100-kilowatt photovoltaic array behind the East Building. What had begun as a reasonably priced, quick-to-build project had run up against typical state bureaucratic ineptness with excruciatingly long delays, cost overruns, fiscal mismanagement, contractor bungling, lack of communication on all sides, and a general cloud of confusion and bewilderment.

No real surprises there.

Nonetheless, all sing hallelujah! A bit shy of eternity later, there emerged on the south-facing hillside a wonderful harbinger of the new world: 100,000 watts of emission-free solar-generated electricity.

It was a great beginning.

I had been a thorn in the administration's side since the day I was hired, advocating, cajoling, pressuring, begging the college to put our money where our mouth was and begin the long and arduous process of weaning ourselves from fossil fuels and going solar. The problem that reared its ugly head again and again was, while we had a shitload of mouth, we had a pitiful amount of money.

The Development Office had put in a tremendous amount of work and patched together a hodgepodge of funding that included federal stimulus monies and state grants, but it still wasn't quite enough to install the size of the solar electric system we wanted. Finally, after much animated discussion, they had convinced a private funder to step forward to put the project over the top.

The knight in shining armor just happened to be Sendak Oil, the major distributor of fuel oil in Franklin County.

"Oil whore!" Jesse cried, a look of mock horror on his face. It was perhaps the fortieth time he had accused me of that. Each time he seemed to get off on it just a little bit more. If anyone could work a joke to death it was Jesse.

"Who would have thought you'd turn into Satan's slut. After all this good work, to see you prostitute yourself to . . ."

"Stop!" I begged. "We got the money. The project's finished. How about congratulations?"

"Congratulate you while you suck on the tit of fossil fuels? Go on—slurp, slurp, slurp away. Oooohhh, give it to me, baby!"

"Are you finished?"

"Who's your daddy? Come on, tell me?" he asked.

"Jesus, it's not funny. Particularly after the millionth time."

"Tell that to Satan. He's laughing his ass off. Counting the days till he fries yours in hell!"

"This is what I love about you!" I told him. "You're so supportive. I work my tail off getting funding for a solar project and this is what I get."

Jesse danced around the room with finger horns on his head.

"Kiss me, darling! Smooch, smooch! Come on, baby! I have such a hard-on!"

Sigh.

I had to give him credit. He did, after all, have a point. It had taken a considerable amount of angst and a good bit of wallowing in guilt for me to finally get on board with the idea of extracting blood money from the devil. Not exactly my cup of tea, but what's a guy to do? Take the money and go solar, or stick to your guns and remain a 100 percent fossil-fuel addict?

Sigh again.

For all the high-level talk from President Obama on down, community colleges always seem to be a tuition check shy of insolvency. Forever doomed to teeter on the fiscal cliff. Politicians from both sides of the political aisle wax eloquently about the importance of community colleges, their bright future, their remarkable opportunities and vocational pathways and saving graces. But when it comes to funding we always seem to be last in line. It's hypocrisy at its best.

Go forth and do good work, but just don't expect us to pick up the tab.

So we end up having to take money whenever and wherever we can find it. Beggars can't always be choosers.

And it wasn't like Sendak Oil was any Shell or Exxon. They were a pretty dinky local player, a family-owned business with a wonderful reputation for community involvement. It was awfully hard to look a gift horse like that in the mouth, even if they had blood on their hands.

Given my involvement, I had been asked by the dean to give a short speech at the dedication of the solar array.

Which is where we were on that sparkling "let the sun shine" October day.

Quick joke: What do you call it when there is a massive spill of solar energy?

A nice day!

It was noon on a Wednesday, the only time at the college that offered a possibility of getting people out for an event. On one level, I was really pleased. There were quite a few faculty and staff present, including all of my colleagues in the science department, the dean and even the college president. There was a local state representative and an aide to our U.S. congressman, both of whom had helped secure funding. A reporter and a photographer from the *Glenfield Recorder* were there.

And for all his bitching, Jesse, in a great show of support, was also there. I knew he would be. And I was pleased to see he had Sarah the nurse with him.

A date or another outing? Hmm . . .

The bulk of the crowd seemed to consist of the entire extended Sendak family, from the patriarch in a wheelchair to the great grandkids in strollers, pleased as punch to be the celebrities of the day.

Try as I might to get pumped for my speech, I was bumming.

There were no students there. None.

I couldn't believe it. I had talked it up in all my classes. The Climate Changers had put up flyers and assured me they'd be good to go. We had done reasonable Web and e-mail publicity. I had even fantasized about you-know-who showing up on her lunch break.

But there were no students.

I was pissed. Pissed and disappointed. If not even a single member of the undergrad set could even bother to show up on a beautiful day to welcome in the solar age, we were totally screwed.

Damn!

Well, I thought, what are you going to do? Even without students it was a decent crowd.

I took a last glance at my notes as the dean droned on and on about philanthropy and civic engagement and community support and what an inspiration the Sendaks were to all of us, blah, blah, blah.

There was, of course, the speech I was going to give and the speech the Roommate had written for me to give.

Frankly, his was much better. I smiled as I thought about it. That speech went something like this:

Hey—Sendaks. Yeah, I mean you! Wipe those shit-eating grins off your faces, assholes. Now! You've had years making obscene profits at the expense of the entire planet and you want to be thanked for this piddly shit? Are you fucking kidding me? Let me tell you Sendaks, if you think this one act of hypocritical generosity is going to get you a special place in heaven, think again. You're going down, bro. All of you. You're going to be the ones Down Under rolling this stinky, gooey ball of oil up the flaming hill of hell only to have it explode in a fiery mass and roll back down again. And again, and again. For eternity. Eternity! That's almost as long as it's taken to build this damn solar array! Even Sisyphus had more laughs than you're going to have! I can just see it now, bro—the damn Devil hootin' and hollerin', laughing his fool head off with his pitchfork up your ass. Burn, baby, burn!

This was to be immediately followed by a rush of the crowd at the mini–oil barons who would then be tarred and feathered and run out of town on a rail. Not that I was quite sure what any of that actually meant, but I figured that whatever it was they had it coming.

Jesse had nailed it. Short, to the point, totally capturing the essence of my feelings. Also, unfortunately, quite certain to get me fired on the spot.

And, to top it off, they'd probably want their solar array back.

I opted for a different tactic.

The dean finally shut up and sat down to a smattering of polite applause, so now it was my turn. Hiding my disappointment over the MIA students, I cleared my throat and stepped to the mike.

"Thank you, Sendaks [blah, blah, blah]; thank you, Development Office [blah blah blah]; thank you, State and feds and dean and everyone else involved [blah blah blah]."

Boring, but safe.

I did manage to get an impassioned paragraph or two in about The Issue and the imperative to *move* and that this was a *first step along the path to a carbon-free campus* and how *solar was the way to go* and that the *time to act was* NOW!

I was almost done, just wrapping up my last *This is our moment!* when, lo and behold, from behind the East Building came a rumbling, ragtag mob of students. Dressed in solar yellow, holding signs that said "YES!!!!!," they came racing up the hill singing, dancing, tumbling, somersaulting! They circled the crowd, grabbed the mike from me, and, who else but Hannah and Trevor, led us all in a chant:

"What do we want?"

"Solar!"

"When do we want it?"

"Now!"

"What do we want?"

"Solar!"

"When do we want it?"

"Now!"

They were out in full force—the Climate Changers, students from my classes, ex-students, students I had never seen before. There must have been a hundred or more of them including—gasp!—*her!*

They'd been there all along, hidden behind the East

Building, timing their arrival for maximum effect. And it had worked. Really worked!

The crowd loved it. Most of all the Sendaks. The old one lifted himself up out of his chair, grabbed his cane and began dancing with the little ones.

"Yes!" we all shouted. "Yes!"

I had tears in my eyes. It was absolutely beautiful!

"Great to see you!" Samantha smiled, as the festivities wound down. "Great speech. And congratulations! I gotta run, got someone to cover for me during lunch. See you tomorrow!"

She gave a wave and waltzed away, sunshine in a woman's body.

It was, as I said, absolutely beautiful.

15

TUESDAY WAS TRAVELING DAY, and just our luck, the weather was absolutely perfect. Blue sky, sunshine, the nip of fall newly in the air. How many days in a row could it be like this? There was no better time than fall in New England.

A fabulous day for a solar home tour.

Each semester I take my students to two solar houses.

The first is a modest, newly constructed home in Montague Center—three bedrooms, two baths, walk to town. It has all the efficiency features and renewable technology so essential for conscientious new construction: extreme insulation, passive solar, photovoltaics, a heater the size of a hair dryer. The owners are passionate and gracious.

The second house on the tour is Bramble Hill Farm, a renovated farmhouse, a stereotypical back-to-the-land, down-home, funky kind of place, dripping with old New England grace and charm. Not old-and-in-the-way but completely renovated, with the latest in high-efficiency retrofits and solar installations.

No solar McMansions on this tour. No millionaire estates, no houses priced obscenely out of the realm of anything but my students' wildest financial fantasies. Just two wonderful homes that emphatically demonstrate how the future of renewable energy is now.

My students liked the first house. They learned a lot. They got how it all fit in. They clearly witnessed the profound relationship between how we live and The Issue.

They liked the first house but they absolutely loved Bramble Hill Farm.

Bramble Hill Farm is the home of the garlic lady and her hippie husband from the farmer's market. I first met Lonnie and Jacob, Bramble Hill's farmers, at a climate change conference in Worcester three years ago. Lonnie's the one the Roommate says I have a thing for. They came loaded with a basket of newly picked greens to share—lettuce and arugula and radicchio and spinach—plus a few garlic cloves to chew on, and words of practical, down-to-earth wit and wisdom that absolutely blew me away.

I've taken my students to their farm every semester since.

The two worked in the health care field in Boston for almost thirty years, he as a medical researcher, she as a nurse practitioner. Then, about five years ago, they up and fled the big city for the dinky hill-town hamlet of Conway, population 1,800. There they bought an old, run-down, dirt-cheap farm, planted a market garden and an orchard, got a few hives of bees, twenty chickens, and three geese, and hand-built an enormous, 3,000-square-foot commercial passive-solar greenhouse. They have a little Community Supported Agriculture (CSA) setup and sell at two farmer's markets and Glenfield's Market, the local food coop. While garlic is their main gig, they grow and sell all sorts of wonderful organic produce. Lonnie and Jacob are just about as happy and content as two people can possibly be. The move fulfilled a lifelong dream for them, a welcome goodbye to all those sick people back east, and a happy hello to a new life and a healthy earth.

Their homestead is a showpiece of energy efficiency and renewable energy. A testimonial to possibility. You can't walk off their property without a fervent belief in the power of good people to do good work in the world. You leave brimming with hope. Inspired.

My class drove to the two sites. I was desperately hoping to carpool with Samantha, the thought of which had kept me tossing and turning, sleepless, the previous night.

I had rehearsed witty, off-the-cuff remarks I would make to her that would reveal the depth and breadth of my knowledge on an incredibly wide range of fascinating non-Issue-related topics. I had planned to lead with a fascinating tidbit or two on European classical architecture, deftly move into a non-pretentious commentary concerning the ongoing crisis in Syria, and then close with women's sports trivia. With help from Jesse, I had spent two and a half hours googling in preparation.

As always, reality reared its ugly head, and I was stuck transporting the usual assortment of social outcasts: those carless, odd-duck misfits too shy or socially awkward to ask for rides, their only recourse being to bite the bullet and tag along with their professor.

And by now Samantha had developed quite a fan club and her posse of young fellow women students had insisted that she ride with them.

This trip in my car I had an interesting mix: an autism-spectrum genius with no social graces, an underage dual-enrollment student (high school and college) whose youthful know-it-all-ness and naïveté had alienated all of his classmates, and a first-year overeager brownnoser who laid on the crap thick and fast at the drop of a hat.

"I just love this class, Professor," she began.

I turned my head and rolled my eyes. I had figured

out years ago that anyone who called me "Professor" had motives to be scrutinized very carefully.

"I can't believe how much I've learned already. I mean, who knew, you know, about the environment and stuff? You have such a gift for teaching."

I cracked open the car window to let out the stifling stench of bullshit.

We were greeted at the farmhouse by Lonnie and Jacob, baskets on their arms, offering us, you guessed it, choice greens and cloves of garlic to munch on during our visit.

It was hard to imagine these two ever having lived anywhere else. It was if they were born on this very farm, an image straight out of Grant Wood's American Gothic, he with overalls and a pitchfork, she with black boots up to her knees, a checkered flannel shirt, and a feather in her cowgirl hat.

My students took to them instantly.

We got a tour of the 17 kilowatts of photovoltaic ground-mount arrays producing enough solar electricity to power not only their house but their greenhouse as well. Anyone who squawked that solar was ugly had never been to Bramble Hill Farm. The glistening arrays, set against a backdrop of family, farm, and field, were hypnotizing. One student had a fly buzz right into her mouth, it was open so wide.

"This place rocks!" Brownnoser gasped, seriously meaning it this time.

We strolled through the passive solar greenhouse and stared in awe at the twelve-foot-high tomato plants bursting with blazing balls of plump, juicy red deliciosities. The greenhouse used no outside imported sources of energy. Nothing was burned, nothing went up in smoke. But solar energy kept it toasty warm even on those chilly February days. And when the sun got really cranking on sunny winter afternoons, warm air was blown from the top of the greenhouse to a rock-filled bed below, where heat was stored and then fanned out during the night. Against the north wall were 150 or so 55-gallon drums, filled with water, that would absorb heat during the day and slowly release it at night. No wild temperature fluctuations here.

In the summer, the pitched height of the greenhouse made for a chimney effect that allowed warm air to rise up and out the top north-facing ventilation windows.

Amazing!

It was like a living thing, the greenhouse. Breathing on its own. An endotherm, able to control its own temperature and keep itself in equilibrium, in harmony, in balance.

Lonnie and Jacob had even given it a name.

Alice. Alice the Greenhouse.

"Named after Alice in Wonderland, of course," Lonnie explained. "Precocious little girl that she was. Alice, meet the class."

"Hi Alice!" my students replied in unison, unprompted.

We went inside their 200-year old postcard-perfect farmhouse. Not one of these drafty and dreary relics from the dark ages but cozy as could be, with attic and walls and foundation now superinsulated. Triple-glazed windows with window quilts to hold in the heat at night. Thermal-siphoning air panels on the south-facing walls, solar hot water, and even more photovoltaics on the south-facing roof.

"Does the house have a name?" a student asked.

"House," Lonnie said, passing around another bowl of garlic.

"Hi House!" chorused my students.

Priceless.

We went down to the lower gardens, a smorgasbord of everything you can sell in a farmers' market. A cornucopia of fall produce. Terraced slopes of chard and broccoli, sugar snap peas, yummy pods and all, and five types of bizarre, crazy-colored, winter squash. No monocultures, not even mini ones, here; the sweet potatoes were nestled in with the cauliflower, its brainy white head touching roots with rutabagas, carrots, and enormous, almost scary-looking leeks. Everything was mulched to the max to save water and weeding. Christmas lima beans wound their purple tendrils up a wooden tepee fifteen feet high, fully loaded with enough protein to feed the entire class and more. Edges of grapes and black raspberries, high- and low-bush blueberries, some picked out or gone by, some still bursting with fruit. Five hives with manic worker bees rushing out in a frenzy to sip the last of the fall goodies from goldenrod and aster, and then returning to regurgitate it back into their miraculous combs as liquid gold, nectar of the gods, wildflower honey.

And, of course, the garlic. Bed after bed of wondrous garlic. The air was thick with its potent smell.

I read somewhere that garlic is the third-most-powerful aphrodisiac in the world, next to oysters and honey. Bramble Hill Farm had two of the three covered. Here I was, chewing on a piece of Purple Stripe garlic while bees buzzed through the air and Samantha was bending over one of the beds . . . oh yeah, the garlic was certainly having an effect on me.

"Come on," Jacob said. "The best is yet to come. On to the animals!"

And they were the cutest animals. Goats that they milked to make three kinds of cheeses, butting heads and leaping into the air like jumping beans on steroids. Baby bunnies that we all got to hold, which nestled under our shirts and stuck their quivering noses out at us, much to the delight of the entire class, who let out a collective "ooohhh!" over their off-the-charts cuddliness.

It was fall food heaven, a locavore's dream come true.

All had been awe and wonder till we ventured to the chicken coop for the last leg of the tour.

The best laid plans . . .

"It's not often you see one of these," bragged Jacob, patting himself on the back. "Designed and built by yours truly. A passive-solar chicken coop, guaranteed to keep these girls happy. And a happy chicken is a laying chicken. Water drums in the back, thermal mass to hold heat, even their very own PV."

"Do the chickens have names?" asked one of my students, continuing the theme of the day. As he spoke he leaned back, accidentally unlatching the henhouse door, which swung free and wide open.

"Whoa!" yelled Jacob. "Shut the—"

Too late. Before you could say "Down the Rabbit Hole," out raced three geese, which, for whatever reason, had made themselves at home in the chicken coop.

"Don't panic!" yelled Jacob, clearly panicking. "They can smell fear!"

The worst thing you can yell in a difficult situation is "Don't panic!" Those two words are about as terror-inducing as they come. When someone yells "Don't Panic," people panic. It's human nature, for Christ sake, and my students were certainly no exception.

Geese are birds with issues. Big birds. With big issues. Never the most pleasant of creatures, they seem perpetually pissed off, down on themselves, down on each other, and down on the whole damn world. Releasing them into a group of scared-silly college kids was an absolute recipe for disaster. At least for us.

The geese were pumped.

The three burst out of the confines of the chicken coop, hissing and squawking and aggressively flapping their wings.

Chaos ensued. Absolute total chaos.

"Run!" yelled the brownnoser, high-tailing it for the greenhouse. Students scattered, laughing and shrieking.

The three geese, a heckling, taunting, triangulation of trouble, made a beeline toward Samantha and her posse.

There was something about that woman that was irresistible, even to the friggin' geese.

Her dander up, Samantha instinctively stepped in front of her gaggle of girls (the human ones, not the geese), stiffened her back, and protectively held her hand up in a stop sign.

"Halt!" she cried, staring down the geese.

Middle-school matron or not, she failed to impress the geese, which clearly couldn't give a shit.

The lead one, a big, white bully of a bird with an evil eye and a diabolical hiss, reared up and pecked her right between the breasts.

A stunned looked on her face, Samantha took three steps backwards, stumbled over the pitchfork, and toppled head over heels into the farm pond. She disappeared for a moment and then came up sputtering, muck and ooze dripping off of her.

In situations like this, what is a guy to do? Take control? Shout out commands? Calm his unruly herd? Gallantly rush to the rescue of his maiden in distress and slay the beastly dragon, or in this case, goose?

Far from it! The whole time the crisis was brewing, this guy stood stock-still, rooted to place, mouth agape, silent, paralyzed with fear.

Students had barricaded themselves in the greenhouse. One was on top of his car. The brownnoser had climbed a tree.

Meanwhile Jacob, pitchfork in hand, had corralled the three troublemakers and herded them back, squawking and hissing, into the chicken coop, latching the gate securely behind them.

Lonnie, quick to the rescue, had rushed into the pond and helped Samantha out of the water and onto her feet. She sloshed her way out to a warm round of applause and audible gasps of relief from the rest of the class.

I forced myself to look away.

One, I was mortified. Here had been a golden opportunity for me to make quite the hero of myself, to show off my masculinity, or at least to come out looking mildly respectable. Instead I had played the gawking statue, not exactly a tribute to manliness.

Two, she had on a white button-down shirt which, when wet, was really quite revealing. Next to nothing was left to the imagination, and, once more, the connections between her and Goldilocks were made readily apparent. With everyone's garlic high just kicking in, more than one pair of student eyes remained glued to that soaking-wet top.

Finally, with superhuman effort, I forced myself out of my daze and confusion, and attempted to reclaim some sort of control over my class.

"Holy shit!" I cried as I turned to Samantha, physically pushing my chin up with my hand in a vain effort to avert my gaze from her breasts. "Are they, I mean, are you all right?"

Everyone laughed, including the geese, who hissed and honked as if they had planned the whole damn escapade just for our benefit. Which they may very well have.

Fortunately, procrastination occasionally has its advantages. I had neglected the night before to unpack my clean laundry from the trunk of the car and, mumbling apologies, I handed the first items I could find to Samantha. While the class huddled in groups, yukking it up and giggling like middle-schoolers, she took a quick trip into the house to change. Apparently none the worse for wear, she soon returned to the scene of the crime with my PVCC spring softball uniform on, a ragged pair of PVCC sweatpants and a T-shirt with my name and number on the back.

I made a mental note never to wash them again.

Once more, there was a warm round of applause from her fellow students.

It's amazing what an incident like this does for class bonding. You can try every trick in the pedagogical book, every ice-breaker, every getting-to-know-you opener, but—mark my words—nothing, *nothing*, brings students closer together than a terrorist attack by manic geese.

On the ride home, my three carpoolers chatted non-stop. The incident at the farm had made them instant best buddies. Much to the delight of the other two, the know-it-all was reviewing highlights of the afternoon festivities, hilariously imitating voices (even the goose's) with remarkable accuracy. The brownnoser was going on and on about the "best field trip ever" and "double, no triple, wow," and I was convinced she wasn't bullshitting. She even referred to me as Casey, not Professor. And, all the while, the autism-spectrum kid had miraculously emerged from his awkward shell and was fast and furiously hitting on her.

And doing it quite well. By the time we were pulling into Parking Lot E he had her phone number.

Emotionally exhausted, I finally staggered back to my office. It was late. The science studio was vacant, my colleagues had all headed home, and adjuncts had yet to come in for evening classes.

Things clearly had not gone as planned, yet, as the brownnoser had said, this could very well have been the most effective field trip on record.

Let's face it: ten years from now, how much were students going to remember from my class? Probably not much. But they sure as hell weren't going to forget Bramble Hill Farm. A fact or two about solar power was bound to get lodged in one of those vast labyrinths of neural pathways, along with geese and pitchforks and wet, white button-down shirts. How could it not?

I was just shutting down my computer and getting set to head home when who else but the dean strolled into my office. Wheezing and huffing, he plopped his heavy frame down in a chair.

"How goes it, Professor?" he asked.

For the most part, the dean and I got along quite well. We weren't exactly buddy-buddy but our relationship was generally cordial and productive. Except, of course, when it wasn't.

He rarely made a visit to my office unless something was up. I anxiously attempted to read his face. Nada.

"Another day in paradise," I answered, my standard reply to authority.

"Another good day I hope?" he asked, his eyebrows edging up. "Or was it, shall we say, something of a wild goose chase?"

I forced a smile—an ashen, pallid smile, more like a grimace that accompanies gastrointestinal distress or severe constipation. He was on to me, he had me by the short hairs, and he was clearly taking delight in my discomfort.

He paused for dramatic effect, just to watch me obligingly squirm.

Bastard. Out with it!

"I just had an interesting encounter with a student in the cafeteria," he continued. "I approached her, thinking it was you, but clearly she was not."

I gulped. I did not like how this was going.

"Red flags always go up when I see attractive students wearing their professor's clothing."

Damn! Why did I have to go and loan her my softball uniform? What was I thinking?

Freud would have had a field day with that one.

"Whoa, whoa, wait a minute." I stood up awkwardly. "I can explain."

"No need to," he motioned me back to my seat. "She already did."

I held my breath. There was no telling with the dean. Sometimes he was as kind as Gandhi, other times more

Attila the Hun–like. I waited to see which side he would come down on.

"Something about a solar home tour and geese from hell?"

"Well," I said, exhaling. "You see, we were just finishing up a lesson on photovoltaics. I thought a visit to the . . ."

He made another hand signal, a slash across the neck that not so loosely translated as "shut the hell up."

"She was quite forthcoming with the details," he went on. "I see no need of additional ones from you."

There was another long awkward silence, he all the while glaring at me, me desperately attempting to once again avoid all eye contact.

"Just when you think you've heard it all," he sighed. "Attack geese! Boy, this is one for the books!" He hauled his massive bulk up and off my chair.

As he reached for the doorknob he turned and shot me one more killer glance.

"She made one rather bizarre comment."

I waited with bated breath.

"She said you're the best teacher she's ever had. The best. Odd, don't you think? One gets mauled by killer geese, nearly drowns in a pond full of chicken shit, and then raves about the one who was responsible for it all?"

He glared at me, eyebrows raised once again.

"Rather, peculiar, no?"

Without waiting for a response he left, shutting the door behind him and leaving me, for the second time that day, frozen in place, speechless.

16

'Conservationist' Told Not to Unscrew Bulbs
Amherst—Police over the weekend issued a verbal
warning to a Gray Street man who they say has been
unscrewing porch lights in his neighborhood for the past
two months.

Police say the man was caught unscrewing a porch light
at 100 Gray Street after residents there set up a video
camera and nabbed him in the act.

Police said that, when questioned, the man admitted to
unscrewing porch lights and stated that he did not want
to see electricity wasted. He claimed no other motive other
than "electric conservation," according to police.
— Daily Hampshire Gazette

No doubt I now grew very pale; —but I talked more
fluently, and with a heightened voice. Yet the sound
increased—and what could I do? It was a low, dull, quick
sound—much such a sound as a watch makes when enveloped in cotton. I gasped for breath—and yet the officers
heard it not. I talked more quickly—more vehemently;

but the noise steadily increased. I arose and argued about trifles, in a high key and with violent gesticulations; but the noise steadily increased. Why would they not be gone? I paced the floor to and fro with heavy strides, as if excited to fury by the observations of the men — but the noise steadily increased. Oh God! what could I do? I foamed — I raved — I swore! I swung the chair upon which I had been sitting, and grated it upon the boards, but the noise arose over all and continually increased. It grew louder — louder — louder! And still the men chatted pleasantly, and smiled. Was it possible they heard not? Almighty God! — no, no! They heard! — they suspected! — they knew! they were making a mockery of my horror! — this I thought, and this I think. But anything was better than this agony! Anything was more tolerable than this derision! I could bear those hypocritical smiles no longer! I felt that I must scream or die! and now — again! — hark! louder! louder! louder! louder!

"Villains!" I shrieked, "dissemble no more! I admit the deed! — tear up the planks! here, here! — It is the beating of his hideous heart!"

— Edgar Allen Poe, "The Tell-Tale Heart" (1833)

"BASTARD!" THE ROOMMATE CRIED as we pulled into our driveway.

I looked over in the direction he was pointing.

There, across the street, in front of the scary neighbor's house, the guy we hated, was a newly installed enormous, inflatable Halloween decoration. It was a ghost, fifteen feet tall, waving its arms, its bloated hideous face lit up from every possible angle.

"Jesus!" I said, grinding my teeth.

"Bastard!" Jesse repeated, slamming the car door and stomping into the apartment.

Jesse and I hated all inflatable yard decorations: Christmas, Easter, Halloween, whatever — it really didn't matter.

We hated them all with a passion, but we hated this one with an unbridled intensity.

Reason #1: The Issue. It was an energy-sucking monstrosity. Stepping out of the car we had been immediately inundated with the droning hum of the ghost's electric fan as it pumped the arms half-full of air so that they could flap at us maniacally. Lights had been installed, illuminating it like the Washington Monument—small Christmassy lights, big spotlights, enormous search lights—enough electricity to power the entire neighborhood, and then some, for the next decade. I was surprised the neighbor hadn't been required to build his own coal-fired electric power plant in the backyard so that he could run the damn thing without overloading the grid. People were driving in from out of town, thinking it was the opening of a new mall. It was probably visible from the friggin' space station.

Reason #2: It looked stupid. Really stupid. Unless you were between the ages of four and seven, or your IQ hovered around the 70s or below, no one could possibly think this piece of crap was in the realm of cute. No one. It was like a gigantic sign in the front of the neighbor's lawn declaring in no uncertain terms that the owner of this humble abode is a total and complete moron and deserves to be run out of town! All of which was true.

Reason #3: With all due respect to parents with little kids, Halloween is supposed to be a scary holiday. Its purpose is to awaken the spirits, let the dead walk, turn loose the zombies. Ghosts are supposed to be terrifying specters from the other world, the undead. The thing waving its arms at us from across the street was the exact opposite. It was a happy-go-lucky Casper with a shit-eating grin, the antithesis of Halloween, a travesty of terrifying. The five-foot-high letters spelling out "BOO!" with smiley faces in each "O" were outlined with excruciatingly annoying blinking lights that induced epileptic seizures from unknowing passers-by.

We hated it.

We also hated the house at which it was installed. It was the scary-man house with the idling car, never-ending lawn mower, and Romney signs. The same one we couldn't possibly even entertain borrowing a toilet plunger from. We didn't know the man, but we hated him anyway.

And now this hideous fiend flap, flap, flapping away.

Bastard!

Jesse was seething. He paced the floor waving his arms, mimicking the ghost but with each of his middle fingers extended. He cursed the neighbor. He used words that made even me blush.

"He's done it now. He's crossed the line!" he cried. "How the hell am I supposed to sleep with that thing mocking us?"

"I don't think you can hear or see it from your bedroom." I answered.

"What the fuck? Are you taking his side? Jesus, the thing is haunting me already and I've known about it for all of five minutes."

"I agree. It's an abomination. But there's not much we can do."

With each passing day the ghost seemed to loom larger and larger. We awoke to its flapping in the morning, we went to bed to its flapping at night. We spent hours getting high, staring out the window, and cursing it. We became obsessed with its presence. It stared straight at us, waved in our direction, that damn smile fixed on its face, its sole purpose to invade our dreams and drive us ever closer to the brink of insanity.

I dreaded coming home from work. Jesse and I went out to dinner three nights in a row, something we had never done before, just so that we could eat with some semblance of peace and quiet.

The situation had become intolerable. Something drastic had to be done.

—

I was at work Friday when a call came in from the Roommate.

"I've got it!" he whispered, desperation in his voice.

"Got what?"

"It. The solution. About the situation."

"What situation?"

"THE SITUATION, you fool!"

"Tell me!" I whispered back, playing along even though I still didn't have a clue as to what he was talking about.

"I can't."

"What do you mean you can't?"

"I can't say anything on the phone. Someone might be listening."

"Look, if you're still going on about her holding hands with some . . ."

"Jesus! Drop it! The ghost!" he said.

"Oh," I replied, relieved we weren't going *there* again.

"Ransom," he whispered.

"What?"

"Ransom!"

I could hear someone in the background.

"Right!" Jesse loudly spoke. "Why don't you try turning it off and then turning it back on again. Call me back if it still doesn't work." He hung up the phone.

—

That night, Jesse, joint in hand, excitedly outlined his plans for the 2012 Great Halloween Ghost Caper.

It was not overly complicated. We were, under the cover of night, going to un-tether the beast, confiscate the illuminating bulbs, disconnect the fan, and hold the whole kit and caboodle hostage.

"That's stealing!" I argued.

"No it's not. It's ransom. There's a huge difference!"

The plan was to leave a note. Outline our objections, highlighting the energy issue. Give conditions for its safe return.

We weren't heartless bastards like he was. We were reasonable. We were open to compromise. We'd allow it to run from 6:00–9:00 p.m. on weekdays and 6:00–10:00 on weekends.

We could have taken a hard line. We could have knifed the son of a bitch. Left it for dead. Deflated, tattered and torn.

But no. We were better than that.

I had to hand it to Jesse. It was a masterful plan. Bold and brilliant.

It recalled the words of a 1960s-era politician I couldn't stand who once famously said: "Extremism in the defense of liberty is no vice."

This was clearly one of those difficult times that called for extreme solutions.

If it had to be ransom, then ransom it was!

—

It was Friday night, two weeks before Halloween. Dressed in black, stocking caps on, high as kites, we waited till after midnight and then silently slunk across the street.

We had spent hours going over our plans. We had made a map of the neighbor's front yard, incredibly detailed, down to the very last light. We were well rehearsed with backup plans and alternative escape routes. We had the timing down to the minute.

Watching for cars, totally paranoid, I disconnected the fan and ran it back across the street while Jesse, gloves on, unplugged and bagged the miles of stringy light bulbs. I slipped the ransom note under the door. We both lay on top of the ghost, deflating it as quickly as we could. Flopping it into a wheelbarrow, we sprinted back home.

Joy of joys! In a matter of minutes victory was ours! Navy Seals would have nodded their heads in approval. The operation had gone off without a hitch. The ghost was vanquished!

Our ransom note, made from words cut out from newspapers, had stipulated that if the owner agreed to our conditions he should show an American flag in the window. God knows he had them. There must have been a hundred or more waving from his yard every Fourth of July.

A little bit of patriotic bullshit seemed to put a positive spin on our action. Show the flag and the victim would be returned.

I was pumped.

That morning, after a fitful sleep with considerably more tossing and turning than snoozing, I awoke to cursing from Jesse.

"Damn!" he yelled. "Damn, damn, damn!"

He burst into my room.

"Get up. Now!" he yelled shaking me. "We are in deep shit!"

There, in front of the evil neighbor's house, was a police car. The neighbor and an officer were talking, the neighbor pointing out the scene of the crime. He was holding what looked to be our ransom note and gesticulating wildly.

Peering out from behind the curtains, barely breathing, we watched with rapt attention. Finally, the conversation ended, they shook hands, and the officer drove away.

"Was that a smile on the face of the cop?" I asked hopefully.

"That was no smile," Jesse whimpered. "That was a serious grimace. That was an I'll-hunt-these-felons-down-if-it's-the-last-thing-I-do! look."

"Well, it's probably all over now," I reassured him.

"Over? Over? Christ, it's just begun. They're on to us! I know they are! What if we left fingerprints on the note? What if they track us down? Christ, why did you talk me into this?"

I decided not to remind him whose harebrained scheme this was to begin with.

"I can't imagine that the police don't have more important things to deal with than something as silly as this," I replied, nervously laughing.

"Are you fucking kidding me? This is the kind of shit they love. Traffic violations, drunken driving, bar fights— Christ, those things are a dime a dozen. This is the real deal. This is the kind of crap that gets their blood flowing. It's probably grand theft larceny or something. I bet it's the talk of the station."

Jesse could be quite the drama queen. He loved to blow the magnitude of minutiae way out of proportion.

But there was something . . . something about that way the cop had looked in our direction.

The weekend was miserable. A cold, driving rain combined with creeping paranoia to keep us indoors, jumping at our own shadows, quibbling with each other over nothing, pacing back and forth, continually peering out from behind the curtain at the house across the street. I was unable to concentrate, nothing kept my attention, my stockpile of grading stared me down.

And then I heard it. A distant noise. At first I thought it came from across the street but then I realized, no—goddamn it, no! It was coming from inside our house. From the basement! I had to cock my head to make sure.

Thump, thump. Thump, thump. Thump, thump.

I fancied it was just a ringing in my ears, but Jesse heard it as well. The day dragged on, the sound grew louder and louder. We put on music, paced the room, covered our ears but the wretched noise only increased. We were too scared to leave the apartment. Too freaked out to stay. An untenable situation.

The pot only made things worse.

Thump, thump. Thump, thump. Thump, thump.

On and on it went until my skin tingled and my goose bumps felt on the verge of popping.

It was late on Sunday. Forty-eight hours since we had done the deed. Forty-eight hours of pure hell.

I hadn't slept. I hadn't eaten. All I'd done was smoke a tremendous amount of weed and endlessly obsess. Jesse, disheveled and wild eyed, paced the floor to and fro with heavy strides, foamed, raved, and swore. I had taken to muttering to myself and jerking involuntarily. Neither of us could even look at each other.

I couldn't hack it a moment more.

Thump, thump. Thump, thump. Thump, thump.

"We've got to do something!" I said. "We've got to do something now!"

Jesse, teary and trembling, wordlessly agreed.

Holding each other's hands we crept down to the basement, sweating and whimpering.

There was the victim, half in and half out of the wheelbarrow, the head eerily cocked in our direction, the eyes wide open and accusatory. There was no more grin on its face. It was a scream. A howl from hell.

And the noise! The god-awful noise!

THUMP, THUMP! THUMP, THUMP! THUMP, THUMP!

We opened the basement door, and not even caring if there were car lights, frantically pushed the wheelbarrow, ghost and all, back across the street. Dumping the victim on the porch steps, we raced back to the apartment, grabbed the lights and the fan, and made another run. Taking the corner into our yard a little too quickly, the wheel of the barrow went right over Jesse's big toe. He stifled down a scream.

"No doctors!" he whispered. "No doctors!"

Not daring to turn on lights, huddling in the dark, we spent a sleepless eternity as his toenail turned a dark, deep, ghostly blue.

"Bastard!" Jesse cursed.

Ghost and neighbor: 1.

The Roommate and me: 0.

17

IT COULD NOT HAVE BEEN A FROSTIER DAY to protest global warming. After a series of spectacularly beautiful and balmy weeks, the third Saturday in October was cold as hell. A biting wind whistled down the Connecticut River as folks gathered at the public boat ramp in Easthampton for the march on the Mount Tom Coal Plant.

The facility sits on a beautiful stretch of the river, a designated National Fish and Wildlife Refuge, in Holyoke. An interesting juxtaposition — one of the most destructive things on the planet next to one of the most gorgeous ones. Go figure.

Every day, 1,200 tons of pulverized coal are shot into Mount Tom plant's thirteen-story boiler to heat water to make steam to turn a turbine to rotate a magnet around a coil of wire to get electrons all hot and bothered and create the magic of electricity. Granted, it's a little more complicated than that, but hey, how much do you really need to know?

The mind of the inventor is a constant source of amazement to me. I mean, seriously—electricity? Who came up with that one? I know Ben Franklin did the kite-and-key thing but for the life of me I can't fathom how they got the skinny on the rest of it. Shocking!

I'm challenged enough figuring out which clicker actually changes the channel on the damn TV.

I used to worry about how little I knew. I used to obsess endlessly about what would go down if my students ever caught on to the profound depths of my ignorance. There are times when I'm teaching and I think to myself, Wow, what a scam! Do they actually think I have a clue as to what the hell I'm talking about?

Once, in a dismal attempt to rectify my intellectual shortcomings, I went so far as to get a CD titled *Electricity for Dummies*. I forced Jesse, my captive carpool, into listening to it on our morning commute. By the end of the second chapter he was ready to rewire the house. The only info I had amassed was an even greater fear of anything with a plug on the end.

As a way to deal with information overload, there are certain topics I've simply given myself permission not to understand. Like electricity. I just go ahead and accept it as scientific magic. It's much easier that way, much less of a brain strain. Plus, I'm thirty-two years old, for Christ sake! There's only so much the old head can handle, only so much room in the Gray Matter Inn. Additional factoids could drive out essential memorized must-knows, such as every crucial line from *The Wizard of Oz*.

After all, we have our priorities.

Magic.

It's oh so much easier to explain complex technological mysteries to my students that way.

The march on Mount Tom was organized by the "No Coal Alliance," a local offshoot of 350.org, an activist group intent on shutting down our local carbon dioxide–spewing monstrosity.

If I had the power to "off" just one of the fossil fools, hands down it would be Big Coal. Everything about it, from the mining to the burning, drips with disaster. Oil and gas are dreadful enough; coal is beyond bad.

I get why we use it. Estimates vary, but it's good for at least a couple hundred thousand U.S. jobs. We're the Saudi Arabia of coal. We sit atop estimated reserves which, if burned (God forbid) at current rates, would get us another 200-plus years of electricity. Coal provides somewhere around a third of the electricity we use in the United States, though that figure is declining.

And, returning to Dr. Seuss's *The Lorax*, electricity, like Thneeds, is what "everyone, EVERYONE, *EVERYONE* needs!"

But boy, is it trouble.

Disregarding all the other shit that goes up the stack (sulfur dioxides, nitrogen oxides, carbon monoxide, volatile organic compounds, mercury, particulate matter—Jesus, the list goes on and on), coal plants release more CO_2 than any other fossil fuel—two thousand pounds of it per megawatt hour of energy, which is double that of natural gas.

It's awfully hard not to put coal front and center in the climate-change blame game.

I bundled up for the weather and got out of the car. Jesse was along with Sarah. I noticed immediately that she grabbed his hand for warmth. Things seemed to be progressing nicely on that front. (She had made a great fuss in the car over his blue toenail, much to his delight.)

Out in the parking lot there was a gathering crowd of a hundred or so, holding signs and carrying banners.

"EVEN ELMIRA GULCH SAYS NO TO MOUNT TOM!" one read, a wonderful picture of the Wicked Witch of the West flying on her broom stick while giving the middle finger.

Yes!

Jesse, Sarah, and I were meeting up with four of the Climate Changers, the usual dynamic duo (Hannah and Trevor) plus two wonderful young women, Meagan and Abbie. Fresh out of high school, newbies to climate-change activism, they already had full-blown OCD.

Once again, therapists throughout the Valley should thank me for my work.

The demonstration was on the young side. It was a great thing to see the college-age crowd making their voices heard. There were a few families with young kids in tow, and a good smattering of old farts with their grizzled faces and clenched fists, but the weather was turning ugly and the faint of heart were staying home.

Snow began to fall. Hard. In October for Christ sake! Another one of these weird weather wonders that was increasingly becoming the new normal.

The problem with days like today was that they gave the right-wing climate deniers an audience as they yelped, "See! Told you so! Snow before Halloween. So much for your global-warming lies!" Of course, on the twelfth consecutive day of 95 degrees in June, they were conspicuous in their silence.

The crowd was being warmed by a local bluegrass group called the Wandering Kind, a wonderful foursome playing fiddle, mandolin, guitar, and stand-up bass. Their repertoire was apropos—old-time coal-mining songs and union anthems. "Which Side Are You On?" got us stamping our feet and clapping our gloved hands. Jesse entertained everyone by screeching out his "Yeehaws" and swinging arms square-dance style with Sarah and anyone else who would join in. His "hurt foot" only seemed to ache when he wanted somebody's cute fingers fondling it.

A few songs and one short talk later, the organizers promised we'd march to the Mount Tom Plant, thankfully, because none of us seemed overly well-dressed for the early onslaught of winter weather. My feet were already feeling the nip.

The featured speaker, an eloquent climatologist from U-Mass (they hadn't asked me! waaahhh!) presented us with an apt metaphor.

"What is your body temperature at equilibrium?" she called out to the crowd.

"Right now, thirty-four degrees and rapidly falling!" a demonstrator responded, his breath rising like smoke. Everyone laughed.

"In other words, I should be brief," the speaker smiled. "Let's hope it's somewhere around 98 degrees. But what happens when it goes up a degree, to 99, or maybe 100? We don't feel so great, do we? But we probably still manage to go to work. We still make it to school."

A few of the students nudged each other, shook their heads, and laughed.

"What happens when we're two degrees warmer? Anything much over a hundred and we're heading downhill fast. It's a stay-at-home day with hot soup and another layer of clothes."

"Hot soup! Hot soup!" a few demonstrators chanted.

"Three degrees?" she went on. "Sweats, chills. You're lucky to make it out of bed out at all.

"Four degrees? Something serious is going on. It's doctor time.

"And pretty much anything above that and life hangs in the balance. When your forehead is on fire, you don't need a doctor to tell you something's seriously wrong.

"Allow me to remind you, my friends, that Mother Earth is not unlike our body. A degree rise in temperature, even two, may be tolerable. Not an ideal situation, but she's pretty adept at rolling with the punches.

"Keep cranking up that climate thermostat and things go south pretty fast.

"Well, I've got bad news for you, folks. We're not talking

one or two degrees Fahrenheit. We're not talking 'suck it up and go to work.'

"The most recent climate projections show a distinct possibility, a real likelihood, of a 7-, 8-, or even 10-degree Fahrenheit rise in global surface temperature."

The crowd groaned.

"Ten degrees," she repeated. "Maybe even as soon as the end of the century.

"Think of your body at 108 degrees.

"It's called death.

"Now think of the earth 10 degrees warmer. Mother Earth's forehead is burning up.

"Tell me good people, is this what we want?" she shouted, pointing toward the power plant.

"NO!" the crowd shouted back, waving their "Shut It Down" signs.

"Is this what we are going to accept?"

"NO!"

"Then what are we going to do about it?"

"Shut it down!" the crowd roared.

"I can't hear you!" she cupped her hand over her ear.

"Shut it down!" we yelled even louder.

"One more time!"

"*SHUT IT DOWN!*"

The march began.

By now the snow had picked up in intensity. Jesse, head cocked back, was attempting to impress Sarah by catching snowflakes on his tongue. The crowd had grown to a couple hundred, maybe more, and spilled onto Route 10 for the half-mile march to the power plant, escorted by police cars. Their flashing lights, the unexpected snow, the chanting, the signs, all made for a very pleasant high.

Thankfully, minus the pot. Whenever I was stoned my body temperature felt like it plummeted 10 degrees. Not exactly what I needed right now.

"What do we want?" an organizer with a bullhorn yelled.

"NO MORE COAL!" we yelled back.

"When do we want it?"

"NOW!"

"What do we want?"

"NO MORE COAL!"

"When do we want it?"

"NOW!"

I felt a tap on my shoulder.

"Unusual weather we're having, ain't it," someone said in a Cowardly Lion kind of voice.

I jumped. It was her! Samantha!

"Hey! Wow! I didn't see you," I said. "Wow! Great to see you. What are you doing here?"

Hmm. . . Such an astute question. I had talked about the demonstration in class and now here we were marching on a coal plant carrying signs saying "Coal is Stupid" while singing and chanting. And I'm wondering what she's doing here? It's times like these that my absolute brilliance around women simply bursts forth.

"Same thing as you are, I hope," she said, smiling through the snow.

"Following the Yellow Brick Road? All right! You were the lion just then. From the *Wizard of Oz*!" I was desperately trying to regain some of my lost feng shui.

"Best movie ever!" she replied.

"Oh my god!" I agreed, perhaps a little over enthusiastically. "Absolutely. Totally. Well, maybe *An Inconvenient Truth*, but, absolutely best non-documentary."

Jesus, how awkward can one guy sound? To make matters even worse, I attempted a spastic mimic of the Oz quartet's "We're Off to See the Wizard" dance. Minus any degree of coordination, grace, or rhythm.

Mercifully, she laughed.

Jesse joined us, putting his arm around me and shivering.

"Having fun?" he asked.

"Oh, hey, uhmm . . . "[long awkward pause] . . ." this is my roommate, Jesse, and his, ahh . . . friend . . . Sarah. This is, ahhh . . ."

"Samantha," she smiled, holding out her mittenless hand.

I hadn't forgotten her name—of course I hadn't. For the love of God, how could I possibly forget her name! I just couldn't get it out. I sometimes have this paralyzing syndrome in social situations where names got lodged in my head, stuck on my tongue, unable to make it from the brain to the voice box. Yet another manifestation of my extreme social awkwardness.

Put me in front of a class of students and I have no fears, no trepidations, no hesitation, no anxiety. I am in my element.

Put me in front of a beautiful woman and all hell breaks loose.

It's like a stutterer I used to know. He would painfully struggle to get certain words out. Yet he had a beautiful, clear, stutter-free singing voice.

In class I sang.

Everywhere else I seemed to stutter.

I gave myself a swift mental kick to the voice box. Sing, damn it, sing!

"Hey," Jesse replied. "I've heard a lot about—"

I zipped him a "Jesus, don't say it!" look.

"—your class," he went on with barely a pause. "Casey seems to be enjoying it."

Christ, I thought. I didn't say she was a student! I didn't say she was from my class! I didn't say anything!

"Yeah," she said. "It's great. Really great. It's such a joy to be a student again."

Once more that beautiful smile.

The four Climate Changers had joined us and somehow I managed to introduce them without bungling their names. The eight of us marched together.

"ONE! WE ARE THE PEOPLE!

"TWO! A LITTLE BIT LOUDER NOW!

"THREE! WE'RE GOING TO SHUT THIS POWER PLANT DOWN!"

The snow was falling more heavily. One of those early ephemeral New England snowstorms, most likely here today, and with any sort of warmth, gone tomorrow. Flakes as big as quarters. Thank God for the police-car escort in front. With the swirling snow it was getting increasingly difficult to even see where the road was.

Given the season, many of the trees still held their autumn-turning leaves, and the snow, clinging to color, was absolutely gorgeous.

Turning the corner we stopped. It was bracing to see the power plant up close for the first time, a sobering moment that briefly silenced the chanting. The stark angles of the power plant emerged from wisps of clouds, and then, just as quickly, disappeared again. An eerie glowing red light atop the huge smokestack blinked on and off, on and off. With the backdrop of snow on leaves and the curve of the Connecticut River barely visible, it was quite a sight.

Strange to think that this was root of so much evil.

Regaining our composure, one of the march organizers with his big baritone voice got us going again:

"IF NOT US, WHO?

"IF NOT HERE, WHERE?

"IF NOT NOW, WHEN?" we chanted.

"It looks like the Wicked Witch's Castle," Samantha shuddered. "There should be a sign: 'I'd turn back if I was you.' She cackled, a wonderful imitation of the terrifying Wicked Witch of the West laugh.

"I use that one with my kids," she said. "Keeps them in line."

"I guess! Release the flying monkeys and I'm out of here!" I said.

Our chanting continued.

"WE DON'T WANT THE WORLD TO BOIL!
"JUST SAY NO TO COAL AND OIL!"

Marching next to her was wonderful. I kept a close tab on my body to make sure I wasn't too close to her, but not too far away, either. I don't know if it was just my imagination but it certainly seemed that if I drifted at all to the side she seemed to sidle right back up next to me.

Absolutely wonderful.

We had gathered at the locked gates to the plant, the crowd swollen to nearly three hundred, chanting and singing, stomping our feet to keep out the cold, raging against the machine.

The organizers, huddling together, looked anxious and unsure as to what to do next. It was clearly too cold for any of the planned speeches. They'd lose the crowd in an instant. The band with frosty hands had left their instruments behind. There seemed to be no Plan B.

Samantha was blowing on her fists.

"You want my gloves?" I asked.

"Nah. I'm good."

"Seriously," I lied. "My hands don't get cold."

Jesse snorted.

"Really? Thanks. Silly me for forgetting to bring my own! Wow! First your clothes, now your gloves. How lucky am I?" One more smile as she put them on, wiggling her fingers to get the blood circulating.

Jesse gave me the thumbs up behind her back. Sarah, having clearly been filled in on the action, bobbed her head in approval.

"These will definitely come in handy!" Samantha said.

Reaching down, she made a snowball. Walking to the

edge of the gate, mouthing a silent prayer, she hurled it in the direction of the power plant.

The crowd, hoarse from the chants and the cold and looking for inspiration, turned to her and watched.

Once more she reached down, made another snowball, kissed it this time, and then let it fly.

A loud *Hurrah!* went up.

"Let's do it!" someone yelled.

"Let 'em have it!" cried somebody else.

Within seconds, three hundred snowballs in a single volley flew over the gate. Then three hundred more. A torrent unleashed against the dark side.

Folks were shouting, yelling, chanting, singing. The organizers, visibly relieved, were jumping up and down, cheering on the crowd, yelling for more.

The four Climate Changers were busy making a snowman. Jesse was hurling missiles fast and furious, and shrieking like the Great and Powerful Wizard of Oz himself. Samantha, Sarah, and I continued a steady barrage.

Okay, maybe it was tilting at windmills, but God, it sure felt good!

The cops, evidently too cold to emerge from their vehicles, had given us a break and let the demonstrators snowball away.

Our half-hour siege finally over, our arms exhausted, my shoulder achingly out of joint, my hands numb and, like Jesse's toe, scarily bluish, we turned to march back to the boat ramp, police escort lights still flashing. The snow had started to lift and blue windows of sky emerged.

Glancing back, the coal castle had become clearly visible. Demonstration notwithstanding, plague and pestilence continuing unabated.

We had, however, left a watchful contingent of snowmen and snowwomen to guard our flank, each silently facing the power plant, each proudly holding a sign.

"SOLAR NOW!"

"SHUT IT DOWN!"

"END THE COAL ECONOMY!"

And, my favorite:

"MOMMY, MAKE THE BAD THING GO AWAY!" (with a picture of the coal plant).

The eight of us made a final huddle in the boat ramp's parking lot where the march had begun. We were cold and tired, but exuberant. It had been a wonderful action. Sure, we were preaching to the converted, but boy, the converted sure needed each other. Jesse had his arm around Sarah, pulling her in tight. Abbie, who had been holding hands with Meagan the entire march, was now neatly folded in her arms. Even Hannah—surprise, surprise—was leaning curiously close to Trevor.

Samantha and I stood next to each other. It wasn't awkward. It wasn't weird. It was . . . comforting. Really comforting. Everyone else was silent, looking at us, watching, wondering.

I glanced at her, and again she smiled. I exhaled a deep breath, visible in the cold, my CO_2 steam rising from my own little mini-me power plant.

"Thanks for the gloves," she said. "Next time the clothes are on me. I promise."

Jesus. Just like the Wicked Witch with the bucketful of water, cold or no cold, right then and there I melted. Simply melted away. Not a horrid kind of melting. Not a "who would have thought a good little girl like you could destroy my beautiful wickedness!" melting. But a marvelous, warm-and-fuzzy, good-to-be-alive-even-with-smoke-stacked-evils-and-climate-changing-catastrophe kind of melting.

Next time the clothes are on me, Samantha had said. I couldn't help but wonder if I'd ever see a time when the clothes would be *off* of her.

—

We were riding home, heat blasting, my hands gripped tightly on the steering wheel. The first snow of the season always made driving an adventure. It took a storm or two to get folks back in the swing of winter-weather travel, and even with only an inch or two of snow on the road, cars were swerving and weaving.

"She seems nice," Sarah said.

"Who?"

Sarah gave me the look.

"Oh, yeah . . . she is. Really nice."

"And she has a great arm," Jesse chimed in. "You see her winging those snowballs? Give me a woman with a good arm any day." I could see Sarah in the rearview mirror, flexing her biceps.

I sighed. "Just like me to go after the untouchables. Anyway, she probably has a boyfriend."

"She doesn't have a boyfriend," Sarah replied.

"What do you mean?" I slowed down behind some idiot going three miles an hour. "How do you know?"

"She doesn't. I can tell. Did you see the way she was looking at you? She doesn't have a boyfriend. Or a girlfriend." She elbowed Jesse.

I could feel myself blush.

"It's irrelevant," I said. "She's a student, it's hands-off. No ifs, ands, or buts. So it really doesn't matter anyway."

"Come January it will," Sarah said.

I gripped the wheel even harder.

18

WEDNESDAY AT NOON was the Climate Changers' weekly meeting. I was dying with curiosity. I loved to endlessly speculate about student relationships, since I lacked any of my own. I had had inklings before that Abbie and Meaghan were interested in each other, and now that I'd seen them so adorable together at the march I couldn't wait to see how they were getting on. And then there were Hannah and Trevor. Will wonders never cease? They had seemed so close at the Mount Tom demonstration that I had even toyed with thoughts that there might be more going on between them than just a working relationship.

When I walked in, Abbie and Meaghan were snuggling in the corner, happily entertained by the fireworks exploding from the opposite end of the room. Evidently cooler heads had prevailed, and Hannah and Trevor were back to being cat and dog.

"It's a fabulous idea," Hannah was gushing.

"I'm sorry, Hannah," Trevor said. "And please don't take offence at this, but are we still on planet Earth here?

I mean, you can't be serious! Three hundred and fifty purple caps?"

"It's a fabulous idea," Hannah said, holding her ground.

"Dude, it's a fabulous idea if you're a fucking moron!"

"Language, Trevor," I cautioned.

"It's a fabulous idea if you're a goddamn moron!" Trevor continued.

"You know, anything that is creative or artsy you go off on!" Hannah said, scowling. "Just because we're not manning the barricades, marching in the streets, smashing the state doesn't mean it's not a good idea."

"Hannah, I'm all about creative and artsy. I'm just not into lunacy and insanity!"

"Maybe you can explain the idea one more time to the rest of us," I offered, clueless as to what they were bickering about.

"All right. So, we get people to crochet 350 purple caps and then hang them up on the wall next to the cafeteria," Hannah said.

"What the hell is 'crochet'?" Trevor asked.

"It's like knitting," Hannah replied. "Only not."

"Go on," I urged.

"That's it."

"What do you mean 'that's it'?" Trevor asked in a mocking tone.

"That's it. We knit 350 purple caps and hang them next to the cafeteria."

"I thought we were crocheting."

"Knitting, crocheting. Whatever."

"And the point again?" Trevor asked.

"Three hundred and fifty purple caps. Get it? Each cap represents one part per million of carbon dioxide. Jeez, Trevor, you know that. It's what we need to get back to in order to save the planet!"

"Knit purple caps?"

"Crochet!"

"Whatever!" Trevor shouted.

"Three hundred and fifty of them," Hannah reiterated.

"And then hang them next to the cafeteria?"

"Exactly."

"And the point?" Trevor asked.

"I told you! Each purple cap represents . . ."

"Dude! I know what each purple cap represents! I just don't have a clue as to what it has to do with anything! And why a purple cap? Why not a pink popsicle stick! Or a blue balloon. Wouldn't that be easier? I mean who the hell knits anyway?"

"Crochets."

"*Whatever!*"

"It's a graphic representation of what we need to accomplish. It's an attention grabber. It's a conversation starter. People will stop. People will talk. People will . . ."

"Laugh their asses off. Think we're clinically insane. Know we've gone over the god damn deep end."

"You know, if this was your idea—" Hannah said.

"Dude, are you kidding me? This would *never* be my idea! Not in a million years. Not in 350 million years! Knitted purple caps?"

"Crocheted!"

"*Ahhhhhhhhh!*" Trevor leapt up, spilled coffee all over his crotch, yelped again, and fled the room.

I felt bad for Hannah. Her idea didn't seem to be gaining much traction with the rest of the group. But it was wonderfully creative, and—who knows?—it could have worked. It really could have.

Three hundred and fifty crocheted purple caps. It could have swept the country like wildfire, changing the entire national debate. Purple Cap societies hanging purple caps next to every cafeteria wall from Alaska to Alabama. Legions of marching, chanting, sign-carrying, flag-waving purple cappers swarming on the capital. Three hundred and fifty United States Representatives whooping it up in the House chambers as they vote to pass comprehensive climate-change legislation, each one proudly wearing a purple cap. The president of the United States signing into legislation the most profound, far-reaching emission-reduction laws ever with a pen topped off with, you guessed it, the cutest little purple cap.

But *damn, damn, damn* if there wasn't that one recurring fatal flaw, that Achilles heel of the purple cap idea.

Who the hell actually knits?

Or was it "crochets"?

Whatever!

19

"You told her what?" Jesse asked incredulously.

"I said I liked how she did her hair," I sheepishly replied.

"Jesus. You are in deep!"

"I couldn't help it. She started it!"

"Started what?"

"It. She said she liked *my* hair," I said.

"Whoa, whoa, whoa. Wait a minute, back up here. She said what?"

"She liked my hair."

"Tell me her exact words."

"'I like your hair.'"

"Jesus," Jesse said.

"It's not a big deal. I just got a haircut. She was being nice."

"It *is* a big deal. It's a huge deal. Cut or no cut, your hair looks like shit. It always has and it always will. Face it, bro, no one could possibly think it looks good. What did you say after that?"

"God, why do I tell you everything?"

"Are you serious?" Jesse asked. "That's what you said to her?"

"No. That's what I'm saying to you!"

"Come on. I'm dying here. What exactly did you say to her?"

"When?" I asked.

"After she said she liked your hair, you moron!"

"She didn't call me a moron."

"She should have. What did you say?"

"Thanks," I said.

"That's it? Thanks?"

"No! I told you already. I said I liked how she did her hair."

"What else?"

"What do you mean what else?"

"What else did you say to her?" Jesse asked.

"Nothing."

"You're lying, you son of a bitch. I can see it in your eyes. You're the world's worst liar! Tell me what else you said!"

I breathed deep, and sat down.

"I told her I liked how it was wavy. I told her it looked good like that. Not that I didn't like it straight. I said she looked great both ways. But I like it wavy."

"Jesus. Wavy! Was that it?"

"That's it."

"You're not holding back?" Jesse asked.

"I'm not holding back," I said.

"Then what?"

"She said thanks. She said she'll wear it that way more often."

"Oh my god. I can't believe this. I honestly can't believe this!"

"Christ, are we in fucking middle school here?" I asked. "I complimented her hair after she complimented mine. It is not a big deal! You are such a drama queen!"

"She said she'll wear it that way more often?"

"Yeah."

"How did she say it?"

"What do you mean 'how'?"

"Did she look at you? Did she smile?"

"Seriously," I said. "I think this might be the most ridiculous conversation I have ever had in my life. Bar none! I'm done. Finished. I'm cooking dinner." I turned my back to him and began rattling pots and pans.

Jesse followed and put his arm around me, resting his head on my shoulder. "She smiled, didn't she?"

I sighed and didn't answer.

"Tell me she smiled."

"She smiled."

"Winked?" he asked.

"No wink," I said.

"Big smile?"

"Pretty big."

"Really big?"

"Pretty big."

"Jesus." He gave me a big hug. "You are in deep!"

20

AT THE HEIGHT OF THE INSANITY gripping the nation preceding the November presidential election, I managed to remain scrupulously nonpartisan in the classroom. While any one of my students with half a brain or even anyone vaguely familiar with presidential politics knew it would be a cold day in hell before I'd ever vote Republican, I saved my rants for those opting out of the democratic process.

"Democracy is not a spectator sport!" I thundered. "You want to whine? You want to bitch? Then vote!" I slammed my fist on my desk for dramatic effect.

"Don't like the Republicans? Don't like the Democrats? Vote Green Party. Vote Libertarian. Write *me* in! But if you don't vote, someone else will. You have a choice: let others decide your future, or let your own voice ring out in the ballot box!"

I know. It was a little melodramatic, perhaps a tad too heavy on the "rah, rah, sis boom bah, go-o-o-o-o democracy!" But students were solemn and seemed to get the point. Who knows, maybe I even guilt-tripped one or two of them who might otherwise have opted out on Election Day into actually voting.

While I wasn't Obama's biggest fan (he didn't mention The Issue in any of the three presidential debates! *Arrrrr!*), I found the alternative unthinkable.

Mitt Romney? Jesus! This was the best the Republicans could send up?

There is a special place in hell for those flip-floppers who radically change positions for reasons of political expediency. Here was an ex-governor, snake oil oozing out of every orifice, who had originally embraced the science of climate change—only to deny it once he began running for president.

Here's Romney snickering during his inauguration speech at the Republican National Convention: "President Obama promised to begin to slow the rise of the oceans and heal the planet." Cue the derisive laughter from delegates.

Laughter! Can you imagine that? *Laugher!* At the mere mention of a president wanting to heal the planet!

"My promise is to help you and your family," Romney continued.

Jesus. Mitt the Flip, it'll be awful hard to help the family when you've stir-fried the planet they're on. Think about it.

I could just see Poseidon, God of the Sea, the Earth Shaker, hanging with his homies on top of Mount Olympus, not taking this shit lightly.

"All right, Mitt my Man," he might say. "You can talk that trash, but can you hang with the fellas? Get a rise out of this!"

BAM! Down comes his Trident and up roars the Atlantic, taking down Romney and all of those other climate-change-denying assholes with him.

You can never accuse those Greek Gods of lacking a rather vicious sense of humor.

Payback's a bitch, Mitt.

In any event, it was hard to teach during the week leading up to the election. The polls were way too close for comfort, my confidence in the American people to do the right thing was wavering, my OCD was raging, and to add insult to injury I was suffering from severe constipation. Nightmares of climate deniers once more seizing the reins of power had left me anxious, exhausted, and totally on edge.

I felt as though ghosts of Halloween past were still lurking in the basement.

Speaking of Halloween, other than the doubling of Romney signs in the neighbor's yard, there had been no news from the scary man. His Halloween ghost was back up and running, on his schedule, not ours, its presence adding to my overall distress and discomfort. Jesse and I still slunk out our side entrance and made a beeline toward the door every time we saw him, but we seem to have escaped from our botched ransom reasonably unscathed.

Back to voting. I hate to say it, but sometimes it seems as though fear, prejudice, and clinical insanity seem to be a prerequisite in many states for casting a ballot. Vast swaths of the American public suffer from a chronic and debilitating epidemic of ignorance.

Perhaps what I was preaching to my students was downright wrong. Maybe democracy really should be a spectator sport for some, with players and watchers. Truth be told, perhaps it would be best to go ahead and purge those climate-change-denying, anti-intelligentsia, anti-science ignoramuses from the voting rolls.

No brains, no vote.

Hell, if it takes throwing democracy to the wolves to bring back sanity, then so be it.

Of course, there is that one ever-so-slight rub.

Who are the deciders? Who gets to choose who plays and who watches?

After smoking a bowl (or was it two?), Jesse and I reached a cataclysmic decision.

We would!

It was a no-brainer. If you answered "yes" to any one of the following questions you were forever expunged from the rolls of eligible voters:

"Number one," Jesse coughed, exhaling deeply and passing me the pot. "Are you now, or have you ever been, a member of the Republican party?"

"Brilliant!" I laughed. "I'm totally there. Let's just ignore the fact that Teddy Roosevelt was the first conservation president. And that Tricky Dick Nixon signed the most sweeping comprehensive environmental legislation ever into law. And that even George W., God bless his tortured soul, created the largest marine sanctuary in history, now off-limits to energy extraction. Lord knows how perfect the Democrats are, free from the slightest bit of corruption by big oil, big coal, and frackin' gas money. Expunge the Republicans from the voting booths. Let's just ignore Welch's ghost from the McCarthy hearings: 'Have you no sense of decency, sir, at long last? Have you left no sense of decency?'"

"Excellent," Jesse responded. "And how about this? Are you a white male who has ever resided for more than one month in any one of the red states, namely those confederate dens of sin that forever go Republican?"

"Yee-haw!" I cried, giving a pathetic rendition of the rebel yell. "Southern good-ole-boy stereotypes. I love 'em! So inclusive. So liberating!"

"Number three," Jesse cried. He jumped up on a chair and began waving his arms from his podium of power. "Do you make more than $200,000 a year?"

"Bravo! Eat the rich! Why stop at $200,000? Let's make it $100,000! Hell. Let's make it 50,000!"

"Wait," Jesse said. "I make more than 50."

"Too fucking bad! You're gone! Later, dude!"

"Whoa, whoa, wait just a minute, mister," Jesse countered. "*You* went to school in Texas for a semester!"

"Yeah, but that doesn't count! It's not like it's actually part of this country. It was more like a semester abroad."

"Try again!" Jesse said. "You're gone too!"

We paused to take another hit.

"I know!" Jesse leapt back onto his chair. "We'll stick with number one! We've never voted Republican! Never have, never will!"

"We're not number one!" I yelled. "We're not number one!" We proceeded to parade around the apartment, sanctimoniously shouting and stamping our feet and singing praises to a voting populace purged of anyone who disagreed with us.

Ah, benign fascism. What's not to love?

—

Two weeks before the election, I had given my class a homework assignment to research the presidential candidates' positions on climate change and energy issues, and then write a two-to-three pager comparing and contrasting. It seemed a reasonable way to highlight the stark differences between Romney and Obama and, in a not-so-subtle way, help get out the vote.

The papers were the usual community college mix of the brilliant and the barely literate.

Samantha took artistic liberties and painted a stark Orwellian portrait of a Romney America. Colleges like ours were mandated to have their own coal-fired power plants, with students' financial aid based on how much coal they could shovel in a day. The government had seized control of the Weather Channel, forecasting cooler temperatures and refusing to broadcast extreme weather events. A dedicated underground of climate activists were sneaking onto roofs in the dead of night to install photovoltaic panels and then heading for the hills, only to be hunted down and persecuted by the climate police.

It was absolutely, publishably brilliant. I photocopied it, brought it home, and taped it to the refrigerator door.

During class, in an attempt at balance, I had asked one of the students who had articulated Romney's position in a somewhat coherent and sympathetic way to read his paper out loud. I asked Samantha to do the same. I was pleased to note that the volume of applause was greater for hers by far.

As she increasingly was wont to do, Samantha stuck around after class.

"Nice paper," I said. "Let's hope it remains fiction!"

"Thanks!" she said. "It's almost beyond belief that this man and this party are to be taken seriously."

I nodded my head, So much for being free of bias.

"I mean, his economic policies are bad enough. Along with his stance on gay rights and abortion and women's issues and immigration and gun control, and God, everything else. But to deny climate change? To deny science? Wow!"

"Wow indeed!" I agreed, noticing how her freckles seemed to stop right at the midpoint of her neck, and how her hair was unraveling from the left pig tail. It was all I could do not to reach out and tuck it back in.

"Sometimes," she continued, "in the depths of my despair, in my darkest moments, I think to myself, why do we let some of these people vote? I mean, if they're that ignorant, that uninformed, that, I don't know, silly, maybe they should be locked out!"

My god, this woman! I stumbled a step backward, closing my eyes to regain balance and composure, and leaned against the whiteboard for support. Talk about being on the same page! Jesus! Everything she wrote or said was perfect.

"You okay?" she asked.

"Fine," I replied. "Just fine."

"Don't tell anyone I said that!" she continued. "About voting I mean. Not exactly a wholesome embrace of democracy!"

I zipped my mouth closed and mumbled, "My lips are sealed."

"Two weeks and I can sleep again. Hopefully!"

"Vote early, vote often!" I said.

She laughed.

"See you next week?"

"I'll be here."

I sat down on my desk and watched her leave, my eyes fixated on that unbelievably attractive zone between her waist and her upper thighs. Next week would be November. November!

Once again I thought about what Sarah had said: January was two short months away.

21

Mistrial Declared When Prosthetic Eye Pops Out
Philadelphia — An assault trial over a fight that cost a
man his left eye ended in a mistrial Wednesday when his
prosthetic eye popped out as he was testifying, startling
jurors.

John Huttick was weeping on the witness stand in
Common Pleas Court as he testified about the impact of
losing his eye in the August 2011 fight in the parking lot of
a bar called the New Princeton Tavern, the Philadelphia
Inquirer reported.

Suddenly, the $3,000 prosthetic blue eye popped out.
Huttick caught it and cried out as two jurors gasped and
started to rise.

"I couldn't believe it just came out," Huttick said.

Judge Robert Coleman, who called it an "unfortu-
nate, unforeseen incident," granted a mistrial motion by
defense attorney Eileen Hurley. He scheduled a new trial
for March 3.

— Associated Press

"DID YOU SEE THIS?" Jesse said. "'Mistrial Declared When Prosthetic Eye Pops Out.' Just when you think you've got the case nailed shut . . . *POP!* I've heard of 'saved by the bell' but this is ridiculous."

"Handy trick to have up your sleeve," I commented after reading the short article on page 2 of the Gazette. "People pissing you off? You'd be like 'Don't make me lose the eye!' Christ, no one would mess with you."

"Truth. You know, there's a lesson here. This could be just the kind of thing the climate-change movement desperately needs."

"A good bar fight?" I asked.

"Yeah, well, maybe that too, but I was thinking of something even more dramatic. Something not just eye-catching but eye-popping. Get the fucking jury's attention. *WAKE UP!* No more business as usual! Mistrial!"

I recounted this conversation to the Climate Changers the following Wednesday at their weekly meeting.

Generally speaking, the group ran their meetings efficiently and productively. They were action-oriented, and they did their utmost to keep themselves on-task and digression-free.

God knows our staff and faculty could learn a lot from them. Our Academic Affairs meetings were notorious for their rich depth of mind-numbing bullshit. Two hours of self-serving blather by the same-old-same-olds, whose gross propensity toward extreme verbal diarrhea, coupled with a profound inability to ever get to the fucking point, made for meetings straight from Hell. What could easily be summarized in a three-sentence e-mail would instead gobble up whole afternoons in seemingly endless, excruciatingly boring, and irrelevant monologues.

You know what they say about college faculty: put six together in a room and give them one manageable task to accomplish. The result? Seven radically different opinions and eight convoluted courses of action, not a single one based on any semblance of sanity. To make matters worse, in the exceedingly rare instance that faculty *could* actually agree on a single course of action, administration would bypass it and end up doing whatever the hell it wanted to do anyway, with the state usually doing its utmost to sabotage even that.

Ahh, the joys of public higher education. Your tax dollars hard at work.

Or was it . . . hardly working?

Whatever.

Occasionally however, even the Climate Changers' best-laid plans strayed from the straight and narrow and lurched off-topic into the twilight zone. After all, meetings are meetings and human beings seem genetically pre-wired for procrastination and lunacy.

They loved the eye-popping article. I had to read it to them four times. (Hannah laughed so hard she had to leave the room to pee.) The unfortunate result of all the hilarity was that the focused discussion on fundraising strategies for new photovoltaics on campus quickly dissolved into a rollicking, irreverent brainstorm unconstrained by reality.

The Climate Changers came up with the following:

FIVE EYE-POPPING EVENTS THAT COULD CHANGE THE CLIMATE DEBATE!

- One: Jesus, Buddha, Mohammad and a few other theological movers and shakers appear together at a climate-change rally. Mohammad wears a tight T-shirt boldly proclaiming "No More Coal." Jesus liberally uses the "F-word" when describing fossil fuels. Buddha sits, Buddha-like, in front of a gas-guzzling SUV and refuses to budge. All three emphatically state that there will literally be HELL TO PAY if we don't get our act together. Now!

- Two: The United States military unleashes a wave of drones that take out the fifteen dirtiest coal plants in the Ohio River Valley. They give a respectable heads-up so that no one is killed. The president defends his actions, emphatically stating "there can be no compromise in the defense of Mother Earth!" The public loves it and clamors for more.

- Three: Oregon invades Nevada, constructing settlements and building huge photovoltaic arrays. The Oregon governor justifies such action by stating "Oregon is just way too fucking rainy, and Nevada has so much more sun than we do. It's just not fair!" The Nevada governor retaliates and orders elementary schoolchildren to occupy Oregon's hydroelectric plants. The U.S. military intervenes with even more drone strikes on random coal plants.

- Four: Three hundred thousand Southern Baptists and born-again evangelicals stage a sit-in on a hill in Appalachia slated for mountaintop removal. They issue a joint statement blasting coal as "the opium of the devil." "Where is electricity mentioned in the Bible?" they ask. They further emphatically announce that "only by rejecting the satanic temptation of fossil fuels can we aspire to ascend the sustainable stairway to the kingdom of Christ." Millions join them.

- Five: A climate-induced mega-storm sweeps across the United States, resulting in seventeen states becoming completely submerged underwater. Again, enough heads-up notice results in zero fatalities. Coincidently, these states just happen to be "red" ones represented by climate-change-denying lunatics in Congress. With those states no longer existing, Congress is reconfigured, the right's stranglehold on sanity is lifted, and comprehensive climate-change legislation banning all fossil-fuel plants is overwhelmingly passed. Just to be on the safe side, the federal government drone-strikes all of the remaining coal plants for good measure.

It was a great meeting. Totally nonproductive but a great meeting.

—

It was strangely prophetic that on the very next Monday, October 29, 2012, Super Storm Sandy, the second-costliest hurricane in U.S. history, slammed into the Eastern Seaboard. Fourteen-foot tidal surges took out homes, business, infrastructure, and anything else silly enough to be in its path. New York, New Jersey, and Connecticut were devastated. Parts of New York City were underwater. Even with relentless advance notice, more than 100 people in the United States died from storm-related causes. Thousands became homeless and millions more were without power, many of them for weeks. Estimated damages were in the $60-plus billion range.

Be careful what you wish for!

Unfeeling bastards that we were, Jesse and I were initially grateful, almost gleeful. Safe and stoned in stormless Western Massachusetts, we had been granted a day off thanks to our governor declaring a state of emergency. That hellhole of an Academic Affairs meeting that I absolutely loathed and detested was cancelled. Hallelujah! I felt like those adolescents in Britain when the Nazis took out their school. Thank you, Sandy!

In the beginning, with the storm pummeling the East Coast and the two of us glued to the telly, we both felt an almost apocalyptic giddiness at her stunning ferocity.

Vindication was upon us! The time had finally come to pay the piper!

"Go, Sandy, go!" Jesse screamed, in a voice usually reserved for a Tom Brady touchdown.

"Come on, Ma Nature, it's payback time! Show the motherfuckers who's the boss!"

"Wake them up!" I cried, pumping my fists. "Give those climate-denying anti-science assholes a one-two punch!"

"Kick 'em in the privates!"

"Just do it!"

It's after times like these, blinkered by OCD and egged on by the Roommate, that I become painfully aware of just how much of a complete and utter fool I actually am. Here we were, cheerleaders for destruction. Applauding devastation. Hooting and hollering as fury unleashed itself on millions.

Clearly not our finest hour.

As gruesome images of the wrath of Sandy unfolded, glee quickly dissolved into guilt. Bodies washing up. Untold death and devastation. Homes, schools, stores, hospitals, and factories destroyed or shut down. No lights, no power. Dreams shattered.

We both felt terrible.

As always, Jesse laid the blame game squarely on my shoulders.

"I knew it!" he said. "You're the devil! The second coming of Satan! You wanted this to happen just so you could say 'I told you so!'"

"Shut up. This isn't funny. Don't joke about shit like this."

He fell to his knees and made the sign of the cross.

"Be gone, devil! Leave this world! Go back to the fiery depths of Hell and make it burn even hotter with your sorcery and wrath! Let the earth live!"

There are times when people carry jokes too far. This was one of them.

I managed to muster one of my rare holier-than-thou faces, got up, and left the room, queasy and nauseated.

—

In the difficult days that followed, a stark, painful possibility emerged that maybe, just maybe, a tragedy of this magnitude could actually get folks to connect the climate-change dots and derive some sort of meaning out of madness. That this horrific kick-in-the-ass could provide a rare teachable moment and prompt real change.

Michael Bloomberg, the Republican mayor of New York City, ended his endorsement silence and threw his support to Obama for president. Climate change was the tipping point, and the stark distinctions between the political parties on The Issue forced his political hand.

The headline of *Bloomberg Businessweek*, a major conservative business magazine, screamed out: "It's Climate Change, Stupid!" For a brief moment, the press was all over the topic.

Even the general public had turned off their reality TV shows and tuned into the real world.

For one brief, fleeting moment . . . and then quickly most of us ducked right back under the veil of denial. Back to business as usual—or unusual, as the case may be. It's stunning how quick we are to accept a new normal, no matter how screwed up it was.

The tragedy of the human condition: the pathetic length of our attention span. Thirty minutes of concern, the length of a sitcom, and then—*poof!* Out of sight, out of mind.

Halloween morning, with Sandy's horrific aftermath making the holiday, for once, a truly scary one, I came down to breakfast to find Jesse cackling hysterically over the morning paper.

"Oh God, what now?" I asked, knowing his sense of humor was continually piqued at the dysfunctional, the awkward, the bizarre.

"Charge-pocalypse!" he laughed, shaking his head.

"Charge-what?"

"You know the most frightening thing New Yorkers say they're dealing with post-Sandy?"

"I'm quite sure you'll tell me," I replied, sitting down and fixing myself a bowl of cereal.

"No fresh water?" Jesse said. "No way—they've got alcohol. No food? Christ, they can stand to lose a few pounds. Apartment under water? You're kidding! Maybe that's what will finally get rid of the cockroaches. Whatever! They're New Yorkers. They'll deal. But there is one thing, one thing, that is absolutely intolerable. Unbearable. Unfuckingthinkable! They can't charge their goddamn cell phones! No electricity. No juice. No cell phones. Anything but this! Anything! The poor fools are going nuts. Charge-pocalypse!"

He laughed that maniacal laugh again.

Whoa, I thought, an epiphany appearing right over the cornflakes. Wait just a minute here. . . . Could this be the marketing tool we were desperately searching for? The prosthetic popping-out-eyeball had finally come home to roost!

I could visualize the propaganda piece. Cameras rolling. Terrifying footage of Sandy ravaging the coastline. Devastation and destruction everywhere. A person straight out of an ad for anti-depression meds sitting on ruined rubble, knee-high in flood water, gnashing his teeth, weeping, clutching his cell phone to his broken heart.

Morgan Freeman's deep, somber voice-over.

"Climate Change. Higher seas. Shifting shorelines. No texting. That's right—no texting! Tell Congress and the president to act now!"

Whatever it takes.

22

SANDY OR NO SANDY, it was Halloween, which meant party time. Every year, Taylor—a guy who lives down the street from us—puts on an unbelievable costume party. He must have money—he renovated this old beat-up Victorian and now it's absolutely gorgeous, open and spacious and party central. It's got peculiar rooms with odd corners and slanted ceilings, walk-in closets as big as my bedroom, a wrap-around porch to die for. He has a backyard with those weird Japanese lantern things on poles that illuminate the trees and the winding garden terrace in a creepy kind of way. It's a perfect place to celebrate Halloween.

Dress-up is mandatory and folks take the party seriously. Some prepare their outfits months in advance.

A few Halloweens ago, at the height of the fright-night frenzy, two guys came in all decked out as cops. They were impeccably dressed in spotless uniforms with name tags, night sticks, handcuffs, the whole works. They looked straight from the precinct.

The booze was flowing, joints being passed every which way. The two announce in a very loud voice that vehicles were blocking driveways and towing would commence immediately.

Everyone laughed.

"Dude," one partier said, toking away and passing a J to one of the "cops." "You two are fucking awesome."

The whole room froze as the cops pulled out their badges.

"Dude," one of the cops replied. "Move your car or it's fucking history." Then they turned and left.

It was a great party.

This year Jesse, Dustin (a good neighbor—not the creepy guy with the inflatable ghost), and I went dressed as a threesome. I took an oversized black trash bag, cut out holes for my arms, and then padded it with crumpled up newspapers to make me plump and puffy. On the front I had taped a huge letter C made out of white cardboard. I painted my hands and face black and completed my outfit with black pants and black shoes. I looked somewhat like a black overstuffed M and M, only with the letter C.

Jesse and Dustin did the same with white trash bags, white pants, and white shoes. Dustin, who is African American, painted his face white. We had decided to mix it up a little.

The other difference between us was that they had big black letter O's taped onto their baggy white outfits.

Off we sauntered down the street to the happening, quite pleased with ourselves.

"Who the hell are you supposed to be?" said Taylor the host, spilling his wine all over my shoe, as our threesome entered. He was dressed as Gandalf the Gray—pointy cap, sorcerer's staff, long flowing beard, and all.

"The scariest thing you can think of!" I shouted, striving to be heard over the deafening din of dance music.

"What?" Taylor screamed, spilling more wine, this time all over my C.

"CO_2—we're CO_2!"

"C O what?"

"CO_2. Carbon dioxide—we're the greenhouse gasses! Scary or what! Get it?"

"What?" he shouted, spilling even more, this time all over himself.

Christ, what were we thinking? Pairing The Issue with Halloween may not have been such an awesome idea after all. It seemed immediately apparent that the political nature of our outfits would most likely be grossly underappreciated.

Nonetheless the party was wonderful, a frightening frenzy of dead brides, zombie ninja warriors, stunningly beautiful wood elves, drag vampire prom queens, and two Cap'n Crunch cereal boxes (yes, there were two! Ah! Costume faux pas!) among a host of others. The closest anyone else had come to being intellectual about their outfit was an elderly woman who wore only her slip and a sign that said "Freudian" draped around her breasts. Perfect.

A couple of pumpkin brews and a shared joint and I was pleasantly spooked. Alcohol being an evil drug, I hardly ever drank, but there was something oddly appealing, and a little bit scary, about pumpkin in a beer.

Self-conscious, awkward spaz that I am, I was usually not one to dance, but it was impossible not to get caught up in the buzz of the evening. Twirling, gyrating, and flopping around, I was able to rise above self and not obsess about looking the fool. Everyone else clearly was doing the same.

Try as we might, it was hard for the three of us to stick together. The place was packed. In addition, we were having severe costume issues. Dustin's O kept falling off. During one of his patented old-school disco moves Jesse had ripped open his outfit and crashed into one of the Japanese lanterns, and now his newspaper stuffing was poking out of his trash bag.

Just as I had feared, our message was clearly getting lost in the shuffle.

Wardrobe malfunctions aside, we were having a fabulous time. And then, at about 11:00 p.m. I walked out into the garden to see Jesse, his arm around the waist of a dazzling sunflower, nuzzling her stalk.

My face dropped. Damn! What was he thinking? I was pissed. He had shown every sign of being seriously attracted to the new lust of his, Sarah the nurse. They were beyond outings and into official dates. He had even brought her home and prepared the only meal he could cook with any sort of creativity and gusto—macaroni and cheese. He had been talking about her nonstop since the apple non-picking. Every night it was Sarah this, and Sarah that. Evidently she could do no wrong, and I was beginning to think, and hope, that she might actually be The One.

I was really happy for him. I liked her. She was smart. She was cute. She was doing good work. She had gone on the march on Mt. Tom with us. She cared about The Issue.

And it seemed pretty obvious to me that she liked him. As screwed up as he was—Christ, as we all were—he really was a great guy.

And he clearly worshipped her.

And now, here he was, flirting away with a goddamn sunflower! Jesus Christ! He was too old for this shit.

I angrily pulled him aside.

"What the hell are you doing?" I demanded.

"What? What are you talking about?"

"You know what I'm talking about! I don't care if you're loaded or not—stop it! Now!"

Jesse gave me weird look.

"You're being a total and complete moron," I continued, "and you know it. Think what you're doing! Think about it!" I gave him a shake, and more of his insides fell out onto the floor.

"Believe me," he said. "I am. And I think I'm actually going to get lucky tonight! Finally, after weeks, she says she wants to photosynthesize! With me! With me! Can you believe it? How can I refuse?"

"Weeks?" I yelled. I was really pissed now. "Christ, you just met her! How can you do this? What about . . ."

"Hi Casey!" the sunflower said, sauntering up and slipping her hand into Jesse's. As she pulled her petals away to kiss him, there emerged, in all of its radiant glory, the flowery face of Sarah.

"Yes!" I said, giving them both a huge, Halloweeny hug.

"I am so glad to see you. Photosynthesize away, my friends. Photosynthesize away! You have my blessing." I did the sign of the cross over both of them.

Sarah gave me an embarrassed look and then they both laughed and walked toward the door, hand in hand, snuggling and giggling, Jesse dribbling a trail of newspaper stuffing behind him.

It was really quite cute.

Dustin and I punted and morphed into carbon monoxide (CO). Still scary, still deadly, but not exactly The Issue.

Closer to midnight, Dustin hooked up with an extremely cute vampire/werewolf hybrid sort of thing and I was left, as always, standing awkwardly alone in the corner, a single C, a quite high atom of carbon.

"Isn't carbon, like, good?" Vampire/Werewolf's friend asked as I attempted to explain the origin of my outfit. She was a totally hot petunia with purple lacey petals cascading over her breasts and fanciful papier-mâché leaves sprouting from her gorgeous rear. Not quite as stunning as the sunflower, but pretty damn close. Just as I launched into a mini-lecture on the heat-trapping properties of carbon dioxide, Gollum (of *Lord of the Rings* fame) swept in.

"There you are, my precious!" he hissed, sweeping

her off her feet and carrying her to the dance floor as she laughed and shrieked.

Note to self: Halloween parties—not always the best opportunity to educate the world and change the course of human history.

I wove my way home and lay awake most of the night, smiling, listening to Jesse blissfully photosynthesizing with his lovely flower and daring to imagine the possibility of next Halloween doing the same with one of my own.

November

23

AFTER WHAT SEEMED LIKE AN ETERNITY, the first Tuesday of November, Election Day 2012, finally arrived. If the presidential drama had continued even a day longer, I would have lost it. After one more "Vote or else!" soapbox rant to my classes, I voted at the high school and then staggered home, anxious as hell, and wolfed down way too much pizza. It was leftover from the weekend and the pepperoni had a greenish tinge which I didn't happen to notice till the very last piece.

Truth be told, I hadn't felt particularly well for weeks. The possibility of a Republican victory, of Mitt Romney becoming the next president of the United States, was way too much to stomach. It seemed inconceivable that anyone with a shred of a brain would contemplate voting for Mister Moneybags from the Monopoly Game, the rancid face of capitalism gone sour, a man whose vision of the future was so 1950-ish. But the scary thing, what made my intestines twist themselves into tangled knots, was that even with the voting public on our side, electoral chicanery in several swing states combined with an unfavorable ruling from the Supreme Court could certainly throw the election to the Republicans, just as it had with George W. Bush. Anything was possible.

Jesse had gone out to dinner with Sarah, his sister Clara, and her sister's boyfriend, a getting-to-know-you introduction to Sarah. I was already on the second joint when they waltzed in the door, elated and energized, Sarah and his sister arm in arm.

"It's in the bag!" Jesse shouted. "Exit polling looks fab. Mitt's going down! Any news in the last few minutes?"

I was happy to see that dinner had gone well.

They all sat down, transfixed, in front of the blaring TV. Jesse grabbed the remote and immediately began obsessively coverage surfing.

"That son-of-a-bitch Romney!" Clara said, wrestling the remote from her brother. "That prick. That fucking asshole! Sorry about my language, sweetie." She gave Sarah a peck on the cheek. "Something you're just going to have to get used to."

Jesse's sister had an even filthier mouth than her brother. She was three years older and had been a marvelous role model for him. She had bought him his first bag of grass when he was sixteen, got the sister of one of her close friends to deflower him a year later, forged him a fake ID when he was nineteen, and was a consistently badass influence on him.

Clara was a second-grade teacher in Glenfield and we loved her dearly.

As much of a motormouth as she was, her boyfriend was solemn and silent. He was a prominent attorney in town and seemed like a nice guy, but it was sort of difficult to tell. When the bunch of us got together it was hard as hell for him to get a word in edgewise. And now with Sarah, who could chat it up with the best of them, in the picture, he seemed destined for silence.

Clara hated Romney even more than we did, if that was humanly possible. The sound of his name brought forth either a blood curling scream or a string of slanderous, raucous filth.

"Christ!" she continued, spittle frothing from her lips. "Fuckhead wins and I'm out of here. Seriously, I'm moving to Canada. I swear to God I am. I refuse to live in a country with a shit-for-brains president again!"

"Hey Clara," I said, giving her a big hug.

"Darling!" she said, hugging me back. "Please tell me everything is going to be okay!"

"Relax!" Jesse said. "As I said, it's in the bag!"

All that did was raise my anxiety level another notch or two. As smart as the Roommate was, his track record on calling elections was mixed at best. To this day, one of my most haunting memories was the Gore/Bush 2000 debacle. Sitting in our dorm room, high as kites, Jesse dancing jigs as he called Florida and the election for Al Gore.

We all know how that went down.

"Shut up!" I cautioned. "Don't jinx it. And stop changing the damn channel!" Between Jesse and his sister we had stuck with one station for no more than half a minute before frantically moving on to another. I was queasy enough without being subjected to the dizzying number of channel changes.

"The polls . . ."

"Quiet!"

"It's as good as . . ."

"I'm serious. Don't say it! Don't say anything. Here, take the Cheetos—if I eat one more I'm going to puke!"

The night was long, as election nights are wont to be. I was the odd one out, with no one to snuggle with. The leftover pizza, the rancid pepperoni, too much crap food, a nervous, over-acidified stomach, channels changing faster than Romney's flip flops, the future of the planet at stake—I was on the verge of pukedom. Every time a state was called for Romney, I grew increasingly nauseous. I had ceased to be entertained by Clara who, whenever Romney's name flashed across the screen, continued to unleash every foul word known to humankind, sometimes in multiple languages, often accompanied by obscene gestures including three full moons at the television, these last high jinks getting huge laughs from Sarah.

It was somewhere around the third joint that the major stations, even the fascist Fox lie-through-their-teeth network, called the election for Obama.

Thank God! Finally, finally, it was all over!

Occasionally, just occasionally, good triumphs over evil. Not great, but at least good.

Jesse did his "Fuck You Romney" victory break dance, getting the cord of the stand-up lamp wrapped around his ankle and bringing the whole damn thing crashing down on his head, much to the delight of Sarah and his sister, who waltzed with her boyfriend around the wreckage singing poorly but loudly.

Nah, nah, nah, nah
Nah, nah, nah, nah
Hey, hey
Goodbye.

I sat on the couch, pretty stoned but not nearly as nauseated, breathing in and out and in again, wondering what Samantha was doing at that very moment and feeling content to know that we would live to fight the good fight another day.

—

With the election finally over, I was once again able to sleep and grateful to shift my late-night fantasies away from the humiliating collapse of the Republican Party to something much more inviting. Like me and you-know-who.

No sex in this evening's installment. Not even foreplay.

Just that warm and fuzzy feeling of contentment and tranquility. Pure domestic bliss. I could so clearly see it. Our passive solar house sitting high on a hill, the green of the Berkshires stretching out forever. Photovoltaics (hmm . . . four kilowatts or five?) and solar hot water on the roof. An organic garden and mini orchard out back. Two cats in the yard, a few chickens clucking away (no geese!). Our bedroom window wide open to catch the twinkling turn-ons of the fireflies.

"Did you plug the car in?" asks Samantha dreamily as I turn out the lights. "Of course, sweetie," I reply, reaching out to pull her close. Ahh . . .

Speaking of plug-ins, I have this fabulous idea for a television commercial starring, —voilà— Samantha and (duh!) me. Guaranteed to sell. A Super Bowl ad, an instant viral sensation on YouTube.

Two vehicles pull into a dusty, desolate South Texas gas station. Tumbleweeds tumble, flies buzz, waves of heat rise from the pavement. Very rural and redneck. An incredibly hot attendant (guess who?) sits out front, decked out in sexy cowgirl outfit with a ten-gallon hat and fantasy riding boots, low slutty shorts and a super-tight top, plenty of cleavage for the camera to lazily pan over. She's fanning herself, bored to tears.

Your Hollywood-handsome cowboy with an eight o'clock shadow and dreamy eyes (no, not me!) gets out of Vehicle #1 (a souped-up gas-guzzling truck, of course). He opens the hood.

"Know what I got in here, darling?" he drawls.

She continues fanning and swatting flies.

"Three hundred and sixty horsepower, six speeds, zero to seventy in three seconds. Hell, I can tow the damn gas station behind this baby. Why don't you and I take her for a spin." He smiles, the sun reflecting off dazzling white teeth.

No response.

Meanwhile, out from Vehicle #2 (just a car) shuffles our hero, yours truly. Nerdy, poorly dressed, flicking fast-food crumbs off his smiley-face sweater, a Doctor Seuss–like hat perched crookedly on his head. He stumbles and barely catches himself.

The cowboy snickers.

The attendant bats her beautiful eyelashes. "Fill 'er up?" she asks.

"Oh no," says I. "I don't use gas. It's all electric. I'm just looking for directions to Dallas."

Wiggling her gorgeous ass the attendant sidles up to him, slides her hand up his thigh, and blows softly in his ear.

"You drive," she coos. "I'll ride shotgun."

The cowboy spits and grimaces.

Voiceover comes in, Morgan Freeman again: "The all-new electric Whatever. Taking you places you've never dreamed!"

I told you. Guaranteed to sell.

Am I brilliant or what?

24

JESSE AND I HAD SPENT the better part of a Saturday afternoon endlessly watching YouTube videos of mountaintop
removal, a.k.a. mountains being blown to shit, to smithereens, sky-fucking-high. We stared, unable to avert our
eyes, helplessly transfixed, as mountaintop after mountaintop disappeared. *KABOOM!* Over and over again.

As if strip mining wasn't bad enough; Kentucky, Tennessee, and the Virginias managed to one up it and find an
even more horrific way to get out the damn coal.

Literally blow the tops off of mountains.

Jesse had celebrated the successful passage of the
medical marijuana referendum question the week before
(hooray!) by heading down to a northern Connecticut
porn shop and buying a bong, still illegal to purchase in
Massachusetts.

Guns yes, multiple rounds of ammunition of course,
but bongs? God, no! What are you thinking?

Christening it "The Head Hunter," we were on our
third bowl, wallowing in our angst and anxiety, mountaintops and minds blown to kingdom come. If the psychotic

effect of watching mountaintops blasted away didn't necessitate a prescription for medical marijuana, nothing would.

"Wow! One more mountain!" he begged, choking on his hit. "Just one more!"

The images were difficult enough to watch stoned, next to impossible straight. Hence the need for pot.

One moment there it was. The most beautiful of all Appalachian hills, draped in a vibrant, forested quilt of beech, ash, birch, and hemlock. Cloaked in wildflowers—trailing arbutus, Oconee bells, heartleafs, and rue anemones. Witness to geologic uplift and eons of erosion. Disturbed by hurricane and fire, flood and drought. Idyllic home to white-tail deer, black bear, and bobcat. Serenaded with the choruses of songbird, frog, and insect. Its back massaged with all of the little folk—plant, animal, fungi, and microbe. Climbed and hunted and gathered and made love on by people for ten thousand years.

One moment there it was. The most diverse, amazing, natural wonder you could ever imagine. A temple to the gods and goddesses. A shrine to all that was sacred.

And then, in a blink of an eye, with one push of a button or flick of a switch or click of a mouse or however the hell else they blow things up these days, *KABOOM!* Mountaintop gone. Forever. Vanished!

We were looping Queen's "Another One Bites the Dust" (and another one, and another one)—music to blow up mountains by.

Who says one can't multitask when stoned? We were blasting tunes, mountaintops, and our fragile little brains, and, frankly, doing all three quite well.

"Wow!" Jesse said. If he were to have said "wow" one more time during this horror-fest I was going to blow his top off.

"What god createth, humans hath destroyeth."

Spoken like a true atheist.

And then, as if reality weren't surreal enough, Jesse had figured out a way to run the videos backwards. We got the heartache of watching mountaintops blown off, but then the joy of watching them sewn back together, all in an instant. Off and on. On and off. Absolutely mesmerizing. Over and over again. My head was spinning. I could feel my brain rattling around in my cranium, loose as a caboose.

"I wonder who thought this one up?" Jesse asked.

"What do you mean?"

"I mean, were a bunch of suits sitting around in a boardroom and some dude said, 'Whoa, wait a minute. Screw those pesky hillbillies feeding us all this shit about black lung and emphysema and tunnel collapse and living wages. Who needs 'em? Let's just blow the fucking mountains up! It's a win-win situation. We make more money, they go back to their hovels and stills where they belong.'"

I couldn't help but laugh.

"I mean, put yourself in their shoes." Jesse continued.

"The last place on earth I'd want to be in is their shoes, either the miners or the corporate hacks."

"Yeah, but think about it. If you don't give a shit, if you truly don't give a rat's ass about anything other than the bottom line, then it makes perfect sense."

Damned if the Roommate wasn't right. Mountaintop removal was the ultimate cluster fuck. But to some corporate fat cat in his mansion a thousand miles away, it all made perfect sense.

Rivers? Streams?

Who needs them? It's not my water.

Hiking? Hunting?

That's for Losers!

Aesthetics?

Overrated!

Wildlife? Nature?

Whatever!

The locals?

Fuck 'em! They're poor!

Those are all externalities. Obstacles to get rid of. Foes to be vanquished.

Coal, on the other hand? Now you're talking the real deal! Shit that matters. Black gold. Get it out of the ground, quick and cheap, and let nothing stand in your way.

We will move mountains to get it. Literally *remove* mountains.

Got a hill of coal? Blow it sky high! Gobble up the good stuff. Burn the son of a bitch and fry the friggin' planet.

And make a shitload of money doing it.

The words of John Muir, high on my list of the Top Hundred Good Folk, echoed through my rattled brain: "These temple destroyers, devotees of ravaging commercialism, seem to have a perfect contempt for nature, and instead of lifting their eyes to the God of the mountains, lift them to the Almighty Dollar."

Written a hundred years ago in 1912 at the height of Muir's battle over the damming of the Hetch Hetchy Valley in Yosemite National Park, these words could have been written today.

Jesse was right. It made perfect sense.

I could see Satan, doubled over in laughter, pissed that he didn't think of it. John Muir rolling over in his California grave, wondering why history is destined to repeat itself endlessly, wondering when, if ever, we'll learn from our mistakes.

"Wow!" I said, taking one more hit. "Wow!"

Just when I thought I couldn't get any more bummed out, or stoned for that matter, there was a knock on the door. We looked out to see two well-dressed twenty-something guys clutching what seemed to be Bibles.

"Don't answer the door," I begged. "Please. I can't handle this. I'm way too stoned."

The bong and pot were in plain view. The house reeked of marijuana.

"Just pretend we're not here!"

My pleas fell on deaf ears. Jesse, a satanic grin lighting up his face, had already succumbed to the inner evil possessing him. Clearly intent on torturing me, he graciously let the two in.

They fit to a T the stereotype of Bible-toting, evangelical, out-to-save-our-desperate-souls door-to-doorers. Men's-underwear-commercial good-looking, with close-cropped hair and athletic builds. Dressed impeccably, as if for a final job interview, smiles wider than the Hetch Hetchy Valley.

Jesse welcomed them to the living room, where I lay immobile, frozen on the couch, Queen still blasting, pot smoke still drifting leisurely overhead.

Jesse wasted no time in getting to work.

"I'm so glad you're here," he said, turning off the music, shaking their hands, and offering them something to drink. "I'm concerned about my good friend Casey." He motioned toward me.

I shot him my evilest eye, bloodshot as it was, but he ignored me.

"He's fallen under the spiritual deception of thinking humans can change the climate. Humans! I mean, how absurd is that?"

The evangelicals glanced at each other anxiously.

"You and I know that environmentalism is just another secular ruse to ignore the real moral issues of our times. He's trying to save the planet. We had someone come here 2,000 years ago to do just that, Casey—and He doesn't need your help!"

Jesse was up and pacing. He had wildness in his eyes.

"God promised Noah after the flood that nothing like that would ever happen again. Humans destroying the planet—blasphemy! The earth will only end when God declares it to be over. When Jesus returns to usher in salvation. Help me to help him see the light!"

Our two guests were speechless. They anxiously gripped their Bibles and remained glued to the couch.

Like a flash it dawned on me—I was being pranked! These dudes weren't evangelicals. Jesse was just messing with my head! He had a long and twisted history of unleashing practical jokes at my expense. And this, clearly, was just another one of them.

Once, when we were camping, I went to take care of business in the outhouse. It was a dilapidated, ancient, run-down crapper. Unbeknownst to me, he had crept behind and somehow inserted a curved branch through a crack in the back. Just as I was about to let fly, I felt this scraping motion on my ass. It literally scared the shit back into me.

Another time we were at a party and he told me to be extra sensitive to the host because she had recently lost her big toe in a chain saw accident. How I fell for that one I'll never know, but I imagine pot had something to do with it. Sitting by her side, I had just finished the last gulp of my drink when, looking down, I noticed a toe staring up at me from the bottom of my mug. It was, of course, a gag mug with a fake toe. But before any sort of rational thoughts could surface in my addled brain, I screamed, the intensity of which made her spill her drink all over my crotch.

Needless to say, I was the hit of the party.

The ruse this time was obvious. I was once again to be the butt of another perverted, obscenely warped gag of his.

I leapt from the couch.

"He speaks the truth!" I cried. "I blaspheme God! I embrace Satan. I have impure thoughts about an incredibly hot student in my class. I obsessively masturbate and smoke way too much weed. But now, thanks to you, I see the light! God gave us carbon dioxide, so it must be a good thing! God left the remains of those ancient plants and animals as a present for us to dig up and burn-baby-burn. If God wants the earth to warm, then warm away, dear planet!"

I knelt down before the startled two.

"I know now the error of my ways," I yelled, kissing one of their hands. "I am born again! Praise be to Jesus!"

I jumped back onto the couch, pumped my arms in the air, and let out a rapturous "Hallelujah!"

Then I burst out laughing.

"God, you guys are good!" I said, lightly punching one of them on the arm. "You friends of Jesse's from work?"

There followed a very long, incredibly awkward silence. I noticed Jesse was nowhere to be seen. Disappeared like a mountaintop. Gone.

"Maybe we should go," the taller one said, standing up and inching toward the door. "Thanks for your time."

"Whoa," I sat back down on the couch. "Wait a minute. You mean, you guys are, like, for real?" I stammered.

"Yeah," the shorter one replied. "We get the message."

"Oh God, I mean, oh gee." I was red-faced and totally flustered. "I am so sorry. I meant no disrespect. Honest to God, I mean, honestly, I thought this was a joke. You know my roommate, he . . ."

The taller one let out another painful sigh. "That's okay. Thanks for the water."

As they walked down the steps, the shorter one turned to me.

"By the way," he said, sorrow in his eyes. "Our faith tells us that when God granted humans dominion over the earth, it was not to be taken lightly. My church is working hard on these issues and I see climate change as a huge threat. It scares the hell out of me."

I felt the knife blade deep in the heart, twisting and turning.

"Yeah," I answered. "Me too."

I shut the door and watched them walk away, talking softly to themselves, taking anxious glances back at me.

Thou shalt not kill? Bullshit!

When I found out where Jesse was hiding, I fumed to myself, his ass was as good as dead!

25

Indoor-Grown Marijuana Factoid: "According to a 2011 report, indoor marijuana growing may account for 1 percent of the entire country's electricity consumption. Specific energy uses include high-intensity lighting, dehumidification to remove water vapor, space heating during non-illuminated periods and drying, irrigation water preheating, generation of CO_2 by burning fossil fuel, and ventilation and air-conditioning to remove waste heat. Substantial energy inefficiencies arise from air cleaning, noise and odor suppression, and inefficient electric generators used to avoid conspicuous utility bills. . . . More growing could be conducted outdoors, thus reducing its footprint."
— Huffington Post, August 27, 2012

ONE OF THE WONDERFUL THINGS about being the advisor to a school club is that you get to see students in a totally different light than in the classroom setting. With all the messy weirdness of grades and grading out of the picture, interpersonal dynamics shift to a much more egalitarian relationship.

I loved being the advisor to the Climate Changers. I got to know students not just as students but as people and as activists. In a world so fraught with cynicism, materialism, narcissism, and despair, it was wonderfully uplifting to be in constant interaction with late-teens and twenty-somethings out to save the world.

It was what gave me hope and fed my optimism.

My role in the group was that of advisor. It was their club, their agenda. I served as a reality check as well as a resource in navigating the sometimes cumbersome bureaucracy of the institution.

Maintaining my integrity and professionalism while juggling these unique relationships with club members was always interesting, but not always easy.

"Do you smoke weed, Mister C?" Trevor asked at the Wednesday group meeting. Side conversations stopped as the rest of the group eagerly anticipated my answer.

It was not a question out of the blue.

With the overwhelming passage of the medical marijuana initiative on the November ballot, Massachusetts was positioned to be one of eighteen states in the country, plus Washington, D.C., to legalize marijuana for medical use with a doctor's prescription. I had walked in on a discussion concerning whether the college, through its Department of Community Education, should offer a series of workshops on growing techniques. These would be credit-free and open to folks in the community interested in entering the marijuana business legally.

The right answer to the "do I smoke pot" question proved to be elusive. I prided myself on my openness and honesty within the group, and they reciprocated in kind. I was continually impressed with the strict observance of one of our major club ground rules: personal issues brought up in the group stayed in the group.

A simple "no" would have made me look the fool. I played the part of the left-wing, authority-be-damned activist professor quite well. That was the niche I proudly filled on campus, and I relished it.

I was always the first to trash excessive alcohol use when it came up in personal discussions. I gave my tobacco smokers, thankfully few and far between, continual shit along with serious urgings to seek out campus resources to help with their addiction. But my conspicuous silence during previous pot discussions had clearly not fallen on deaf ears. I got the feeling that they knew me too well for a no.

An "I have" was a difficult sell in my case. Been there, done that, I used to be young and a pothead, blah, blah, blah was probably not going to fly.

For reasons I couldn't quite explain, a simple "yes" seemed like simply TMI, too much information.

"I'm not sure what this discussion has to do with climate change," I answered. While honesty was generally the best policy, evasiveness seemed appropriate at this moment.

"See? I told you he did!" Trevor turned triumphantly to the group.

"I didn't know that OCD was a diagnosis for medical marijuana," Hannah offered.

My raucous laughter sealed the deal.

"Once again, someone clue me in as to why this discussion is relevant to the mission of this group?" I said awkwardly attempting to change the focus.

Surprise, surprise—Hannah and Trevor had been going at it. The tangling twosome had locked horns over the pot issue, with Trevor advocating for our school's direct involvement and Hannah expressing caution.

"PVCC could be a trendsetter, way out ahead of the game on this issue," Trevor explained.

"You can't be serious!" Hannah said. "People think

we're on the fringe enough already. This will not exactly enhance our credibility."

"Says you of the 350 purple caps."

"Shut up."

"Look. No one is saying we grow it. I'm saying the school should teach people how to grow it. It's a huge difference. You gotta know best practices for growing weed. Very sick people are going to be depending on high-quality stuff. What better place to learn than a community college?"

"I think you've had a little too much of that stuff, high-quality or not," Hannah replied.

"Dude, it's not like you don't smoke weed," Trevor retorted.

"Not as much as you."

"Folks," I chimed in. "Let's keep this productive."

I was, however, intrigued to know that Hannah smoked pot. Aside from climate-change activism, she seemed so . . . straight. I had a hard time imagining her tolerating marijuana use, let alone firing up a doobie. And anyway, how did Trevor know all this about her? Hmm . . .

"Anyway," Trevor continued. "We have an ideal setting. A great greenhouse, the perfect teaching venue."

"God, you are such a hypocrite!" Hannah lashed out. "If we're going to do this then we should do it right. Indoor grows are an incredible energy suck. They use like ten or twenty 1,000-watt grow lamps, 23/7. Crazy climate-change-inducing whack jobs!"

"I'm a hypocrite? Dude, you're not exactly a pot snob. Last time you bought it would have been from anyone. You were totally desperate. You told me so yourself. If the bag had been labeled 'this pot powered exclusively by big coal' you would have still inhaled on the spot."

What? Was he serious? I looked at Hannah with new eyes. Here she was, sitting in her vintage 1950s, Catholic high school girl's outfit waxing eloquently about indoor grows and taking shit from Trevor about her personal pot-purchasing policy. Who knew?

Once again, no judging books by their covers.

"And what, you *are* a pot snob?" Hannah shot back angrily. "That kid you buy from in economics class looks like a Mafia wannabe."

To intervene or not to intervene. I was often in a quandary when the heat got turned up.

"All I'm saying," she continued, "is that we need to think about the carbon footprint of everything we do. Agriculture has a huge impact. We can't address climate change without looking at how we grow things. So if we're going to go out on a limb and advocate something as out-there as this—and I'm not saying we should—it seems to me we should take the high ground, pun intended. Outdoor growing has much less of an environmental impact than an indoor grow. I mean, we teach sustainable gardening, right? If we're going to do this, why not teach sustainable marijuana growing? It makes perfect sense. We could set the standard for growing grass in as ecologically conscious way as possible."

I was beginning to like this girl more and more.

"Organic 101," Trevor said, smiling at her. "Pot that is."

Everyone laughed.

She had a fascinating point, argued with eloquence. I felt gobsmacked to realize that I had never given any due consideration to where my pot came from. To be perfectly honest, I only cared about the size of the buds and the quality of the buzz. But there was clear merit to the sustainability issue. Organic pot, grown only with synthetic-free pesticides and herbicides and fungicides, fertilized by poop from free-range chickens, hand- or horse-sown and cultivated, fossil-fuel-free, brought to your local dealership on the back of bicycles—what wasn't to like? What self-respecting medical-marijuana user wouldn't jump all over that one? I certainly would. Valid diagnosis or not.

And you knew the competition was going to be fierce with legal pot dispensaries clamoring for market share. They'd be desperate for any kind of edge.

Maybe this was why Hannah was a business major.

And it was all true: we had a newly built passive-solar greenhouse on campus and were in the process of setting up permaculture gardens. We had an emerging degree option in farm and food systems, and were already teaching agriculture-related classes. We were rolling out a new initiative called SAGE: Sustainable Agriculture and Green Energy. The idea of teaching business people how to grow marijuana for medicinal purposes in as environmentally sensitive and low-carbon way as possible was far from lunacy. And again, what better place to address the issue than a community college?

I did not, however, for an instant, think the Climate Changers had a chance in Hell of selling this one to the president. She was a wonderfully progressive woman, but teaching as sensitive a topic as this in a state institution before the dust had even settled on the referendum ballots was certainly a stretch, at least at this time. Indoors or out, conventional or organic. I could just hear the acrid tone of her voice as she camped out in my office following a conversation with the Climate Changers, the dean standing behind her, scowling. While I had never heard inappropriate language from her before, in this instance her dropping one or two of the F-bombs would certainly not have been out of the realm of possibility.

Later that evening, I brought up the idea with Jesse. I approached him mid-drink in the middle of a lactose frenzy and, not for the first time, milk shot out of his nose as he exploded in laughter.

"Fabulous idea!" he roared, soaking my students' homework. "I can just see the headlines now!

"'PVCC Takes the High Road.' Or better yet, 'PVCC Puts the High Back in Higher Ed!' Or how about this one:

'Three R's Not Good Enough for College: Reading, 'Rit-ing, 'Rithmatic, and Now Rolling. Joints, That Is.'"

Jesse was certainly on a roll of his own. There was no stopping him, and I had to admit he could be quite quick in his witticisms.

"Okay. I get it. Thanks for the feedback."

"I'm not done!" he said, gesticulating wildly, this time spilling his milk. I quickly gathered up my students' home-work I had been grading, wondering how I'd explain the stains to them. Jesse could be such a spaz when he was over-enthused.

"What about this? 'Looking for Academic Excellence? The Grass Really Is Greener at PVCC.'"

"Enough!" I said.

"How about 'PVCC: Perfectly Voluptuous Conscien-tious Cannabis.'"

"I'm not quite sure about voluptuous, but you've made your point! Anyway, all brilliant ideas are initially met with ridicule."

"Ridicule? Are you kidding me? This is the best idea I've ever heard! Absolutely brilliant! You'll put PVCC on the map! In fact, coincidences abound—I just scored some outrageous outdoor weed."

"The dealer wasn't an economics student, was he?" I asked.

"Does it matter?" Jesse replied.

We spent the rest of the evening happily high watching countless episodes of *SpongeBob SquarePants*, perhaps the best stoner show ever. Voluptuous!

Brilliant or not, I secretly hoped this issue would be one that the Climate Changers would put on hold, or, bet-ter yet, forget all about. Picking and choosing one's battles was a great modus operandi.

26

"DO YOU HAVE A MINUTE?" Samantha asked.

"Of course," I replied.

It was after class on a windy Thursday. She had waited for all the other students to leave, and then sat back down heavily on one of those torturous, ancient wooden chairs, whose only saving grace was that their aching discomfort was sometimes the only thing that kept my students awake.

This would be my seventh time I was alone with her in the classroom—not, of course, that I was counting. I put on my nonchalant, professorial, eager-to-engage-student-on-a-purely-intellectual-basis-even-though-they-are-so-incredibly-hot face, hoping it would mask an overwhelming urge to rest my hand on her thigh.

Pity the boys in her seventh-grade classroom, and a good number of the girls as well. I wondered if she had a clue as to how many crushes students had on her. How many boys were introduced to wet dreams featuring her in a starring role. Christ, there were probably kids deliberately flunking out just so they could gaze in wonder at her for another year.

She was wearing an oh-so-cute skirt with an ice-age-mammal theme. Wooly mammoths and mastodons and saber-toothed cats. She caught me staring.

"The Pleistocene epoch," she said, pointing to a giant ground sloth. "We start tomorrow. I call the unit the Big, the Hairy, and the Bizarre. This skirt is a teaser."

Damn right it was a teaser. I crossed my legs, hoping nothing down there would get the wrong impression and rise to the occasion.

"Anyway, I had a horrible experience yesterday," she began, face downcast.

"Oh no!"

"Just horrible."

My mind ratcheted up to worse-case scenario mode. She knew! She knew! Shit. Jesse, opening his stoned, can't-keep-a-damn-secret mouth must have blabbered away in the downtown donut shop about his ridiculous professor friend who had a continual hard-on around a middle-school science teacher who just happened to be one of his STUDENTS! I uncrossed and then recrossed my legs, sweat beading on my forehead. I prepared for damage control—deny everything. Always the best option.

No, now was the time to confess my obsessive love and lay my heart out on the table.

No, no you fool, deny!

Confess!

Deny!

She looked at me quizzically.

"Are you OK?" she asked.

"Fine," I said. "But you? What's up with you? Why horrible?"

"I was so devastated," she continued. "A parent came in. She told me how upset her son was with what we talked about in class."

"Which was?"

"The Issue, of course."

I let the air out of my lungs and drew the back of my hand across my brow, relieved that she wasn't on to me. I stuck a reminder note in the back of my brain to yell at the Roommate for something he had never done. Preemptive strikes were often a wise tactic.

The Issue. She called it "The Issue"! And I had thought I was the only one who did that. It was just like her. So . . . perfect.

"Why was the mom upset?" I asked.

"I guess she felt he was too young to hear about climate change. It was just too much for him. Too real. Too depressing. He had cried himself to sleep the night before. Didn't want to go to school in the morning. 'What's the point?' he had asked. 'We're all just going to die anyway.'"

"Oh God. That is so hard."

Samantha wiped her eyes. I didn't know what I was going to do if she started crying.

"Yeah. Really hard. It used to be sex ed that brought the parents running. Now it's this." She let out a long sigh.

"What'd you tell her?"

"I tried to be empathetic. I told her we were done with the gloom and doom and were now plowing full-speed-ahead with the 'We Shall Overcome.' I complimented her on raising such a sensitive boy and told her how I fervently wished all my students were just like him and cared so deeply about climate change."

"Sounds like quite the boy," I said.

"Actually, truth be told, he's a royal pain my ass. Always making farting noises. Can't keep his hands to himself. Has the attention span of a banana peel. I was shocked he had heard a word I said!"

I laughed. "Kids. Full of surprises."

"I guess. But it made me question everything. Maybe they are too young. Maybe we should wait until high school to teach them this stuff. Keep them innocent a little bit longer."

"Yeah," I said. "Just like sex. And we all know how well that's worked."

She smiled and blinked away tears.

"I don't know, Casey, I just don't know. Here we are at the tipping point with the whole world hanging in the balance, and these adorable, naïve little kids are going to have to deal with who knows what. My heart goes out to them, even the pains-in-my-ass. It's just not fair. It just isn't."

I wanted to gather her up in my arms, ice age mammals and all, and tell her somehow, someway, all evidence to the contrary, everything was going to work out.

"I give them the facts and of course it frightens the heck out of them. How could it not? It frightens the hell out of *me*. I used to dread 'the big week,' as we call sex ed. Penises, vaginas, intercourse, pregnancy, STDs. I wouldn't sleep a wink until it was all over. Compared to this it's a piece of cake."

"As an ex-seventh-grade boy I wouldn't quite call it that. More like the big, the hairy, and the bizarre."

She laughed.

"What do I do, Casey? What do I tell them?"

I shook my head in response. So hard to hear the truth. So hard to be the ones to tell it.

"What do we do?" I answered. "What do we tell them?"

27

IT HAD BEEN A SHITTY DAY. It had started off shitty, it ended even shittier, and the middle had been full of shit. One of those unmitigated disasters of a day. Best to have stayed in bed.

My morning class slept through my entire lecture. Not a few of them, not most of them, but all of them. Every single one. Even those students who managed to keep their eyes open were sound asleep. If I had known in advance how the morning would go I would have contacted a few sleep-clinic professionals and rustled up some of their clients. I could have made a small fortune off those poor bastards with insomnia. One breath of that toxic classroom air would have sent even the most sleep disordered blissfully down under.

I should have bagged, bottled, or canned the stuff. Sold it on eBay. Made a small fortune.

It was one of those mornings where I could have left the classroom, come back an hour later, and found the same slumped slugs snoring away. No one would have moved. No one would have known I had gone. No one.

After my morning class I graded exams. I love my job but I hate grading. I hate it with a passion. I loathe it. I would do anything, anything other than grade a goddamn exam. ABG my colleagues and I call it—Anything But Grade. I'd go to a day's worth of Academic Affairs meetings, I'd fill out forty curriculum actions, I'd do my E-3s and my E-5s. Christ, if it meant I could get out of grading I'd smile through an All College Assembly!

It's my fault. Most of my colleagues have thrown in the towel and retreated into the dark abyss of multiple-choice, Scantron-graded, quick-in-quick-out grading. For some godforsaken reason, I actually make my students write something on their exams. I do my best to ask thought-provoking questions that actually require critical thinking. Most of them do a fabulous job. But there is something about reading, over and over, the same answers to the same questions, however stimulating or intelligent they may be, that taxes my brain in cruel and unusual ways.

Three exams down, fifty-seven to go. Somebody shoot me.

The science department had booked a prominent scientist from U-Mass to speak at noon about The Issue. He was an active member of the Intergovernmental Panel on Climate Change that had won the Nobel Peace Prize, along with Al Gore. He had been harassed by the Bush Administration for his outspoken criticisms of government policy. He was engaging, edgy, funny, and right on target. With solid advance publicity school and community wide, we had scheduled him in Wakefield, our largest auditorium, which seats 200.

No one came.

A slight exaggeration. There were five of us from the science department, three staff members, one activist from town, and two, count 'em, two students, both of whom slept soundly through the whole presentation. Total: eleven people, nine of them awake.

Eleven! This guy was on the panel that won the Nobel Peace Prize and eleven people show up to hear him! None of them my students. How embarrassing is that!

The week before, we had had a guest presenter on The Mysterious New England Stone Chambers, these curious oddities that dot the rural northeastern landscape. Who built them? When were they built? For what purpose? The speaker's theory—I kid you not—was that these structures were the handiwork of a lost race of giant humans with double rows of teeth. According to him, the Smithsonian Institution, in a desperate act of conspiracy, had suppressed all evidence of them.

Wakefield was packed—not a seat vacant. Girls were sitting on their boyfriends' laps. People crowded the aisles, packed in the back. The speaker was swarmed afterwards like a rock star.

You have to understand, I've got nothing against stone chambers or extinct giants. In fact, I'm all for them. But for the love of Christ, standing room only for *that*, and then eleven lost souls for The Issue. It was almost too much to bear!

The afternoon just got worse.

Samantha had e-mailed me to say that she was missing class due to parent–teacher conferences. I was totally bummed.

I walked into class to find that the previous instructor had left the computer on and some jerk had come in and downloaded a porno. A couple was going at it, hard core, grinding, thrusting, groaning, leaving nothing to the imagination. My early arriving students looked on in amusement while I furiously fumbled to exit out. Expecting the dean to waltz in at any moment, I finally yanked the cord from the damn machine, knocking the hard drive over in the process.

"I never thought global warming could be this hot!" one of my students yelled, to much laughter.

Thank God *she* wasn't there!

The only upside to this was that most of them remained wide awake, hoping for another X-rated faux pas.

Of course, just as I got onto some sort of roll (joy of joys)—*BRINGGGGGGGGGGGGGGG!* A fucking fire alarm! On the coldest, wettest of days. No coat, no hat, no umbrella, my shoes with a gargantuan hole in the left toe. We waited for eternity outside in 36-degree pouring rain while my feet got numb and my hands turned to ice.

By the time we got back to class it was, duh, over.

I left school in spirits as foul as the weather.

I should have stayed.

Back home it was bitch night. Sarah had called and said she was pulling another double shift and couldn't come over, so Jesse was in foul temper. He and I fought over who was responsible for the disaster zone, a.k.a. the bathroom. We fought over culpability for the moldy, bacteria-laden leftovers in the far back corner of the fridge. We fought over the length of time to cook spaghetti, whose turn it was to buy pot, the collapse of the Red Sox, and the role of methane as a greenhouse gas.

If Jesus had returned in all of His infinite glory, we would have fought over the length of His goddamn hair.

I ate dinner, graded some more until I was on the verge of a breakdown, and stormed off to bed.

Sleep was elusive. I was in desperate need of a package of "forty winks in one whiff" from my morning class. But the dreaded Four Horsemen galloped through my brain and trampled through the bedroom, keeping any possibility of snoozles at bay.

Horseman #1: The Issue. Enough said.

Horseman #2: All of the other issues, from school to the general state of the economy to the prospect of spending Thanksgiving with my family to my angst over Samantha to the chances of the Patriots making it to the Super Bowl to the yada yada yada. On and on and on they paraded, demons and devils grinning and smirking. Meditation Lake didn't stand a chance.

Horseman #3: The Roommate's snores. Two doors down and as loud as a dentist's drill. How Sarah could sleep with him was beyond me.

Horseman #3: The farts. Pasta with artichoke hearts did not go down well. My stomach was a writhing mass of swirling gastrointestinal distress. Breathing through my mouth only made me hyperventilate.

When I finally did fall into a fitful slumber, it was about as restful as Hell.

I began with a dream/nightmare sequence starring Al Gore and Bill McKibben (renowned author of *End of Nature*; founder of 350.org; guru on The Issue) grinding it out in the afternoon's porno clip, my students luridly cheering on every move. Bill was dressed all in leather and Al had a dog collar around his neck, and when they emerged from the screen into the classroom and began to come on to me, I awoke with a start. I suppose the idea of a *ménage à trois* with those two idols should have been flattering. Please don't take offence at this, Al and Bill, but . . . it was not.

Another lapse into sleep.

This time a class full of, you guessed it, extinct giants! Fortunately they weren't going at it, and to their credit they were wide awake, but it was still a tad disconcerting. There I was, hammering away at The Issue and there they sat, grinning away at me, evil rows of double-toothed grins. The grins floated up and over their giant bodies like the Cheshire Cat's till they merged into one huge grin, a mocking, spiteful, ludicrous grin of all grins, sucking me into the giant stone chamber that the grin had morphed into.

Thank God for the alarm clock.

A shower, a shave, and on to face another day.

28

Compelling Explanations—The issues director of the fundamentalist American Family Association told his radio audience that God's feelings will be hurt if Americans stop using fossil fuels for energy. "God has buried those treasures there because he loves us to find them," said Bryan Fisher, who described Americans' campaigns against fossil fuels as similar to the time when Fisher, at age six, told a birthday present donor that he didn't like his gift. "And it just crushed that person."
— News of the Weird

I WORKED LATE ON A WEDNESDAY EVENING, doing a formal observation of an adjunct professor, something required for all first-time faculty. It was an inorganic chemistry class and he was droning on and on about something to do with hydrogen bonds, but then again I wasn't quite sure. I was slumped in one of those god-awful chairs in the far corner of the classroom, pinching myself to stay awake amidst the stifling heat of the classroom (turn down the thermostat! Ahh!) and the relentless monotone of the professor's voice.

The best thing about classroom observation is that it makes me much more empathetic toward the plight of the student. Sitting in the back of the class gives me great insight into:

One: How boring most of us really are.

Two: How difficult it is to pay attention when it's late at night, you're exhausted, the temperature is 105 degrees, and you frankly couldn't give a shit about the subject.

Three: How amazing it is that students actually hang in there as well as they do without going stark raving mad and bolting out of the classroom screaming gibberish and tearing their hair out.

The only thing that kept me from slumping over was the shoulders, back, and hair of this gorgeous brunette in the second row. That got me fantasizing about all of the attractive students in my classes, which led to a fabulous daydream about a certain student dressed in sweet pirate garb (minus the parrot) on a deserted beach; a significant step up, mind you, from the Al and Bill debacle. By the end of the lecture, I couldn't recall a single damn thing about . . . what was it? Oh yeah, hydrogen bonds.

My notes, which I was supposed to submit to our administrative assistant, consisted entirely of intricate doodles around the number twenty-nine, which, truth be told, were quite inspired. Much better, in fact, than the professor's lecture.

In any event, on getting home I found Jesse semicomatose on the couch; as always, the pungent odor of pot wafted through the air.

"Howdy-doody stranger," he said, handing me a joint.

"I can't," I replied. "I still have grading to do. It's been one of those days."

"Oh, but you must! You have to! God's feelings will be hurt if you don't!"

"Jesus," I said. "What are you, a born-again Rastafarian?"

"Genesis 1:11 — 'And God said, Let the earth bring forth

grass, the herb yielding seed, and the fruit tree yielding fruit after his kind, whose seed is in itself, upon the earth: and it was so.'"

"What the fuck?" I said.

"Psalms 103:13 — 'He causeth the grass to grow for the cattle, and herb for the service of man.'"

"Jesse, you're freaking me out here!"

"Proverbs 15:17 — 'Better is a dinner of herbs where love is, than a stalled ox and hatred therewith.'"

"Enough! Stop already!"

Jesse threw me over a copy of the *Valley Advocate*, a weekly publication he had picked up that morning.

"Read it and weep, bro. *News of the Weird*, so it's got to be true. If God buried coal because he loves us to find it, just think how he must feel when we harvest ganja? Fucking ecstatic! Take a hit or crush God. Heaven or Hell. Your choice, bro!"

I read the "news" clip, collapsed next to him on the couch and relit the joint.

With a decision of that magnitude, grading would have to wait.

29

THANKSGIVING DAWNED UNSEASONABLY WARM, 61 degrees and not a cloud in the sky. Thanks to climate change, the English word "unseasonable" may soon become obsolete, along with glaciers, polar bears and most of Florida.

It was the fourth week in November and I had yet to wear a winter jacket. Most days, I dressed for work with only my uniform on: jeans and a T-shirt. I enjoyed flouting the traditional professorial dress code and opting instead for an outfit that screamed out my politics on my chest. "Renewable Energy = National Security" (with a picture of a wind turbine). "Compost Happens!" (an apple core). "Make Lunch Not War" (a raised fist holding a carrot). And, my favorite, the one the Climate Changers had designed and sold as a fundraiser: "Polar Bears Against Global Warming!" (an adorable baby Polar bear with sunglasses on). I did make it a point to leave at home the shirt Jesse had given me one year for my birthday: "A Day Without a Buzz Is a Day That Never Was."

My attire inevitably annoyed my colleague Doug, who taught anatomy and physiology. He was a brilliant professor, a retired physician's assistant who had a great presence in the classroom and terrific command of his material. As sympathetic as he was to The Issue, he was forever lecturing me about crossing the line between facts and policy, between what he referred to as straight science and activist science.

"Look," Doug would admonish me. "Our role is to present the facts. Give students the data and let them interpret it. They need the knowledge and tools for critical thinking. Leave policy for sociology or political science classes. If you confuse that with hard science, then you're doing our students a grave disservice. Blindly moving forward your agenda makes you just as guilty as the right-wing zealots you seem so fond of criticizing. You're politicizing science."

"I do have an agenda and I am politicizing science," I deadpanned.

"Casey, this is no joke. Indoctrination is not education."

"For the love of Christ, Doug, do you actually think I'm indoctrinating them just because I wear a T-shirt with a fucking polar bear on it?"

"I think you're pushing your politics."

"Of course I'm pushing my politics." I said.

"That's my point exactly!"

"I happen to like teaching, Douglas." He hated to be called Douglas, but I was getting riled up.

"What does that have to do with anything?" he asked.

"If the temperature continues to do what it's doing, there's going to be no more teaching. You know why? There's going to be no one to teach. No one. Society as we know it will cease to exist. It's all going to come crashing down. Now that seems to me to be worth pushing politics for. It seems to me. . . ."

"Don't exaggerate," he interrupted.

"A 4- to 10-degree rise in temperature by the end of the century is no exaggeration."

"I'm not disagreeing with you about the severity of the situation. Show them the science, with facts not slogans, that's all I'm saying."

"Look, you teach about lungs and the respiratory system, right?"

"Your point?" he asked.

"What's the worst thing you can do to your lungs? Smoke, right?"

"Smoking is correlated with a significantly higher incidence of cancer, yes."

"Have you seen my shirt with two tyrannosauruses, or is it tyrannosauri, with butts in their mouth? The caption reads, 'The real reason the dinosaurs became extinct.' Would you wear that to school?"

"No," Doug said.

"No? Why not?"

"Because it's juvenile, that's why."

"It's funny as hell!" I said.

"It's unprofessional."

"Unprofessional? Smoking kills what, 300-plus thousand people a year in this county?"

"Something like that."

"The number-one cause of preventable death."

"Where are you going with this, Casey?"

"Where am I going with this? Jesus Christ, Doug, I'll tell you where I'm going! Not very long ago we invaded two countries. Right? We spent over a trillion dollars and we're still spending billions more. We killed God only knows how many people."

"I've got class in five. Get to the point."

"Here's the point: why did we go to war? Because of 9/11. How many people died? Nearly 3,000. That's less than four days of smoking deaths. Four days! And you won't wear a goddamn T-shirt shouting that out because it's 'juvenile'? Unprofessional? Indoctrination?"

"That's not what I said."

"Then what the fuck did you say?"

I was so mad I could spit. The world was going down in flames and I get slammed for wearing a shirt stating the obvious?

Just then our beautiful botany colleague strolled in to check her mailbox.

"My my," she said, rolling her eyes. "Better wipe your mouths, children. The testosterone is practically oozing out. Why don't you two head right down to the little boys' room and see whose is bigger."

"And here's another thing," Douglas continued, ignoring her. He was as pissed as I was. "I don't like the way you monopolize the copy machine every Tuesday morning when you know I have a 9:30 class. Every Tuesday morning it's the same thing. And frankly, I'm tired of it!"

"Don't change the subject," I said.

Anyway, I digress. Back to Thanksgiving.

I was off to see my family. Sarah was going to meet Jesse's parents for the first time.

"How do I look?" she had asked, twirling around in an adorable, low-cut, crimson dress.

"Beautiful!" I smiled. "As always. They're going to love you!"

"Jeez!" she scowled. "What's with you two? Are you in cahoots or something? Can't I get a straight answer out of anyone?"

"What are you talking about? What did Jesse say?"

"'Beautiful. As always.'" She stormed back into the bathroom to redo her hair for the fourteenth time.

Jesse shrugged. "Women," he said.

"I wouldn't know," I replied.

Thursday morning, I drove the Pike an hour and a half east to Route 128 and then north to the small town of Hamilton, where my parents lived. It was one of those wealthy North Shore enclaves with more horses than people. Romney lawn signs still littered the landscape, the poor wealthy white folk still reeling from one of their own getting knocked down in the general election.

I parked the car, steadied my nerves, spent a moment in mindfulness meditation (breathe in the positive, let go the negative) and prepared for the holiday onslaught.

It wasn't that I didn't get along with my family. I did. I loved them all, dearly, and they loved me unconditionally right back.

They were just . . . so different from me. I had fled the country-club, silver-spooned, upper-crust, snooty scene a decade and a half earlier, and never once looked back. I was proud that I had survived that debutante culture reasonably scar-free and morally intact.

The usual suspects would be there: Nathan, my younger banker brother, flanked by whoever his latest hottie was, most likely fingering her the whole time under the table the way he did the year before, winking at me all the while. My older sister Cheryl, anxious and stressed as always, doing her best to keep her Winnebago-dealing husband Winnie and their four, count 'em, four kids in line.

And, of course, my parents.

My father was an investment consultant for Merrill Lynch. Money said "Jump!" and all his life he had replied, "How high?" Of course, it was his financial astuteness, and generosity to boot, that had allowed me to emerge from college and grad school debt-free. It was hard to trash the hand that fed you.

My mother was a professional volunteer. There wasn't a philanthropic organization within fifteen miles that she didn't have a hand in running. The symphony, the arts council, the museum — those were her forte. All wonderful organizations to work for — safe, elitist, all good work, nothing that rocked the boat, nothing that upset the status quo.

They were terrific people. Terrific, but so wrong in so many ways.

Being home reopened my privileged past and made me anxious and put me on edge.

My cross to bear. The black sheep of the family.

I pulled up their long driveway and had barely stepped out of the car before being blind-sided by my oldest nephew, the nine-year-old hellion they called "The Hammer," who decked me with his definition of a "playful" punch to the gut and a knee to the groin while his father—Winnie, my brother-in-law—watched in amusement.

"That means he's happy to see you, bro-law," Winnie said, helping me up.

"Remind me to piss him off so that next time his meet-and-greet isn't quite so painful," I said, reaching for my testicles and hoping, if they were still there, that they'd eventually descend to their rightful spot.

My brother-in-law laughed. Winnie sold Winnebagos—I kid you not. He had an "I love my Bago from Winnie's" bumper sticker prominently displayed right next to "Impeach Obama." He was a jumbo of a man with a shocking tangle of unruly red hair and a bristly red beard to boot.

"Dog on a stump, I'm surprised you're here," he shouted, slapping me on the back. "I would have thought you'd be whooping it up over at the Indian reservation protesting us white devils! Giving thanks the Indian way!"

He let out a war cry and danced spasmodically, chugging what was left of his Budweiser. Same goddamn awful oppressive joke Thanksgiving after Thanksgiving for as long as I could remember.

I pointed to his monstrosity parked out front. "So what you got there, Winnie my man, three miles to the gallon? Or is it gallons to the mile?"

I could tell Winnie was thinking the exact same thing: same tired joke, year after year.

Winnie grinned, turned, and embraced the vehicle,

frantically humping it. "Don't let mean Uncle Casey make fun of you, darling," he said, thrusting and grinding his pelvis into the Winnebago's hood.

"He's just jealous because his Prius doesn't put out. Daddy loves you, baby!"

I gritted my teeth, steadied my loins, and prepared to endure another marvelous holiday.

The theme of this year's gathering centered mainly around how, for the love of Christ, this country could continue to spiral down, down, down and then go and re-elect "that black man" again. Bush had never been "that white man," nor had Clinton. Nor anyone down the line.

References to Obama were always prefaced by his color. Usually with my family, things were so clearly black and white. With Obama they were only black.

Winnie, as always, was the first to go off.

"I just don't see it. Four years of socialistic meddling, skyrocketing unemployment, and we elect the bastard again? Has this country gone *completely nuts?*"

It was hard to say with the brother-in-law just how much of his right-wing proselytizing and relentless Obama-bashing was simply a ploy to piss me off or an actual reflection of his true feelings. Beneath all the bluff and slander, Winnie was really not such a bad guy. He was a fabulous father, he worshipped the ground my sister walked on, he was incredibly solicitous and helpful to my parents. But his politics seemed to be a discombobulated blob of libertarian gobbledygook mixed in with an unhealthy dose of the same-old, same-old nonsensical Republican mantras and hypocritical hysteria.

And this is what really got me. Just when I'd be ready to completely write him off as a card-carrying lunatic, he'd pull a 180 on me. Earlier this fall he had taken advantage of those socialistic federal tax credits he bitched so much about and went out and put 23 kilowatts of photovoltaics on his Winnebago dealership roof. Twenty-four kilowatts! That's a hell of a lot of solar! Without renewable-energy tax incentives from the Feds he would never have dreamed of doing such a thing.

"Smartest business decision I ever made!" he boasted. "A fuckin' no-brainer!"

And this from a Republican who believed that no government is good government—unless, of course, that government benefits him and his! Demonize Washington until they give you give an offer you can't refuse. Government is evil, evil, evil . . . until you get your chunk of the change.

It drove me absolutely bonkers. The sheer hypocrisy made me gag.

I had this desperate need to pigeonhole *all* Republicans as fascist Armageddon-welcomers. It was so much easier that way. And then my damn sister's hubby blows it by going out and solarizing his business. Absolutely infuriating.

It was totally true: the world was so much clearer in black and white. Good versus evil, right against wrong, Satan or God. It was these damn shades of gray that drove me insane!

Fortunately, we did have common ground. One of the few things we could agree on was the recent medical marijuana referendum question. My Libertarian/ Republican family, at least the younger generation, was quite clear about the need for weed.

"Christ, I could use some right now," Winnie said. "My back has been killing me. You holding?"

We waylaid my brother, who willingly left his latest, and we snuck out back behind the house and hid away from the folks, my sister and the kids to smoke a joint.

Pot considerably enhanced my ability to hold on to my sanity (what tattered remains of it there were) while interacting with family during the holidays. Without that altered state of reality, without that bit of a buzz, things could go south pretty damn quickly.

I used to lose it with regularity, rising to the bait each time it was offered and often when it wasn't, and then fighting my family with tooth and claw over every twisted comment.

Thanksgiving dinners of the past were like the classic game Battleship.

"Snowed today, didn't it, Casey?" Dad would say, searching out my weak link and going straight for the kill. "So much for global warming, huh?"

C-3. *BOOM!* Sunk your destroyer!

"Seventh hurricane in the last four weeks," I'd retort. "Wow! I wonder what's up with that? Still in denial?"

E-9. *WHAM!* Say goodbye to your aircraft carrier!

On and on and on until there wasn't a ship on either side still afloat, all of us drowning in recriminations.

Right or wrong, it was much easier to be around them when I was high. It took the edge off, calmed me down, kept a lid on my OCD. I was much more prone to pick and choose my battles, much less likely to go down with the ship.

We slunk back into the house and I immediately walked into the study to find my youngest nephew, the one they called Minnie Winnie, who was still in the throes of potty training, urinating all over my work bag full of exams to grade.

"Cheryl? Winnie? Mom!" I screamed, reverting back to acting like the two-and-a-half-year-old that he was.

"Minnie Winnie is peeing all over my work. Somebody get in here! Somebody do something!"

Mom came giggling to the rescue.

"You come right over here to Grandma, you little rascal," she cooed, folding the little guy into her arms, his thumb in his mouth, his penis still wet and dripping.

She looked up at me, grinning.

"You shouldn't leave your work lying around where little ones can pee on them, honey."

Big Winnie stuck his head in the door.

"Smooth move, little man!" He picked his son up and gently rocked him upside down, the toddler laughing like crazy, clearly relishing all the attention.

Winnie turned to me.

"At least it wasn't number two!"

"Thank God!" I said. "I have to hand these back to my students."

"Give them all a P. P for perfect."

Everybody laughed. The little guy in particular.

After dinner there was the usual round of harassment about how I'm thirty-two and still single, an issue my mother, who as a non-Jew could hold her own with even the most Jewish of moms, has difficulty handling.

"Nathan has a girlfriend." Mom smiled at my brother.

"Nathan always has a girlfriend." I looked over to see what shenanigans the two of them were up to.

"So why don't you?"

"I'm busy, Mom. School takes a lot out of me."

"What about that cute professor you introduced us to the last time we visited? Why not ask her out?" She was referring to my botany colleague.

"She's married, Mom. Her husband is a farmer and has biceps bigger than my waist. She has two kids. She's ten years older than me."

"Does she have a sister?"

"Mom."

"What about that synagogue you go to. Aren't there any cute girls there?"

"Synagogue?" I asked.

"That place you get on your knees at."

"My meditation class? At the Y?"

"That's the one. There must be some single girls there."

"Mom. It's meditation. You have to be silent! It's not exactly the place to pick up women!"

"Well, that doesn't sound promising. Jesse said you're interested in one of your students. He said she's a science teacher and she's twenty-nine, very intelligent and attractive. He says she seems to like you a lot. Why don't you ask her out?"

Jesus! Just wait till I got back home. I was going to kick his ass. Anything I didn't want divulged to my parents was sure to reach them via the Roommate. My mother adored him for that.

"I love my job, Mom. I don't want to get fired!"

"Fired? But she's your age!"

"She's still a student."

"Fired! Hmph! With all the work you do for that school they would do no such thing. I've half a mind to march right on over there and talk to that dean of yours."

God help me! Once again, praise the Lord for the pot.

After dinner, there was the usual uproar over who got do the wishbone. Family tradition was that she or he who found it claimed one end, and the other was fought over by everyone else. Superstition has it that when you pull apart the wishbone, whoever comes away with the bigger half has their wish come true.

My brother's "girlfriend" got the first half.

"I know what I'm going to wish for," she said, staring straight into my brother's eyes. "You know that outfit I saw online? The one I absolutely can't live without?"

She gets one chance, one wish, and she goes for the fucking dress? Really? This was the best she could come up with?

"The Hammer," he who busted my balls earlier, won the rock-paper-scissors shoot-out for the other pull and then wrested the bigger half from the girlfriend. He announced his wish for the Patriots to win the football game this evening. Again, totally unimaginative, uninspired, silly and superfluous—but I could see his point. At least it was something for the common good. A far cry better than the dress thing.

After dinner, suffering from the post-turkey-meal sinkers, we collapsed on the living-room couch to watch the game. Midway through the first quarter, I snuck out to the back refrigerator for a surreptitious gnaw on a leg bone—cheap thrills for the supposed vegetarian that I claimed to be. The score was 7–0, Pats ahead. I came rushing back in to find everyone in ecstasy as the Patriots scored 21 points in less than a minute.

"Holy crapoly!" The Hammer shrieked, still clutching the victorious wish bone in his hand. "It works! It actually works!"

Wow, I smiled. If it was only that easy.

—

On the long drive home I thought about it. I mean, when it comes right down to it, is it really all that wrong to wish for a dress or for the Pats to roll to victory? Isn't it the littlest things that make us the most happy?

If I could get one wish to come true, like the genie guaranteed in Mr. Condom's wonderful presentation, only one wish, I'd be hard-pressed not to go for a chance with Samantha. There was nothing I desired more. Let's face it, if all of the world's problems were suddenly solved, we'd all be battling furiously to keep it that way, neurotic and psychotic that things would revert back to the way they were in a snap of a finger. Fighting like hell to keep heaven intact. And if all the world's problems were suddenly solved, I'd probably still be left single and loveless, down on myself, awkward and alone.

If The Hammer could make magic with the Patriots, maybe there was hope for me!

To hell with climate change! Be gone, guilt! I was going to put me first. Well, me and Her.

OCD or no OCD, I needed that woman! Maybe Jesse had brought home leftovers from his feed, containing, treasure of all treasures, the wishing bone!

Sad and pathetic as it was, it seemed much easier to put my future in the hands (or was it the breast?) of a dead turkey than in my own.

Sigh.

30

Well if you go carrying pictures of Chairman Mao
You're not going to make it with anyone anyhow.
Don't you know it's gonna be (shooby doo)
All right.
— John Lennon, "Revolution 1"

I'VE ALWAYS BEEN A FAN OF MORAL DILEMMAS. Options that don't always have a clear right or wrong are fascinating. The Climate Changers were wrestling with a good one.

Pioneer Valley Community College had a foundation, an independent, nonprofit, tax-exempt institution whose sole mission was to support the college. Because the college was a state entity, when people or businesses wanted to donate money to PVCC, it was the foundation that accepted the gift.

The foundation had an endowment of around three million dollars, not even remotely in the same ballpark as private colleges but still nothing to sneeze at. Three million dollars is, after all . . . three million dollars.

The endowment was invested in a mutual fund. The principal remained untouched, and the interest income was distributed yearly to the college for numerous scholarships to be given to deserving, low-income students. The money these students received had a huge impact on their lives. Scoring a scholarship was a major deal; for some it meant the difference between staying in school or not.

So where was the dilemma?

Like so many other colleges, the endowment's portfolio contained investments in fossil-fuel companies. Needless to say, these were doing quite well; they were investments with a high rate of return, which meant more money for more scholarships. That was the sole purpose, the whole point of the endowment.

There had recently begun a national movement spearheaded by the environmental activist organization 350.org to follow the money and get academic institutions like PVCC to divest their holdings in fossil fuels. Companies would hardly feel the pinch from institutional divestment, but the organizational and educational efforts that went into the campaign, the elevation of The Issue to front page news, was priceless. As an academic institution focused on sustainability, we had an opportunity to put our money where our mouth was. Modeled after the very successful anti-apartheid divestment campaign in the 1980s, which put the squeeze on companies doing business with the racist South African government, the hope was that this, too, would help spark a revolution.

Ignoring the nuanced shades of gray, in strictly black and white terms it went like this: divest in fossil-fuel companies and take a potential loss of income, which meant less money for low-income students, or cede the moral high ground and hope to hell that the details of our investments never get out.

As always, Trevor (*¡Viva la revolución!*) was blissfully unaware of anything but the stark reality of his truth. I was mildly jealous. It was so much easier to live that way.

"The time to act was yesterday!" Trevor shouted, with a thrill in his voice as if he had just won the lottery rather than revealing the "fossil-fuel blood" (as he called it) on the foundation's hands.

"Let's jump on this. Out now!"

As opinionated and biased as I was, I had a decade-plus of life experiences that grounded me, at least marginally, in the real world. Moreover, my father had taught me a thing or two about investments. Getting out of one portfolio and into another, I knew, wasn't exactly a walk in the park. The devil was in the details.

"I suggest a little more homework before you enter the fray," I cautioned. "See what kind of hit, if any, the scholarship fund would take. You've got to know the economic impact on students. Maybe get some additional support from other campus groups, see what other schools have done, research the status of alternative investments—you know, stuff like that."

"I beg to differ, padre," Trevor bowed in my direction. ("Padre"? Where did that come from?) "The time to strike is when the iron is hot!"

He raised his fist in the air.

"And it's sizzling now!"

This got a loud "huzzah" from most members of the group.

Trevor was a great kid. A terrific organizer. Occasionally a little hot under the collar, a little too quick on the draw. Effective action, in my opinion, required some degree of patience.

Either that or I was just getting old and losing the edge. I shuddered with the thought.

On the flip side, I could see his point. He was twenty years old. You see something wrong and you want to right it and you want to do it now. Not in a few months or a few years but *now*. Throw caution to the wind. Sometimes getting bogged down in real-world minutiae was the kiss of death for action.

And it was, after all, *their* group. Ultimately, they were responsible for doing their own thing.

"I am only an advisor . . . I am only an advisor . . . " I repeated the mantra to myself.

"And why stop at fossil fuels?" Trevor ranted on. "Let's get the hell out of all of this bullshit—the gun makers and bomb droppers, the sweatshops, and Walmarts—"

I looked away, embarrassed.

"—and all their evil minions. Dude, the foundation shouldn't be playing the capitalists' crap game to begin with. They should be investing in the community! They should be keeping the money here, not throwing it in the troughs for the corporate pigs and fat cats to feed off!"

It could be awfully hard to resist Trevor when he was on one of his rolls. Another few minutes of this would whip the Climate Changers into a fearful frenzy. They'd be marching down to the foundation office and taking it over, sitting in, hunger-striking, shutting it down.

Channeling my inner blinking yellow light, Hannah, always the voice of reason, pulled back on Trevor's reins.

"Whoa, Trevor, chill-pill time. Remember the purpose of the endowment. It's for us. For our scholarships. Remember how pumped you were when you got one last year. This is a little like the pot calling the kettle black."

Trevor ignored her. I could see his annoyance at having his own complicity thrown in his face.

"Maybe we should maintain the focus on fossil fuels and keep Marx and Lenin in the bag until further notice," Hannah continued.

"Pulling out of fossil fuels is the tip of the fucking iceberg! We've got to pull out of everything! Everything! It's capitalism that's leading us to the brink of chaos!"

"Oh God!" Hannah said, groaning loudly. "Here we go again!"

"Carl Sagan said, 'It is far better to grasp the universe as it really is than to persist in delusion, however satisfying and reassuring.' I say: fuck this capitalist bullshit. Let's bring the whole system down!"

"Talk about going delusional!" Hannah shot back. "The foundation getting out of the stock market will bring capitalism to its knees? Economic collapse is the only solution to the mess we're in?"

"I'm dead serious, Hannah. Let's push the whole damn thing over the cliff."

"We're not lemmings, Carl!"

"I'm Trevor, not Carl."

"Whatever."

"'Those who are able to see beyond the shadows and lies of their culture will never be understood, let alone believed, by the masses.'"

"Who said that?" Hannah mocked. "Spiderman?"

"Plato," Trevor replied.

"Don't be a moron, Trev. Total and complete economic collapse is not exactly an option that people are going to buy into. You're off in La-La Land again. There he goes. Everybody, wave goodbye to Trevor. Bye-bye!" Hannah blew him a kiss.

The other folks in the group, mesmerized by this debate, tried to hide their smiles.

"Don't you get it?" Trevor continued, undaunted. "I don't want people to 'buy into' anything. *Buying* is the problem, Hannah. Did you see what happened on Black Friday?"

He was referring to the Friday after Thanksgiving. The biggest shopping day of the year.

"Some dude was stabbed at a Walmart 'cause he cut in line! Stabbed, for Christ's sake. We are on an insane path.

Growth, commercialism, buy, buy, buy. It's the antithesis of the solution."

I couldn't help but smile. Carl Sagan? Plato? Antithesis? This was the height of intellectual discourse. I was digging it. Unless the usually mild-mannered Hannah pulled a knife on Trevor—a distinct possibility given the killer looks she was shooting his way—this was exactly what college was all about.

"Look, Plato."

"Stop it, Hannah! It's not funny."

"Carl, Plato, Trevor, whatever! You've got to get real. I mean, I agree that growth is a problem. But not all growth is bad. We want people to buy. We just want to change what it is that they're buying. Photovoltaics, insulation, warm clothes, decent housing, books and music, organic food. We have to live, Trevor. We have to eat and drink and have some sense of community."

"We're not living, Hannah. We're consuming. There is a difference. We're parasites, an invasive species, gobbling up the planet! Munch, munch, munching away. And then spitting out enough CO_2 to send us into oblivion. There will be no community if there is no world to put it on! What's it going to take for people to notice and begin to resist?"

"For God's sake, Trevor, don't go socialist on me again. If I hear that 'workers united' crap one more time I'm going to puke. I swear to God, Trevor, I mean it. Projectile vomit all over you. And I guarantee it will not be pretty!"

Trevor ignored her. "The world's got this burning, gushing wound in its side and we're just mopping up the floor while we look around for a goddamn band-aid. As if that's going to solve the problem. It's bullshit."

"So what do you suggest? Get rid of the endowment so we don't have a scholarship fund? Throw kids out of school? Make them add a fourth shit job to their crazy week? Wow! That will really help! You'll have all us students on your side for that one. That's sure to bring on the revolution!"

"Status quo is over. Reject the dominant paradigm!"

"I am so sick of the same tired old bumper-sticker bullshit!" Hannah had fire in her eyes. I had never seen her so worked up, nor heard her language so crude. "Damn, Trev, we drive to school together. You're texting me all the time. You can't live without your phone. You buy a new hippie hat every week!"

"Deep breath, Hannah," I cautioned. "Let's keep this civil." You could attack a man's politics to your heart's desire but what he wore on his head was off-limits.

"Dude, if I thought for a moment I could change things by not driving, by not texting, by not getting stuff, I would do it in an instant!"

"Then what's your solution? Come on, Trevor. You're the brilliant one, name-dropping Sagan and Plato. Come on, tell us what to do? Short of which way to slit my wrists."

It was a tense moment. To butt in and say something . . . or keep my distance and hold my tongue. The perpetual dilemma.

On cue, Abbie, always the vibes watcher, always the one to bring us back together, always catching folks as they fell, softly raised her voice and began singing the classic Beatles song:
You say you want a revolution
Well, you know
We all want to change the world . . .

Hannah's face relaxed and she chimed in:
Shooby doo wop, oh, shooby doo wop.

Abbie and Hannah continued, their voices beautiful together:
You tell me that it's evolution
Well, you know

We all want to change the world . . .

With the exception of Trevor with the downcast eyes and slumped head, we all began singing. All of us. It never ceases to amaze me how everyone, no matter what generation, reveres the Beatles.

But when you talk about destruction
Don't you know that you can count me out . . .

Suddenly Trevor leapt up, shouted a loud "In!" put his arm around Hannah and added his deep bass to what was really quite a spectacular *a capella* mix.

The whole lot of us joined him, out of our seats dancing, swinging arms, holding on to each other, and singing at the tops of our voices for all the college to hear—like it or not!

Don't you know it's gonna be (shooby doo)
All right.

God, if only life could always be like this. Engaged intelligent conversation, activism, a little bit of edge and tension, and then all ends happily in song and dance and hugs and joy. A Hollywood musical with a happy ending. Glee on TV. Utopia.

The song ended. I turned and glanced out the meeting room window and there, wouldn't you know it, was the dean peering in, a quizzical, bemused look on his face. His timing, as always, impeccable.

Another day in paradise.

31

SAMANTHA HAD A LESSON PLAN on oceans that she was developing for her class. With complex vocabulary and high-level math, she was looking for advice. Her concern was that it might be fatally plagued by TMI—Too Much Information. That her students' attention would stray, that the project was doomed for failure.

"I want their minds to wonder, not wander," she said. We were standing at the door after class, looking at the fading end of November light and the soft beginnings of snow sticking to the white pines behind the greenhouse.

"Fact. They're in the seventh grade. Their minds do both. Given the ride they're on I find it incredible that you ever get them to stay on track at all."

"It's not much different from what you do."

I shook my head. "A lot harder."

"I'm not so sure."

"God, I can't imagine, even for a day, teaching middle school. That age is so insanely out of my league. Believe me, college is a much easier gig. Absolutely no comparison."

"You'd be surprised. Students are students," Samantha said.

"I still don't see how you do it. As it is, I can barely hold this age. Case in point: one of my students last week told me I had a significant 'Cassandra complex.'"

"Cassandra complex?"

"Yeah. CC. Just what I need; a new acronym to worry about. Do you know who Cassandra was?"

"I don't. Should I?" Samantha asked.

"I had to google it when I got home. Terrible thing to be labeled a classical reference by a student and not have a clue as to what they were talking about."

"So who was she?"

"A princess of Troy from Greek mythology. Stunningly attractive. The second-most-beautiful woman in the world," I said.

"Who was the first?"

"Not a clue," I said as I looked away, avoiding her eyes.

"Go on."

"So Apollo, the sun god, had the hots for her and granted her the gift of prophecy. The power of foresight."

"Uh oh. If I know anything about Greek mythology this is not going to go down well."

"Bingo. There was a catch," I said.

"Duh."

"Apollo, of course, wanted her to sleep with him." Self-editing was never my forte. I could feel myself straying into TMI land.

"I could see that coming," she said.

"And she wouldn't."

"Of course not."

"Which did not make for a pleasant situation."

"Why am I not surprised?" Samantha said.

"So Apollo placed a curse on her. Her predictions, all of which would still come true, were never to be believed. Never. For her and all of her descendants. She foresaw the tragedy of the Trojan Horse and warned her people, and they were like, yeah, whatever, you may be hot but you're crazy. Bring it on."

Samantha was silent.

"The girl in the back evidently thinks I'm an arrogant know-it-all jerk who is convinced that if the world just believed me all would be saved. I was smacked down by a student."

"I'm not sure it was a smack-down. It may have been the opposite."

"It was a smack-down. And anyway, what if she's right? I'm forever cursed. Destined to be a vocal Cassandra."

"Nonsense. *I* believe you. So do your students. You're a good teacher. In fact, you're a great teacher. All the great teachers I've ever had passionately thought they were right. Most often, it turned out they were. And, unfortunately, not everyone always believed them."

Once more I avoided her eyes and looked down.

"So," she said. "Back to ancient Greece. She was given the choice to sleep with him, keep the gift of foresight, and have the world believe her. And she just said no?"

"So the story goes."

"Wow, and to think I gave it up to Harvey Moshman on his living room floor just because he knew all the words to the new Cold Play album."

Don't ask for details, my brain screamed, neon signs flashing "TMI" growing stronger and stronger.

"I certainly would have done Apollo," she continued. "I mean, being the sun god and all, he must have been hot. Probably a little full of himself. Lots of women, goddesses even, fawning all over him. But goodness, the gift of prophecy. Tough to turn that one down."

"I don't know," I said. "Curse and blessing."

"So would you have?" she asked.

"Would I have what?"

"Would you have slept with him?"

Please, dear God, don't have the dean walk in on this conversation.

"Apollo? I don't think so. I mean, sun god or not, I'm just not that kind of guy."

Samantha laughed. "Okay. If you were Cassandra, and you could keep the ability to see the future and, most importantly, be believed. *Then* would you have slept with him?"

I took one deep breath and two steps backwards and came down hard on the front desk, sitting on my hands. I was terribly afraid of where they would go if I left them to their own devices. I looked at Samantha. She was wearing her hair in pigtails, braided with blue and red yarn—courtesy, I was sure, of one of her adoring students. Her freckles ran down her face like drops of rain. Rivers of freckles. As always when I was around her I was completely, totally unhinged.

I didn't want to sleep with Apollo. I didn't want to sleep with Cassandra. I wanted to sleep with *her*. How obvious was that?

"Think about it," she continued. "If you knew what the future held, if you truly knew it, and everyone believed you. Everyone. Think of your power to do good in the world. To change history. Think about The Issue. You'd be a superhero!"

It really didn't seem like much to ask. One roll in the hay with the sun god and I save the world.

Or do I? What if I see the future and it's one of devastation and war and famine and hot, hot, hot, and I tell people, and they believe every word I say, but then they go right on doing what they're doing, right on riding the wave to the end of the world. Cassandra Complex or not, how was that any different from where I was right now?

"Do I really have to sleep with Apollo?" I asked. "Can't I at least have Cassandra instead?"

She laughed and glanced at her cell phone. "Jeez, gotta run. See you Thursday."

I watched her walk out the door and into the swirling snow, pigtails bobbing, promising myself to download every Cold Play album that evening, and wondering how the hell Harvey Moshman could ever have let her get away.

32

On Wednesday afternoons after teaching, my colleagues and I unwind by playing darts. We set up a board at the far end of our science department's conference room. To make it more interesting and to put a pseudo-intellectual spin on the game, we make our own targets and place them over the real board. That way, we're not throwing at numbers, we're zinging darts at things we despise.

We're very proud of ourselves. We consider it a creative way to take out our aggressions, at least some of them, while cultivating the always-important co-worker bond.

It's not for everyone. What started off as a somewhat friendly way to unwind, has taken a serious turn toward the cutthroat. Our competitive juices flow, testosterone levels rise considerably, and trash-talking reaches astronomical heights.

The botany professor used to play but she's recently bowed out, citing the obscene amount of "manly mayhem" that the game has devolved into. The real reason is that she sucks at darts.

Three of us play regularly: the natural history professor (a.k.a. the Lunatic), the anatomy/physiology professor (smartest guy in the school), and yours truly.

Each week we take turns making the board. There are a few set rules. No images of students, no colleagues, nothing that could be construed (by us, of course!) as overtly offensive.

Other than that, we're good to go.

The targets used to be simple, something that took little thought and even less time to make. Perhaps a few words, a picture from the net, a page cut out from a magazine. Nothing more. Arranged on a round sheet of paper and pinned to the board with point values stuck in random places.

Those days are O-V-E-R, over! Target making has assumed a life of its own. What used to take a few minutes now requires drafts, prototypes, even feedback from the art department. Those who don't play poke their heads in after class on Wednesday just to see the week's image. Last semester, the natural history professor skipped out on an entire lecture because he was physically unable to drag himself away from his board making.

We've come up with names for our dart-throwing alter egos. The A/P prof is "The Grim Reaper." The natural history prof is "Dartwin" (get it? "Darwin"?) Given his incredible inconsistency and overall inaccuracy, I suggested Dartlose. He told me to fuck off.

I keep changing names. I haven't found one yet that I'm truly comfortable with. If I lose a few weeks in a row, I blame the name, cast it aside, and think up a new one.

"Dartagnan" (named after the Three Musketeer's wannabe D'Artagnan) got me through most of last semester until I went into a tailspin. "Doctor Dioxide" was meant to intimidate, which it did at one point for five consecutive Wednesdays. Currently I'm "Methane Man," which, particularly after a lunch of leftover bean burritos, can instill fear in the hearts of my fellow players.

We keep the targets in a formal binder, autographed by the week's winner. The natural history prof is talking up developing a website. He's convinced it could go viral.

As previously noted, he is certifiably insane.

This semester has been an exceptional one for targets.

The A/P prof did fabulous work with "Bad Things That Begin with the Letter D." He had graphic pictures, assigned a point value to them, and arranged them with great artistic flair onto the board. It was an instant classic—dysentery, diphtheria, deafness, degenerative optic myopathy, delusional disorder (wow—a double D!), dementia, delirium, dengue fever, dermatitis, depression, Down syndrome, distemper, and dwarfism all came to life with terrifying images.

My suggestion to add the three climate-change D's (delay, deny, and dismiss) was met with derision. Mixing of issues was a definite don't.

So much to worry about with the letter D! Who would have thought?

I had a stunning come-from-behind victory courtesy of three Diarrheas in a row, each worth fifty points.

The natural history prof spent hours on a marvelous "Aquatic Invasive Plant Species From Hell" board featuring such ne'er-do-wells as purple loosestrife, Japanese knotweed, water chestnut, and phragmites, plants that take over wetlands and drive down biodiversity. He turned around and used it in class the very next day, flinging darts while loudly cursing their names, much to the delight of his students.

My focus was always on, who would have guessed it, The Issue. Given the overwhelming amount of climate-change shit there is to hurl darts at, I'm never at a loss for material.

I'd have to say my best work yet was last semester's three-part series entitled "Dire Consequences," which I spent most of winter break working on, with wonderful assistance from Jesse. His computer proficiency, along with excellent pen and ink skill, created collages of compellingly destructive images that you couldn't wait to have a go at. Drought, famine, sea-level rise, hurricanes, typhoons, and mass extinction all had a prominent place.

The only thing more depressing than the board was my complete inability to hit it. I came in dead last on every one of those games. Curses!

This weekend, with Jesse's and a good bit of weed's help, I devised a fab "Darts to the Deniers" board. It featured some of the many villains, those climate–change-denying Neanderthal corporations, politicians, and pundits who perpetuate the myths and misinformation so prevalent.

Fox News: Their motto? No lie too big to air!

Exxon/Mobile: We don't care. We don't have to care. We're Exxon!

Shell Oil: Three cheers for the melting of those pesky glaciers! Now we can drill wherever we want!

Keystone XL Pipeline: Aquifers be damned. We'll ship that dirty tar sands oil whether you like it or not!

ABC News: One feature (count 'em, one!) on climate change in the last year.

Wall Street Journal: Four fifths of their last year's letters, op-eds, editorials, and articles misleading on climate change.

Mitt the Flip ("I Love Coal") Romney: what more can you say?

Senator James Inhofe (Republican, Oklahoma): Global warming is "the second-largest hoax ever played on the American people, after the separation of church and state." Whoa, bro! Is there any gray matter left in there?

The entire right wing of the Republican Party: What's not to love? I don't want to stereotype, but it's oh-so-hard not to!

Last on this board (and we're just scraping the surface of bloodsucking leeches here) was my hands down favorite. For sheer lunacy, audacious impudence, and unbridled ignorance, it's hard to top the Heartland Institute.

A leading climate-change-denying organization, they launched a crazy billboard campaign in the Chicago area featuring the convicted Unabomber, Ted Kaczynski, and the mass murderer Charles Manson. Next to their billboard-sized pictures, making them look somehow even more insane then they actually were, was the text "I still believe in global warming. Do you?"

I kid you not.

If I was driving and I had seen that sign, I would have run off the fucking road.

I had worked hard on this board and I was damn proud of it. It was my shining moment, my *Mona Lisa*, my *Venus de Milo*. Just looking at the images made my fingers quiver and my pulse race.

"Prepare to be annihilated," I announced in as menacing a voice as I could muster.

It was epic struggle, a game of games. With one dart to go, the three of us were tied. Tied! I had driven myself into a frenzy, which, combined with seething rage against the deniers, had left me shaking.

The last dart. Winner take all.

The A/P prof got a direct hit on the evil empire, Exxon. Good for 30.

The natural history prof landed one right smack dab in that asshole Inhoffe's ear. Also good for 30.

Tie score. I hadn't won in weeks. The pressure was excruciating. All I had to do was hit that infuriating Heartland Institute logo and the game would be mine. One dart to close it out. One dart to seal the deal.

Focus. Focus. I took a deep breath, leaned back and . . . shit!

The dean walked in.

He hated our dart games. He thought it unprofessional,

inappropriate, and nasty. He had no appreciation for our creativity, our artwork, our dart-throwing dexterity.

We, however, knew the true story. Just like the botany professor, the dean totally sucked at the game.

He glared at me. I was startled, unhinged, and in mid-throw. I turned, tried to check my arm, but before I knew it the dart, with a mind of its own, lazily arced out of my hand.

My colleagues gasped.

"Holy Christ!" the dean yelled, hopping up and down. "Mother of . . . Jesus! What the hell, Casey!"

There was the dart. Sticking straight out of his shoe, imbedded in his foot, sunk deep into the big toe.

He reached down and yanked the sucker out.

"For the love of . . ." He hopped, slammed shut the door, gave a final terrified look through the window, and limped out.

There was a stunned moment of silence while I realized the extreme severity of the situation. What had happened was catastrophic, calamitous, unthinkable. With a sudden burst of inspiration I divined a way out.

"Do-over!" I cried. "No fair. I was distracted! I demand another throw!"

"Bullshit!" my colleagues yelled in unison, already psyching themselves up for sudden-death overtime.

"He walked in! That game was mine!"

"Bullshit!" they yelled again.

"Bastard!" I fumed. "Son of a bitch!" I slumped into a chair, crisscrossed my legs and hunched my shoulders, totally depressed by the injustice of it all. I watched as the natural history prof's dart struck straight to the heart of Heartland, and begrudgingly high-fived him as he ran his victory lap around the conference room table.

Toeless boss or not, the games must go on.

33

I DON'T LAY AWAKE AT NIGHT WORRYING about too many of my students. Most enter PVCC with a solid educational foundation, they're not too deep in debt, they talk lovingly about their families, and they have a clear vision of where they want to go. They see their community-college years as a stepping-stone to a better and brighter future. They're already off and running.

Then there are those students who can't quite seem to make it out of the starting gate.

This semester, once again, I had Warren in my class. It was his third time taking my Intro to Climate Change. I had flunked him twice, and he was hard at work on a third F.

It wasn't that he was stupid. Far from it. He was an extremely bright, personable kid with exceptional writing skills. When in class he was an active participant, articulate, vibrant, full of life and energy.

Outside of class, he was a walking disaster.

Anything bad that could possibly happen to a human

being, short of paralysis or death, happened to Warren with alarming regularity. He was a magnet for misfortune, a connoisseur of catastrophe. Calamity stuck with him like flies on turds.

I'm pretty adept at sniffing out BS, teasing out truth from fiction. Generally I give students the benefit of the doubt, but there are times when I have to call them on their sob stories.

Not so with Warren. There was no way he could possibly make this shit up.

His excuses for missed work, classes, and exams were definitely not your boring, run–of-the-mill, lah-dee-dah, crap-happens scenarios. They were a significant cut above. They hovered in the Hall of Fame of the totally bizarre, almost too strange to be true. He deserved his own column in "News of the Weird". If his life were a reality TV show, he'd be a megastar.

Of course this wasn't why he had flunked my class twice. Along with his uncanny bad luck, he had profound issues with procrastination. He had a remarkable inability to get work in on time, if at all. His ongoing bouts with the law and the ludicrous resulted in far too many absences, making him impossible to pass.

While I'm not one to gossip about my students overmuch, it was hard not to tell Warren stories.

"I saw that your favorite student made the paper yesterday," the botany professor said, cornering me at the copy machine. "Care to fill me in on details?"

"This is a good one," I replied, closing the copy room door, happy to oblige.

A herd of Australian fainting goats had fled their farm enclosure and made their way into the open door of a neighbor's apartment, wreaking havoc on house and home. Damages included a chewed-up laptop, belonging to—you guessed it—Warren.

There was even a picture in the *Glenfield Recorder*.

Warren, a broad grin on his face, holding the remains of his computer in one hand, petting one of the culprits with the other. Certainly a one-up on the classic "dog ate my paper" routine.

Last semester, he was attempting the Heimlich maneuver on some poor soul choking on a pork chop in the restaurant where he worked. The guy's wife, returning from the bathroom and thinking Warren was some punk gangsta attacking her husband, tased him. He fell over backwards and smashed his head, requiring fifteen stitches. As they say, no good deed goes unpunished.

The semester before, he was mistakenly arrested for indecent exposure and charged with urinating on baby Jesus in a Christmas crèche scene. The real culprit turned out to be the priest, who had imbibed a little too much of the communion wine and then mistaken the King of All Kings for the holly bush behind the church. How anyone could mistake Warren with his tattoos and piercings for a man of the cloth was beyond me.

Not surprisingly, all of this had led him to a rather delusional world view, which he was fond of sharing with me and anyone else whose ear he could bend. His somewhat scattered knowledge of The Issue, all three partial semesters of it, fit rather nicely into a paranoid paradigm.

It was a Tuesday afternoon. We were in the middle of a discussion on the albedo effect and how loss of glacial ice meant less reflected sunlight leading to greater warming and then even more loss of ice. A classic positive feedback loop.

I asked if there were any questions.

"Then I guess the Mayans really were right," Warren volunteered.

"About the melting Arctic ice?" I asked.

"About the end of the world. Looks like we really do have only a few weeks left!"

"Oh my god," said Jenny, one of my more outspoken

students. I could see her rolling her eyes. "Please tell me you're joking!"

"I'm dead serious," Warren continued. "December 21, 2012. It's the end of the Mayan calendar. They saw this shit going down thousands of years ago. Time to pay the piper."

"More like time to change the channel, Warren," Jenny replied. "Too much sci-fi TV."

Warren, along with the rest of the class, laughed. Remarkably, though incessantly reeling in his world of chaos, he maintained an astonishingly cheerful countenance. He would recount his frequent flirtations with disaster with a shrug and a smile. He was a popular kid. The ribbing he received from fellow students was good natured.

And one ever really knew how seriously to take him. Like with the Mayans. It was unclear whether or not he really was a true believer, or just out to pull our collective legs.

It was totally true that the Mayan end-of-the-world thing was the talk of the town. All the rage. Jesse had kept me up to date with the daily projections of impending doom, from the earth getting sucked into a black hole at the center of the galaxy to our imminent collision with a planet called Nibiru. December 21 was the last day of the Mayan long-count calendar, something going back 5,000-plus years. According to some, and Warren seemed to be one of them, this meant that the end was near. Climate chaos had only fanned the fires.

"You don't seriously buy that bullshit do you, Warren?" Jenny asked.

"I am," Warren announced proudly, "a Catastropharian."

"Catastro-who-ian?" I asked.

"Catastropharian. I'm into the Apocalypse," he said, smiling good naturedly.

"How can you be into the Apocalypse?" Jenny asked. "No one's 'into the Apocalypse.'"

"I am," Warren countered. "And so will you in three weeks."

As luck would have it, Warren was always present when the focus in class was on the catastrophic consequences of unchecked climate change. He was always absent when we dealt with solutions. He got the despair without the hope. His read on The Issue had gaps big enough to drive a Mayan temple through.

I felt a wave of guilt, knowing that, sometimes, a little bit of knowledge was not always the best thing.

"People are continually falling for crap like that," Jenny continued, her dander up. "Remember last year, October 21, 2011. You were freaking out, Warren, when some lunatic radio show host predicted the Rapture. People quit their jobs, sold all they owned, waited for the stairway to heaven. Beam me up, God! Jesus, Warren, remember? Last I checked, we're still here."

"My brother is a Jehovah's Witness," Jessica, one of the quiet ones, chimed in. "They're always going off on the Apocalypse. No such luck. I'm still stuck with him."

"I'm old enough to remember Y2K and the Millennium Bug," Samantha spoke up. She was sitting behind Warren and rested her hand gently, comfortingly on his shoulder. "All the computers were supposed to crash on New Year's Eve 1999. Planes were going to fall from the skies. The government was going to crumble. Warren, nothing happened."

"I think, Warren," I gently cut in, "as dire as the situation is, with concerted efforts by all of us, we can go a lot longer than three weeks. I have complete faith that great minds, such as those in this classroom, are going to be the ones to make the Mayans eat their words."

Warren looked mildly disappointed.

Sticking around after class, he asked, "So you don't think there's anything to this Mayan prediction?"

"I don't," I answered, almost following with a "sorry" that would have been wildly inappropriate.

"Damn," he said.

"Excuse me?"

"I was sort of hoping for a reprieve. I have a court date on December 23."

"Oh no."

"Oh yeah. I hit a fire hydrant."

"A fire hydrant?"

"I was driving this kid home and his ferret got under my foot. I couldn't find the brake."

I should have known. Who else but Warren would get a ferret under his foot?

"Wow. I'm so sorry. But, all things considered, it does beat the end of the world."

A smile crept over Warren's face.

"You don't think climate change is going to do it?"

"Not on my watch!" I exclaimed, somewhat arrogantly, inflating my power and ability about fifty zillion times, my newly named Cassandra Complex in full swing. "I'm not a great fan of the Apocalypse, Warren. Just not my thing. And, if I may be so bold, I'd encourage you to look elsewhere for inspiration."

I could see the wheels turning in the kid's brain.

"You really think there's hope?"

"I don't think. I know."

Warren smiled that winning smile.

"See you next class." I told him. "That is a command, not a suggestion."

"Aye, aye, captain."

He turned and left the room.

And, surprise of surprises, next class there he was.

Anyway, the Mayans couldn't be right. They just couldn't be.

After all, January was less than a month away.

34

"SHE ASKED YOU TO DO WHAT?" Jesse asked.

"Go to the middle-school science fair."

"Oh my god. Sarah! Did you hear that?" Sarah came in from the kitchen. "She asked him out!"

"Stop! She did not ask me out!"

"How did she say it?"

"What do you mean 'how did she say it'?"

"I mean what exactly did she say?" Jesse asked.

"What is this? The Inquisition? Why do you always do this to me? Jesus, she asked if I could go to her seventh-grade science fair. She said her kids would get a kick out of having a professor look over their work."

"Bullshit. Kids don't give a flying fuck about whether or not a professor shows up. *She* wants you there!"

"Oh my god, will you chill! You are so full of it!"

"What'd you say?" Jesse asked.

"What do you mean 'what did I say'? Is this a trick question?"

"What'd you say?"

"I said yes. Of course."

"How'd you say it?"

"Stop!"

"This is a date. She's asking you on a date."

"Are you nuts? It's a middle-school science fair!"

"It's a date," he reiterated.

"It's not a date!"

"Sarah?" Jesse asked. "Date or no date?"

"Could be an outing," Sarah answered, smiling at me.

"See?!" Jesse shouted. "Date. Outing. Same difference."

"Will both of you please stop!" I said.

"What's the longest river in Egypt?" Jesse continued.

"What?"

"You heard me. The longest river?"

"Am I missing something here?"

"Answer the question."

"Oh god. The Nile," I answered.

"Exactly. Denial!"

"Christ. Will you leave it?"

"Date, date, date!"

—

On Saturday morning I spent an inordinate amount of time choosing my T-shirt. I even stooped to asking Jesse what he thought.

He gave me the look.

"Don't open your mouth," I said. "Don't say a word. Just tell me which fucking T-shirt to wear!"

After about seventeen unsuccessful try-ons I eventually settled on the polar bear. A solid choice. I figured her kids would like that one the best.

I circled the middle-school parking lot at least five times before getting up enough nerve to finally park the car. Focusing on my breath, I did the usual before class routine.

Nose clear? Check.

Zipper up? Check.

Hair not too crazy? Lost cause. Don't even go there.

The middle-school gymnasium was buzzing with science fair activity. Students stood in front of their projects with parents proudly looking on. Parents chased after students' younger siblings. Siblings chased after siblings who were already bored to tears and were pinching and whacking each other and crawling under tables and causing general havoc and mayhem. The noise level was deafening.

"Hey!" Samantha greeted me, a kid hanging on each arm. "I'm so glad you made it!"

"Hey!" I answered. "So am I."

"Natalie, Tony, this is Professor Casey," she said. "He's my teacher at my college. He's come to look at all of the wonderful science projects you've worked so hard on!"

"Awesome!" the kids said, letting go of her and fleeing the scene. Jesse was right. They clearly did not give a shit.

The science projects were arranged on tables in tidy rows in the middle-school gym. I walked down the aisles, reading the posters and asking questions of the little science dweebs. I was bowled over by their enthusiasm, intensity and intelligence.

For the most part the projects were beyond terrific. Middle schoolers aren't yet versed in the art of academic bullshit, so their work cuts to the quick in an incredibly appealing way.

"Boy, I wish your students could see the work my kids have done," Samantha bragged.

"I wish my students could *do* the work your kids have done!" I replied.

She laughed.

All of the projects had an environmental theme, and I was pleased to see there were quite a few that dealt exclusively with The Issue.

One pudgy boy with a buzz cut had built a miniature greenhouse and measured how trapped infrared radiation effected temperature. He still retained a hint of a little kid lisp, and he bounced up and down as he talked. It was all I could do not to hug him.

There was one project graphically illustrating the incredible inefficiency of incandescent lightbulbs and the amount of heat waste they generate. An adorable girl with braces and braids had built a box around an incandescent lightbulb and a similar one around an energy-efficient compact fluorescent, and recorded temperatures in both.

"Lightbulbs should be just that," she explained. "Lightbulbs. Not heat bulbs! That's just wasted energy!"

I applauded.

She had altered an old-time Smokey the Bear anti–forest fire poster portraying a burnt-out forest which now read, "Only You Can Prevent Climate Change!" Brilliant!

There was another on the effect of acidification on ocean life, measuring the impact of pH change on the physical integrity of clam and scallop shells. The boy was like a mini-Einstein, with an enormous slanting forehead and outlandishly unruly hair. I was convinced he'd have absolutely no difficulty making a seamless transition from middle school straight to PVCC.

"You are one smart dude!" I told him. He grinned ear to ear and his hair seemed to twist and twirl and grow another inch.

My hands-down favorite, however, was the experiment determining the effect of climate change on sea-level rise. The presenter was not an inch over four feet, if that, and she had shockingly red hair. She looked about seven.

"Tell me about your project," I prompted.

She stood stock-still, back straight, hands folded, looking me straight in the eyes, and launched into her well-rehearsed spiel.

"Well," she began. "As we all know, release of carbon dioxide from the combustion of fossil fuels is causing the planet to warm."

She totally had me at the "as we all know." None of this "scientists theorize" or "the experts agree" but instead "we all know." Absolutely no wiggle room there. You're either with us or you're anti-science. Take that, climate deniers!

"The warming of the planet is causing Arctic ice to melt," she continued. "What effect do you believe that will have on sea levels?"

"Umm . . ." I hesitated. "It will cause them to rise?"

"That's exactly what I hypothesized," she continued. "Let's see what the reality is."

My god, this girl was good!

"In this container with water and floating ice I marked the water line and put it next to a heat lamp.

"In this next container, also with water but with a pre-tend island in the middle, I marked the water line and put the ice on top of the island."

It was next to a heat lamp as well.

"The first container represents Arctic ice like at the North Pole. Did you know there is no land under Santa's workshop? It's ice floating on water."

Jesus, did this brilliant little girl, a budding climatologist, still believe in Santa?

"The second container represents glaciers on land, like in Greenland or Antarctica. It's different from ice floating on water, isn't it?"

"It is," I agreed.

"So what do you think will happen when the ice melts?"

Samantha looked at me and winked.

It was a great little experiment. I took notes so that I could replicate it in class. You had to think about it. Most folks would say both would cause a rise in sea level, but she explained icebergs melting had no direct effect whereas glaciers melting caused a dramatic increase.

"I do hope you've learned something!" the girl closed, thanking me for my time.

"I certainly have!" I answered, my eyes practically tearing.

—

"Your kids are amazing," I complimented, as the fair began to wind down. "They are so smart. They really are. I had no idea these projects would be so sophisticated. They are brilliant. Absolutely brilliant. I am so impressed."

Samantha beamed as though they were her very own flesh and blood.

"And they love you. It's so clear they worship the ground you walk on! You should be very proud. I remember my middle-school science fair project. It was a leaf collection. There were like four leaves, and two of them were the same. I even think I screwed up the identification. Extremely lame. But *these* projects! These kids are little Einsteins and Einsteinettes."

"It's a good crop this year," she agreed.

"I guess. That one over there. The little guy with the Bart Simpson shirt. I swear I had a ten-minute conversation with him about methane emissions from permafrost. He knows more about it than I do. I asked him to be a guest speaker in my class. He laughed but I'm serious. I really am."

"He's a smarty!"

"He is. If one of my college kids did a project like that I'd have thought I'd died and gone to heaven."

"He is a wonderful boy."

"And that girl over there. The one with the methane hydrates and positive feedback loops? Jesus, she is so bright. And she's the same age as the little dweeb?"

"Both twelve. Both seventh graders."

"You're sure?"

Samantha nodded.

"Wow. Who would've thought? The girl looks like a

high school homecoming queen, the mini-dude seems too young to be allowed on the monkey bars. It's like night and day."

"Tell me about it," Samantha replied. "That was me at their age."

"Which one?" I asked. "The Monkey or the Queen?"

She drew my attention to a little girl, one wearing a teddy bear jumper with striped leggings. Another cutie and smart as a whip, but it was nothing shy of outrageous to think of her as a peer of the Homecoming Queen.

"Monkey bars," Samantha sighed. "My goodness. I was so out of it in middle school. So undeveloped. It was not an easy age. It just wasn't. All the other girls' bodies were changing except for mine. At least that's what it seemed like to me at the time. I remember crying myself to sleep at night wondering what was wrong with me. I didn't get breasts until my senior year in high school."

I caught my breath.

"Wow!" I exclaimed, and then, my inability to self-edit rearing its awkward head, added, "things sure turned out beautifully."

Samantha turned and looked me straight in the eyes.

"What do you mean?" she asked.

I took a staggered step backwards, practically poking my eye out on some sort of contraption sticking out from one of the kid's projects.

"Umm, ah, well, you know, I mean, late bloomers are always the most . . . you know, whew, wow."

If she had only stopped smiling at me there would have been a remote possibility of finishing my sentence in some sort of reasonably coherent way.

But she didn't. She just kept smiling. A beautiful, full–lipped, luminous smile that lit up the gym.

I was dazzled, dazed, and confused. My usual state of affairs around her.

She gave me another wink.

It was all I could do to beat a hasty retreat, mumbling something about an exhibit I had yet to visit.

God, if it wasn't like seventh grade all over again.

—

"She winked at you three times?" Jesse asked during the mandatory debriefing session following the science fair.

"Twice."

"Once with the cute kid, but that one doesn't really count. Once when you complimented her boobs . . ."

"I didn't compliment her boobs!"

"You did," Jesse said.

"I didn't."

"Whatever. And when was the other one?"

"There was no other one!"

"I thought you said . . ."

"No. There was no third time! Christ, aren't two winks enough?"

"No argument here. Two winks. God. You better put the brakes on fast!"

"Brakes? What are you talking about?" I asked.

"Slow the flow, bro. Keep this up at this pace and you'll be holding hands by this time next year. Jesus, we could see a first kiss by the end of the decade!"

"Ahhhh! Why do I tell you anything?"

"You don't tell me anything," Jesse said, putting his arms around me. "You tell me everything! That's why I love you. I can relive all of my teenage angst and awkwardness vicariously through you. And whenever I feel like a spaz around women, whenever I'm on the brink of despair, I listen to you and think, Wow! You're so much more fucked up than I am! And then, presto chango, I feel so better about myself! It's like therapy, only without the co-pay!"

"Anything to oblige," I grumbled.

—

The next Tuesday in class, I managed to revisit that awkward adolescent faux pas and once again publicly humiliate myself.

"Here is your breast," I announced loudly, handing back to Samantha the exam she had taken last week.

"Thanks," she said, "but that won't be necessary. I already have two. I don't know where I'd put a third."

Ahhhhh! Curses to Freud and all of his slips!

"Test! Test!" I cried, turning a brighter shade of red while the class laughed. "I'm handing back *tests*!"

Like I said, thirty-two going on thirteen.

35

THE CLIMATE CHANGERS Had made up posters and blanketed the Main and East building walls with them. They had the Office of Student Life send out the following e-mail to all PVCC staff, faculty and students:

HEY ALL YOU BUDDING POETS, ENERGY SAVERS, AND ENVIRONMENTAL DO-GOODERS!

Here is your chance to have your poetry published! Please join the First-Ever PVCC Climate Changers Poetry Slam (kind of)!!!!

We are looking for submissions of poetry (haikus, rhymes, free verse, you name it) with the theme of **TURNING OFF LIGHTS WHEN NOT IN USE!** Winning submissions will be published, printed, and placed on light switches throughout campus!

Why take part in this contest? As a published poet you can:

1. Brag to all of your friends at boring holiday parties, speak really pretentiously, and make casual references to esoteric things that only other poets could possibly understand.

2. Put "published poet" on your résumé.

3. Save the world, one light switch at a time.

4. Win a valuable prize, but we haven't decided what it's going to be yet—or, frankly, whether or not we're even going to give one!

WRITE NOW!

The Climate Changers put out the call on a Tuesday. By Wednesday they were inundated with verse.

I had thought that there might be a bit of an interest, a few pompous verses from some of the English majors, maybe an iambic pentameter or two from an English faculty member, but nothing approaching the avalanche they received. I was shocked at the response.

Their e-mail was absolutely flooded with entries.

"Dude!" Trevor yelled. "This is crazy! There must be a hundred of these mothers in here!"

"Poets, poets everywhere!" Hannah answered. "Who would have thought? This is awesome!"

"Are there any good ones?" I asked.

"Depends on what you call 'good,'" Hannah answered diplomatically.

"Hey," Trevor said. "Quantity over quality. It's the thought that counts!"

"In other words, most of them . . ."

"Suck!" Trevor answered. "Afraid so."

The next meeting was devoted to picking the winners. I was not surprised when what started out as a celebration of the written word quickly turned, as was so wont to happen in Climate Changers meetings, into yet another all-out slug fest.

It never ceased to amaze me how like-minded people, good friends all of them, could squabble with such spite for so long over next to nothing.

I came in late to find the battle lines already drawn along predictable lines.

Hannah standing firm with the pragmatic and the literate, Trevor wildly flying the flag of the proletariat.

"I don't get it," Trevor said. "Tell me one thing that is wrong with these?"

"Oh my god!" Hannah said. "Are you serious? Number one, they aren't poems. Number two, they're stupid. Number three, they suck. Do you actually need more reasons than that?"

"How can someone so smart be so wrong?" Trevor argued. "These are friggin' brilliant!"

"Read some," I suggested.

Trevor obliged.

"Sometimes history needs a push."
—Vladimir Lenin

"Sometimes light switches need a push-off."
—Anonymous

"Without a revolutionary theory there cannot be a revolutionary movement."
—Vladimir Lenin

"Without a light off, there can be no darkness."
—Anonymous

"A lie told often enough becomes the truth."
—Vladimir Lenin

"A light turned off long enough becomes the darkness."
—Anonymous

I laughed.

"Trevor, no one even knows who Lenin is!" Hannah said derisively.

"What are you talking about?" Trevor replied. "He's the godfather of Communism, for Christ sake!"

"I'm not sure I would categorize him quite that way," I offered.

The two hotheads ignored me.

"I know who he is, you moron, but your average Joe probably thinks he's John's little brother, the long lost Beatle."

Trevor continued:

"Let a hundred flowers bloom."
—Mao Zedong

"Let a hundred switches be turned off."
—Anonymous

"In waking a tiger, use a long stick."
—Mao Zedong

"In turning off a light, use a finger."

—Anonymous

"Wait just a minute," I said. "Who wrote these?"

"Who do you think?" Hannah replied, glaring at Trevor.

Trevor laughed and raised his fist in the air. "All power to those who turn off the power!"

"You're 'Anonymous'!" I said, realizing I should have figured that one out after the first poem. "I thought this contest was all about getting other folks involved?"

"Do you actually think 'other folks' would be capable of composing so-called poems like this?" Hannah said. For whatever reason, Trevor's literary works of art were working her into a frenzy. "Trevor stuffed the ballot box! No wonder we got so many entries. It's the greatest hits from his favorite dead revolutionaries. Listen to this one!"

"A revolution is not a dinner party, or writing an essay, or painting a picture, or doing embroidery."

— Mao Zedong

"Notice how he didn't mention turning off the light."

— Anonymous (a.k.a. Trevor)

"Not only is it total crap, but it doesn't even make sense!" Hannah was practically screaming.

"It does too," Trevor replied, his voice hard to hear over my and the rest of the Climate Changers' laughter.

"It does not!"

"Oh," Trevor countered. "So this one's a Pulitzer Prize winner?"

Roses are red
Violets are white
Please when you leave
Turn out the light

"I'd give that poem fifteen minutes tops before someone writes some smart-ass comment on it."

"And I wonder who that smart ass will be," Hannah said. "Hmm. . . . Let me guess!"

"And anyway, violets aren't even white!" Trevor yelled.

"They are too!"

"They are not!"

"Are too!"

I didn't have to ask who wrote the last poem. Hannah certainly had her dander up.

I was having a hard time understanding why such passionate speeches and emotional outbursts would come from such smart, witty college kids. *I* thought these poems were funny as hell. So did the rest of the Climate Changers. Was there something else going on under the radar here?

The night before Jesse and Sarah were having a spat and they sounded just like these two. Going at it over trivialities. Hmm . . .

"That poem gets posted," Trevor said. "This one gets posted!"

Roses are crap
Violets they suck
Turn off the lights
Or we're shit out of luck

"Or better yet, how about this?"

Roses are gross
Violets are crass
Turn off the lights
Or I'll kick your ass

By this time even Trevor and Hannah were laughing.

"Why not!" Hannah said. "Just make sure this one goes next to it!"

Holding hands
They wandered into the light of the classroom
Flipping off the switch
She turned, pulled him close, and kissed him

"You know," Trevor said, sidling up to Hannah. "That one is actually pretty cute."

"Darn right it's cute," she answered. "'I want bread, but I want roses too!'"

Wait a minute. Were their bodies actually touching?

"But please," Hannah continued, batting her eyes at Trevor. "Can we just leave this one out?"

Mountain tops
Blown sky high
Burn the coal
The earth will fry
Oceans rising
Children die
Hear the sobbing
Mothers cry
Please turn the lights off when you leave.
Have a nice day.

"That does not make me want to have a nice day," Hannah said. "It just makes me want to kill myself, with the lights on!"

Ultimately the Climate Changers picked a nice bouquet of flowery verse, some dripping with gloom, others bursting with color—quite an eclectic mix of good and not so good, but all with a point and a concrete take-home message. Some were even written by students other than Hannah and Trevor.

We left the meeting, each with a stack of poems, searching out light switches to tape them under, mouthing silent prayers that even the little things like these would change the world.

Watt you say?
That's right.
It's watts.
And kilowatts.
And megawatts.
And on and on.
It's just not right!
So when you leave
Turn off the light.

36

Every semester I invite a panel of professionals to talk to my class about employment opportunities in the renewable-energy field. It's part of the "what the hell I am going to do with the rest of my life" exploration I attempt to bring to my students.

The point of the panel is to highlight the diversity of local, well-paying jobs in clean energy. Academia can be so damn theoretical that students often lose track of the awesome fact that the knowledge they're (hopefully!) acquiring in class can actually have real-world applicability. It's always good to bring things back down to earth, to get students to understand that, believe it or not, wonder of all wonders, with a little bit of luck and a lot of effort you can actually get paid to do good work. Aware of my OCD as they are, not all my students buy that line from me. Hence the need to bring in a bunch of folks from the field to demonstrate that I'm not as full of shit as my students may think I am.

This semester's panel consisted of an energy auditor,

a photovoltaic installer, and a small-business owner who sold and installed solar hot-water and photovoltaic systems. I had a geothermal engineer scheduled as well but his car broke down, his kids were sick, and his mother-in-law was going in for surgery, which sounded an awful lot like the bullshit excuses for missed assignments I got from my students.

I had chosen the panelists carefully. They were pragmatic, easygoing folk who related well to the college crowd, had reasonably good stories to tell, and, most important of all, could keep their audience awake for an hour and a quarter. They spoke eloquently and passionately about the work they did, and they were very encouraging to students looking for entry-level jobs, even those who had no intention of going any further than an associate's degree.

The take-home message was YES YOU CAN! Yes you can save the world while putting a roof over your head and feeding your family! Hooray!

Each panelist spoke for about ten minutes, showed some PowerPoint images of their worksites and the jobs they had done, talked about their background and how they had arrived at their professional destination, and offered tips for students so inclined to enter their profession. It was interesting and useful, nothing overly dramatic. I sat in the back, once again struck by how difficult it is to be a student and how goddamn uncomfortable those chairs were.

I struggled. Try as I might to focus on the panelists, my eyes were constantly lured to the nape of the neck of you-know-who. I'd force myself to turn away, only to twist right back again. It got so bad that I had to physically put my hand on the side of my head, push it in a forward direction, and hold it there.

Eyes front and center! I kept commanding myself, mostly to no avail.

Every move of her body, every twitch of her shoulder,

every time she rearranged her hair, I was all over it. Once she turned around and glanced in my direction, which startled the hell out of me. My pen flew out of my hand and hit the student in front of me in the back of his neck.

She smiled.

I caught my breath.

The panelists went on speaking.

How anyone could listen to anything the speakers were saying while sitting in a class with her in it was way beyond me.

Eyes forward! I demanded.

Yeah, right. Whatever! the eyes responded, wandering back to the nirvana-like nape of the neck.

After about half an hour of presentations, the speakers took a short break while I reiterated that these panelists represented only three of the myriad possibilities for green employment, that the venue was wide open. I brought out the fact that teaching was a viable option, that we had a middle-school science teacher amongst us doing great work in the climate field (she stood up and curtsied—so cute!), and that there were loads of opportunities to make a difference in the world.

Then I opened up the discussion for questions to the panelists.

Most of them were run-of-the-mill, routine, what you'd expect students to ask.

"What was your background?"

"Do you like your job?"

"How much do you get paid?"

It was getting toward the end of the class, backpacks began rustling, the natives were getting restless.

Finally, with time running out, I asked for one final question.

"What's the weirdest thing that's ever happened to you on the job?" Warren the Catastropharian asked. Yes! He was in class that day!

"So," the PV installer, a guy by the name of Brad, began. "We were doing this job down on Vernon Street. Putting up 3 kilowatts of photovoltaics on this really funky old house. Great project.

"I was having lunch on the roof. Which actually is not weird at all. We do it all the time. The views from roofs are outstanding!

"Anyway, there I was, relaxing, sitting up there on an old chimney. It was for a fireplace that hadn't been up and running in decades, so I knew I'd be safe. At least I thought I would."

This last line got the student's attention.

"There I am enjoying the view and my ham and cheese when suddenly *KABAM!*" Brad brought his hand down hard on the table with a loud noise. Definitely an attention grabber.

"My ass feels like it's on fire! Literally, on fire! My immediate reaction was: 'Damn, I sure as hell was wrong about that chimney!'"

The students laughed, hanging on to every word. Even my eyes were focused on the speaker.

"I stand up screaming, and throw my ham and cheese to the four winds. My co-workers are freaking out.

"'Dude!' they yell. 'Are you okay? What's up?'"

It was clear Brad had told this story before, probably dozens of time. The grin on his face made it equally clear that he relished the retelling. He had the timing down perfect.

"'My ass!' I yell. 'It's on fire! Somebody do something!' I'm jumping up and down, balancing on the pitch of the roof, yelling and screaming, waving my arms like a friggin' lunatic, and suddenly they all start laughing. I mean, they're busting a gut, going absolutely nuts. All of them. My boss is laughing so hard I can see a pee spot forming in the middle of his pants!"

Appropriate or not, there was no way I was going to stop this story from unfolding.

"I'm yelling, 'What the frig! I'm on fire! *HELP!*' and they're keeling over with laughter. Think about it. My ass is on fire and they're laughing their asses off! It was like the world's worst nightmare!"

He paused for dramatic effect.

"So what happened then?" Warren asked, right on cue.

"Come to find I had a squirrel stuck on my ass. It had bit right through my pants and got one of its gnarly little incisors lodged right into my butt cheek. Stuck there. Hanging on for dear life. Evidently the old chimney was being used as a squirrel's nest and one of the little buggers had bitten me right in the ass!"

Now it was my class's turn to go nuts. They were laughing and laughing. The other two panelists had tears in their eyes.

"There I am, jumping up and down on the roof with a damn squirrel chewing me out!" Brad leapt out of his seat and demonstrated his squirrel-jerking, ass-jiggling move.

The class erupted.

"Finally the damn thing gets tired, alarmed, bored, whatever and leaps off, scampering back down the chimney. That, my friends, was weird!"

"Then what?" Morgan managed to ask through his giggling.

"Boss gave me the rest of the day off. I told you. I have a great job!"

All right, so the take-home message probably got a little lost in the shuffle. All they'll remember from the panel was the guy with the squirrel on his ass. Hell, all they'll probably remember from the entire semester was the guy with the squirrel on his ass.

That and the Twenty-Nine-Year-Old being attacked by geese.

But hey, what are you going to do? It was a great story. I'll definitely invite him back next semester.

37 ❦

THERE WAS LESS THAN THREE WEEKS to the end of the semester. Less than three weeks and she wouldn't be a student anymore. I could barely stand it.

Once again Samantha stayed after class. I so looked forward to these times alone with her. If other students needed me or wanted my time I was resentful and edgy. I knew it was totally inappropriate, but I just couldn't help myself.

This afternoon she was wearing a flowery skirt with a Caribbean-blue top that brought out the ocean in her eyes. I was lost in the waves of blue washing over me.

"I took your advice and registered for a class yesterday," she said.

I sat down hard on my desk, the dry-erase marker slipping from my hand.

"You what?"

"Registered. For the spring semester. I still need PDPs, Professional Development Points. I thought that Adolescent Psychology might come in handy. Do you know the professor who's teaching it?"

"Here? You registered for a class here?"

"Yeah. This class has been such a great experience. And if I get three more credits I should be good to go for a few years."

"Here?" I repeated like a moron. "You registered for a class *here*?"

She looked at me peculiarly. "Remember last Thursday in class? You read us the riot act about registering early so we could get the courses that we wanted. I'm glad I did because I got one of the last seats in that psych class. And it's perfect. It meets Tuesday and Thursday late afternoons, just like this one. And God knows I could use a little extra insight into why my students are so weird."

I could feel my throat tightening, overwhelmed by a rapid onset of psychotically induced anaphylactic shock. My tongue had instantaneously swollen to the size of an English cucumber, my skin crawled, my nose dripped, I was terrified I would lose control of my bladder.

Sure, I had told my students repeatedly and in no uncertain terms to register for spring classes, but Christ knows I didn't mean her! Not here! Not now!

She had told me about the need to keep her teaching certification current, how college classes counted . . . but damn, damn, and double damn!

I conjured up the lake image, desperate to keep from passing out. Wavy and wild on the outside, calm and collected deep within. *I am the lake*, I told myself, focusing on the breath while frantically trying not to swallow my tongue. *I am the lake.*

"Do you know who the professor is?" she asked again.

"Lake," I croaked. "Lake. No, not lake, I don't know. Wait, wait, yes I do. Burk, Gail Burk. Very good. Very dynamic. Students love me, I mean, love her. It's a great class. A really great class."

Samantha gave me another funny look. I turned my head to avoid her eyes.

"Are you okay?" she asked.

"No," I said. "Yes. I don't know."

I was in shock. Total nightmare, world-spinning-out-of–control, nothing-matters-anymore, bring on the Mayan end-of-the-world shock. Whether she was in my class or someone else's class, she would still be a student. No matter how "nontraditional" she was, whether she was just in it for the PDPs or not, whatever the reason, she was still a *student in my school!* There for all the world to see. Strictly verboten! GAME OVER!

It was a sledgehammer to the cranium. A shattering of the skull with the contents of my pathetic brain spewed grotesquely on the classroom floor and no one, no one, could ever mop it up. All thoughts of a future with her annihilated, blown away, *POOF*, vaporized in an instant.

It all became crystal clear to me. I mean, what had I been thinking? That in any way, shape, or form she had ever been even remotely attracted to me? That she wanted any kind of relationship outside of the classroom? That I meant anything more to her other than a quirky, climate-obsessed, pitiful professor?

Earth to Casey: WAKE UP! Who was I fooling? This had been one cosmically cruel delusional joke at my expense. To have misinterpreted her flirtations as anything other than idle banter had been clinical insanity. What a vain, narcissistic ass I had been. I had been viewing this relationship from an absurd angle that was nothing short of madness.

What had I been thinking? *What had I been thinking?!*

"I gotta run," I whispered, barely keeping my urine in. "I've got a meeting with a student. I mean a colleague. Whatever. I'll see you next week."

I turned my back on her and fled.

—

I came home to find Sarah and Jesse in the kitchen, cuddling and cooking. I flung my students' lab work to the floor and crumpled along with it in a heap.

They exchanged glances.

"Let me guess," Jesse said. "Bad day?"

"Bad? Bad? This is way beyond bad. This day made bad look good. This day was catastrophic, monumentally horrific, one for the record books. Google disaster and there'll be a picture of me in my classroom an hour and a half ago."

"Dean on your case again?"

"God, I wish. Worse. Way worse."

"Let me guess," Sarah chimed in. "Something to do with her?"

"Bingo!"

"Oh no. She has a boyfriend?" Sarah asked.

"God no."

"A girlfriend?" Jesse asked.

I ignored him. "She told me she registered for a class next semester. She's going to be a student again! At PVCC!"

"In another one of your classes?" Sarah asked.

"No. Adolescent Psychology or some shit like that. It doesn't matter. A student's a student. Christ Almighty, I'm doomed. I finally find the woman of my dreams and she doesn't even know I exist."

"Don't be melodramatic," Jesse said. "She knows you exist."

"Not in the way that I want her to! To her I'm just a professor. A professor! To think, even for a moment, I ever actually thought there was anything more to it than that is absurd. I'm totally fucked. I'm destined to walk the planet, sad and lonely and forlorn for the rest of my days. Maybe the nihilists are right, maybe life has no purpose, no meaning, no nothing. This is my wake-up call, the nail in my coffin. God, maybe I'll just end it all. Jump off the French King Bridge or something."

"You can't," Jesse replied.

"Why the hell not?" I asked.

"You're afraid of heights."

"All right. Then I'll stab myself with one of these knives."

"Good luck with that," Sarah said. "I can't even find a blade in this house sharp enough to slice this tomato."

"God, why me? Why me? I just want a woman, like Sarah, to occasionally cook me dinner. Is that too much to ask?"

"Whoa, whoa, wait a minute, buster," Sarah said. "I'm pulling an evening shift tonight. I'm cooking my own damn dinner. You two fools are on your own."

Jesse had scooted up to her and they were doing that snuggling thing again.

"There!" I cried. "That's what I want! To put my hand on the rear of the woman I love!"

"Don't go insulting my lady!" Jesse shot back. "That's an ass, not a rear!"

Sarah playfully slapped his hand away.

I put on the best pouting look I could muster. "I appreciate the support. The empathy. The kindness and open hearts and soothing words. I really do! The absolute worst day of my life, and you treat it like some silly sitcom."

"Casey, sweetheart." Sarah stopping scrambling eggs and came and sat down beside me, gently massaging my neck. She had taken to calling me "sweetheart" in the last week. While up until now I had found it soothing and comforting, at this moment I had the horrible sensation that she might be the only one to ever call me that.

"You are a wonderful man. We all know it. I am absolutely convinced that Samantha feels the same way. I saw how she looked at you at the march on the coal plant. We've heard your stories about what she's said to you."

"Then why is she taking another class? Why?"

"She probably doesn't know the rules. She probably thinks that if she's not your student then it's okay to date."

"But it isn't. I can get screwed!"

"I thought that's what you wanted?" Jesse asked.

"Stop it, Jesse!" Sarah glowered at him, making threatening gestures with a spatula. "Stir the eggs. Look, why not just take the leap and ask her out. I know she'll say yes. I know it! You'll just have to keep the whole thing a little under wraps for a few months. No one needs to know. It wouldn't be that hard to do."

"I don't want to keep it under wraps!" I said, my voice rising an octave or two and crackling like a thirteen-year-old's. "I don't want to be scared walking down the streets of Glenfield for fear of being seen with her! I just want a normal relationship!"

Sarah turned and faced me. "I'm scared every day to walk down the streets for fear of being seen with him," she pointed to Jesse. "And our relationship is far from normal."

"Thank God for that!" Jesse replied, placing his hand back on her rear end and giving it a pinch. "Anyway, there's always the end of next semester. May is not that far away."

"May? Are you kidding me? *May?* I'm not going to make it to the weekend let alone May. I'm fucked. That's it in a nutshell. I'm totally fucked."

I turned and shuffled to my room.

"Wake me up in six months," I called back to the two of them, collapsing onto my bed.

38

"WE'RE FIRED UP!

"We can't take it no more!
"We're fired up!
"We can't take it no more!"

The Climate Changers were totally psyched. They were huddled together out in the middle of Parking Lot B, chanting and stomping and pumping themselves up. No cold/sleet/freezing rain weather crap was going to dampen their spirits. No way, no how! We were carpooling over to the Downtown Center where the PVCC Foundation's finance committee was ready to meet with us on the Divestment from Fossil Fuel campaign.

My spirits, on the other hand, couldn't have been any damper. It had been less than a day since Samantha had dropped the "by the way I'm taking another class so DON'T EVEN THINK ABOUT ASKING ME OUT EVER!" bombshell, and I was wallowing in depression.

Elisabeth Kübler-Ross was a famous psychiatrist that Samantha was sure to study in her adolescent psychology class. While Kübler-Ross's work focused extensively on death and dying, she elaborated in an articulate and helpful way five predictable stages of grief that people routinely go through following traumatic loss. The acronym she proposed was DABDA: denial, anger, bargaining, depression, and acceptance.

Since yesterday, I had zipped through the first three stages and was now completely immersed in the fourth. I was pretty pleased with myself; some people took years and never made it past stage one.

Denial for me had lasted all of about thirty seconds. I'm way too insecure to think that something terrible isn't actually happening to me.

The anger stage was also brief and fleeting; I mean, who was I going to get angry with? Her? She was way too perfect for that. Me? Pity maybe, but I just couldn't seem to get to anger. Try as I might to blame the Roommate, even that was a no-go.

I had spent most of the night tossing and turning over the bargaining stage, but that too simply wasn't cutting it. While I wasted a good part of an hour wrestling with the decision to accept Jesus Christ as my Lord and Savior if only she'd drop the goddamn class, that was really quite a stretch.

So I cut to the quick and moved right into stage four: depression. I was really much more comfortable there. I figured I could take that one and run with it for years—Christ, maybe for the rest of my life.

I'm not one to think that there's only one soul mate out there, a predetermined chosen one waiting just for his counterpart—but in my case I wasn't so sure. As previously noted, my track record around women was far from stellar. What were the chances of someone like Samantha popping into my life again? Plus I was thirty-two, for Christ sake. I was beginning to think like my mother. My days were already numbered.

Acceptance be damned! Depression it was going to be.

Thankfully, OCD carries with it a few perks. One was that I could shed my OSD (Obsessive Samantha Disorder), at least momentarily, adequately mask stage four, and rise to the task at hand if it meant something to do with climate change. With a precise goal in mind I could free my mind of her, sometimes even for entire minutes at a time. And this divestment thing was a big deal.

The Climate Changers had definitely done their homework. Per the norm, Hannah and Trevor had taken the lead and accomplished the lion's share of the work, but everyone had chipped in. If students in my class could accomplish in one semester half of what the Climate Changers had done in a week, I'd be as happy as a pig in shit. Maybe even happier.

The Wednesday previous, Hannah had been like a drill sergeant, barking out orders, assigning tasks, setting priorities and due dates, not taking no for an answer.

"Abbie, I want that list printed of the dirty 200 immediately. And I want ten copies made, collated, two-sided, stapled, one in each of the trustee's folders. We've got to get them out today. Got it?"

Abbie gave a salute and happily went off to do as she was told. Some are leaders, some are followers. Abbie was definitely the latter, perfectly content in her role as a foot soldier in the war on fossil fuels.

Following their "We all want to save the world" meeting, the Climate Changers had jumped onboard 350.org's Divestment Campaign, targeting the top 200 publicly traded companies that held the vast majority of the world's proven oil, gas, and coal reserves. 350.org's campaign was simple, and the Climate Changers were all over it.

Immediately freeze any new investment in fossil-fuel companies.

Divest from those 200 companies within five years.

"Five years?" Hannah had said. "That's baloney. I want them out now!"

"Come on Hannah," Trevor had cautioned. "Be realistic. You can't just sell off everything on a moment's notice. It takes a while to check out. Don't make demands that you know can't possibly be met."

"OMG, have you gone over to the dark side? Remember the last battle we had over this issue? Since when are you all about 'slow the flow, bro'?"

"I'm just saying . . ."

"Wow! Wow! Who would have thought?" Hannah said. "Mister 'throw caution to the wind, man the barricades, full speed ahead' now bitching about moving too fast. I didn't see that happening in my lifetime!"

It was, I couldn't help but notice, quite the switch—a role reversal if there ever was one. Just when you think you've got everyone pegged, shit like this happens and screws it all up. Life can be so complicated.

"Look," Trevor continued. "My point is—"

"Meagan, have you got that information on socially responsible investment strategies summarized? We need it. Today. You're on it!"

Another salute, this time from Meagan, and off she marched.

Hannah turned back to Trevor.

"Darling, make yourself useful. Is the PowerPoint from my laptop loaded on to the flash drive? And check to make sure that last slide has the 350 website."

"Darling"? "Darling"? Was that a diss or a slip? Was there really something else going on here?

Chagrined, Trevor, like the others before him, dutifully trotted off to save the world.

Fast-forward a week and we're back in Parking Lot B. The weather had taken a turn for the worse and I was anxious about students driving. The Downtown Center where the finance committee was meeting was only a couple of miles from the main campus, but the roads were getting slick. My worst nightmare: students getting into an accident on my watch.

By this time, everyone had arrived in the parking lot but Trevor. He was only a minute or so late but Hannah was freaking out.

"Where is that boy?" she said, alarm in her voice. "When I left him this morning he was just finishing dishes. He said he was going to do a quick vacuum and he'd be on his way."

My mouth dropped.

"Wait a minute," I said. "You've got Trevor vacuuming your apartment? And doing your dishes?"

"Our apartment," Hannah replied.

"Your apartment?"

"Yeah. And our dishes. We just moved in together and it's still a mess."

"You moved in together?"

"Just this past weekend."

"So you're like . . ."

"Yeah," Hannah said, smiling. "Who would have thought, huh?"

I took a step backward and braced myself against my car.

Who would have thought? Who would have thought? Jesus! That was the understatement of a lifetime. While there had been plenty of hints and teasers liberally thrown our way, I still had not seen this one coming. I always thought that "opposites attract" was bullshit, but here, clearly, was a case in point. Not that they were really opposites, but still.

Hannah and Trevor? A couple?

Just on cue, Trevor came driving up, skidding on slush, and Hannah raced to the car. He opened the window, she yelled at him for being late, he gave her the finger, and then they kissed. Not a peck on the cheek kiss. Not an "I'm sort of happy to see you" kiss. But a deep, passionate, intimate kiss. A Hollywood movie kind of kiss, when the music rises and the camera moves in for a close-up and then pans away and the credits begin to roll and the audience stands and applauds and applauds and applauds.

I awkwardly stood, along with the nine other equally stunned Climate Changers, and gawked away, all of us unable to avert our eyes.

It was a totally unexpected, beautiful sight.

Wow, I thought.

You witness something like this and it makes you realize that anything is possible.

First the Roommate and Sarah. Then my two favorite students (next to She- Who-Now-Will-Not-Be-Named).

Double, even triple Wow!

And then the Climate Changers began to laugh. A deep, raucous, collective laugh that rocked the parking lot and drowned out the freezing rain.

Trevor had emerged from the car, his arm around Hannah, holding her tightly. Over his long, shaggy hair was the sweetest purple cap you've ever seen.

He took it off and tipped it to the crowd, bowing dramatically.

Another sparkling Hollywood highlight.

Hannah joined in the laughter, just for a moment, and then instantaneously switched gears.

"Let's move!" she ordered, reverting back to drill sergeant mode. "Time's a-wasting. We'll meet up in the lobby. Everybody drive safe."

The drive to the Downtown Center where the foundation's offices were was a quick seven minutes. I sat in the back seat of Trevor's car and listened in amazement as Trevor went on and on about how he thought the best places for dishes was the cabinet to the left of the sink, not the cabinet to the right, and Hannah, with her hand on his thigh, was giving him the most adoring of looks.

Abbie and Meagan, sitting hand in hand next to me, gave me a surreptitious nudge and smiled.

Once again. Who would have thought?

And then we were there.

Assembling on the front foyer, Hannah barked her final commands, and marched us into the building.

Filing up the stairs and down the hall, signs and petitions and information folders in hand, pumped up, roused and ready to do battle, we rounded the corner into the conference room.

There was no one there.

Empty.

Nobody.

Not a soul around.

"Shit!" Hannah said, despair in her voice.

"You sure you have the right room?" I asked.

She shot me the evil eye.

"Of course I have the right room. Here is the e-mail. December 13. Downtown Center. 3:00 pm. Room 206. *Shit!*"

We rushed back down the stairs to confront the foundation's work-study student, who was busily updating her Facebook status.

"I'm so sorry," she said. "The meeting was changed at the last minute to the main campus. I was so swamped I must have forgotten to tell you."

I could see Hannah clenching and unclenching her fists, a look on her face that was the opposite of forgiving.

She was about to open her mouth when Trevor grabbed her hand.

"It's okay. We can deal. Let's go."

One more look to kill from Hannah and off we rushed.

On the ride back to campus, Hannah gave the universe an earful. And I thought Jesse's sister's language was bad. I didn't even know some of the definitions of Hannah's, but I assumed the worst.

Not that I could blame her. The Climate Changers had put their hearts and souls into this divestment endeavor, and to have it sabotaged by an incompetent work-study student was beyond belief.

We parked illegally and ran into the main building, up three flights of stairs to the president's conference room.

Just in time to hear the motion for the meeting to adjourn.

"Shit," Hannah muttered once more.

Entering the room, still breathless, she explained the screw-up to the foundation's board president.

"That's Celeste for you!" he said, rolling his eyes. "I can't tell you how many empty rooms I've entered thanks to her. Given all the members' schedules, we just couldn't delay the meeting for you. Please accept my apologies."

"So . . ." Hannah began.

"Forgive me for interrupting. Let me explain where we are with this," Mister Foundation continued.

"We've read all that you've already sent to us. Quite impressive. You've done a wonderful job making your case. It seems to all of us that socially responsible investing is an idea whose time has come, particularly given the threat of climate change and those bastards running the damn energy companies."

Did Mister Foundation actually say "bastards"?

"Anyway, Ted here, our treasurer and investment analyst extraordinaire, has done a good bit of research himself on this. He seems to think that we should be able to make as much money from socially responsible investments as we can from fossil fuels, so student scholarships won't take a hit. We might even be able to make more! Given that, hell, it seems like a no-brainer to us. We're all in agreement. It'll take a while to move the money, but I shouldn't think more than a few months. Anyway, great work. I'm sorry to run but I've got to get to another meeting. Hopefully it'll be in the right place."

He smiled at Hannah.

"Hats off to all of you," he said, giving a wink to Trevor, "for a compelling, well-researched argument." He pointed to the divestment folders. "You've done outstanding work. It's students like you who really make a difference. Great for the foundation to put our money where our mouth is. We're with you all the way. And we'll be in touch. Don't worry. Next time, I'll be the one e-mailing the room number to you."

He shook hands with Hannah and scooted out the door, followed by the rest of the committee.

It had barely begun and, just like that, it was over.

One would have thought that the Climate Changers would be on the rapture side of euphoric. I had thrown my relationship (or lack thereof) depression out the window and was a stroke away from orgasm myself! I was floored that the foundation would acquiesce so quickly to a proposal with such significant economic implications. To act as decisively as this was, for a board known for its inertia, nothing short of amazing.

Far from being ecstatic, the Climate Changers were oddly silent. All of them. As the last of the foundation board members left, they collapsed around the conference-room table, looking deflated, morose, defeated.

You would have thought they'd just gotten a definitive NO rather than a resounding YES!

"Am I missing something here?" I asked, incredulously. "You guys just did an unbelievable thing and you're looking like something the cat dragged in. Talk to me!"

"I don't know," Hannah stammered, her fingers intertwined in Trevor's. "I thought it was going to be much harder than this. I thought we'd have to fight tooth and nail for it. You know, refuse to take no for an answer. Picket and petition and rabble rouse and do all that cool stuff.

Sit-in at the foundation office. Maybe even get arrested. I never expected them to just say yes! And now, just like that, it's over. It's weird. I'm like, I don't know, disappointed. It sort of took the fun out of it."

I couldn't help but smile, but I got it.

It was a bloodless victory, triumph with no casualties, a successful storming of the Bastille without ever having taken the sword out of the scabbard. Adrenalin was flowing, blood was boiling, hackles were up . . . and the enemy had ruined everything by not being the enemy! By being on our side. A win handed to you on a silver platter seemed somewhat less deserved, less fulfilling.

Oh to be young again! At my age, I took the victories, few and far between as they were, any way I could get them.

Damn the foundation! Why did they have to go and do the right thing so quickly? What were they thinking?

Bastards!

"Well, if you'd like," I suggested, "I could ask them to reconsider? Would that make you feel better?"

Hannah sheepishly shook her head.

There were glasses from the meeting still on the conference room table along with a pitcher of water, all untouched.

I poured a round for everyone.

"I propose a toast!" I announced. "To the greatest student activist group in the country. I take that back. To the greatest student activist group in the world! To a group who cares not only about their Facebook status, their reality TV shows, their wardrobe, but about shit that actually matters."

"To shit that matters!" Hannah and Trevor and the rest of the Climate Changers repeated to the clinking of glasses.

"Thanks to all of you, we may well be the first community college in the country that will divest our endowment from fossil fuels. Think about it. The first in the friggin' country! That's huge. Really huge. Gigantically huge!"

"To shit that's gigantically huge!" Hannah yelled. More glass clinking. The Climate Changers were perking up considerably.

"I sympathize. It would have been way more fun to hunker down in the trenches and take fire from all sides, and ultimately come out victorious. But don't forget, you worked your asses off on this. You gave them what they needed to make the right choice. And they did it. They did it!"

"To all of our asses!" Trevor yelled, his hand straying down from Hannah's back to her rear end. Clinking, laughing, smiling.

I was on a roll.

"Seriously. I have so much respect for all of you. You're amazing. There is nothing, nothing you can't do. It's because of all of you I have faith in the world. It's because of you I can get up in the morning and do the work that I have to do. It's because of you I can cast off this bout of . . ." I caught myself and stopped short.

"Thank you," I continued. "From the bottom of my heart, thank you!"

Hannah paused for a moment trying to find a segue into yet another toast, but it proved too elusive.

"To shit that matters!" she yelled once more.

In no time at all, the Climate Changers were patting themselves on the back, pounding and high-fiving, telling each other how wonderful they all were.

Hannah and Trevor gave each other another long sensual kiss, much to the delight of the rest of the gang, who hooted and hollered.

We marched out of the conference room down the hall, and back to class or work or home or wherever.

To shit that matters!

Here here!

39

WELCOME TO THE PVCC PHOTOVOLTAIC ARRAYS!

Look behind the East Building. These are solar electric or photovoltaic (PV) modules that convert sunlight directly into electricity to provide lighting, power computers, and maintain proper ventilation in our buildings. Photovoltaic modules harvest a renewable, inexhaustible, and free source of energy: the sun. They do not burn any fossil fuels—coal, oil, or natural gas—and do not release any harmful pollutants or greenhouse gasses (such as CO_2) into the atmosphere. Installing photovoltaic modules is one way to decrease our reliance on nonrenewable forms of energy.

Photovoltaic modules have no moving parts, require very little maintenance, and last for decades. They act like electron pumps. On one side of the solar cells that make up a module there are atoms that produce a surplus of electrons, and on the other side there are atoms that produce a deficit of electrons. This establishes a voltage difference between the two sides. When the sun is shining, bundles of light energy, called photons, strike the cell. Electrons get "excited" and begin to flow down the voltage difference,

much as water flows down a slope. This flow forms an electric current, producing electricity. Photovoltaics provide us with electricity without contributing to climate change.
— From the signage next to the PV panels at PVCC

JESSE'S SISTER, CLARA, the second-grade teacher with the mouth, was developing a rather acute case of OCD. I took total credit for it, thank you very much. I prided myself on my ability to pass on this crippling, devastating, mind-numbing, incurable condition to those whom I cared deeply about.

"You bastard!" she chided me. "How am I supposed to stay sane with all this shit reeling around in my head? It's your fucking fault!"

"That's why I'm here," I said, giving her a hug.

As far as I could tell, Clara was a wonderful teacher. She cared deeply about her students and was always envisioning creative, out-of-the-box strategies on teaching and learning. She had a fabulous sense of purpose and spirit, and her presence had been a great stabilizing force in my life. Her passion for teaching was contagious and was a major contributing factor to my entering the profession.

For a brief moment, a number of years ago, Jesse had somehow gotten it into his crazy head that we would be a good match, but both us knew otherwise. There was zero chemistry, never had been, never would be. It was one of those things that was instantly apparent. As great a friend as she was, girlfriend material she clearly was not. Plus, the possibility of having the Roommate as a brother-in-law, and perhaps having children that shared his genetic material, was a profoundly scary thought.

Clara had been coming over routinely on Sunday nights for dinner, always a great treat for the two of us kitchen-challenged non-cooks. Sarah was working nights this week so we were on our own in the evenings. Clara's talents in the kitchen were phenomenal, and now that her lawyer boyfriend was on some weird minimalist diet, she was in need of a culinary outlet and was sure to wow us with some scrumdiddlyumptious Sunday-night dish.

To further accentuate the positive, Jesse and I had gotten into the habit of always smoking a joint before her arrival, in anticipation of the fabulous feed to come. Before she had her coat off we'd swoop down upon her like jackals on a kill, ravenous with pot-induced munchies.

"There is a god!" I said, barely containing my drool as I opened the door to let her in. I immediately took the cover off of the pan she was balancing.

"Spinach lasagna. I swear I had a dream about this last night."

Jesse was jumping up and down and clapping his hands like a three-year-old.

"Goodie, goodie, goodie!" he cried.

Dinner was like one of those carrion-beetle-on-road-kill nature clips you see on YouTube, only in faster motion. Now you see it, now you don't. Fifteen minutes after she had knocked, there wasn't a noodle left.

"Amazing!" Clara said, shaking her head. "Have the two of you even eaten since the last time I was over?"

I let out a long, low rolling belch that rattled the glassware.

"You're welcome," she replied.

Here was another great thing. She would actually do the dishes. Check it out: she would come over to our house, serve up two stoned fools a home-cooked gourmet dinner, and then do the damn dishes. It was nothing short of spectacular.

"I love you!" Jesse called out as we collapsed, bloated and semicomatose, on the couch.

"Me too!" I seconded.

"You better!" she called back.

Dinner over, dishes done, she joined us in the living room.

"So, Casey," Clara said. "I need your advice."

"As long as it's not about women I'm good to go."

"Oh no. I thought things were promising with that teacher in your class?"

I told her the sad, sad story.

"There's always May," she said soothingly, trying to be supportive.

"If I hear the word *May* one more time I'm going to have a nervous breakdown. Anyway, enough about me. What's up?"

Clara put a reassuring hand on my shoulder. "I do hope it works out. I really do. Anyway, I drove over to PVCC and was pretty inspired by your photovoltaic panels." I had told her all about the October event when we dedicated the new photovoltaic array at school.

"I'd like to do some work with my little ones on solar energy." She always called her second graders her "little ones." So cute.

"I can't go too deep—remember, they're only seven and eight—but I do want to introduce them to the basics."

"Go for it," I agreed, burping again loudly. "Never too early to start!"

"And I want it to be positive. Upbeat. Hopeful. I don't want to overwhelm, but I do want to . . ."

"Turn them on?"

"Exactly! But how?" she asked.

There is nothing like a little bit of pot and a huge pan of spinach lasagna to get those neurons firing away. Not always productively, not always in sync or on task, often seeking tangents or alternative routes that lead to dead end after amazing dead end, but firing, damn it, firing!

It's one of things I love about marijuana. Never a dull neuron.

By the end of the evening, just in time for the closing credits of *Downton Abbey* ("Damn," Clara's sister cursed. "Damn, damn, damn! How am I to know if Ethel the prostitute gave up her illegitimate son to his grandparents?"), we had written, performed, and perfected The Great Photovoltaic Puppet Show!

Cast of thousands (well, three sock puppets and a PV panel crudely fashioned out of a lasagna pan, to be exact), characters to die for (although no death allowed, the target audience being, after all, six years old), drama, action, laughs, pizzazz! And, to top it off, educational!

Of course, writing a puppet show by committee was not exactly the easiest thing to pull off, particularly when two-thirds of the authors were bloated beyond belief and still really high.

The plot, if you could actually call it one, went something like this:

Freddy the Photon travels all the way from his home on the sun to visit his good friends on earth. . . .

"Why's Freddy a 'he'?" Jesse asked.

"Because it rolls off the tongue well with photon," Clara answered.

"Why not Fanny?"

"Jesse, no one's named Fanny."

"How about Felicia, or Felicity."

"Jeez, stop. Whatever."

"I'm just trying to be sensitive to women's issues," Jesse said. "You know, strong girl stuff and all that."

"It's a fucking photon, for crying out loud!" Clara yelled.

. . . So Freddy the Photon travels all the way to earth. He meets his friends Sam and Morgan on their way to school.

"Hello," he says. "My name is Freddy the Photon, but you can just call me . . ."

"THE MAN!" Jesse yelled, clapping his hands.

"Stop acting so stoned!" Clara groaned.

"I'm serious. It's funny. Puppet shows should work on multiple levels. You've got to throw an occasional zinger to the adults in the crowd."

"What adults? This is for my class, remember? The only adult in the room is me, and even that's pushing it! We're not taking this show on the road!"

"You never know," Jesse said.

"I know! This is not leaving Room 112 of Glenfield Elementary School! Ever!"

"That's what they said about *Les Misérables!*"

"Please, someone tell me we don't share the same genes!"

"Humph!" Jesse humphed.

. . . *"You can just call me Fred," the Photon says.*

"Wow," reply Sam and Morgan. "We've never had a photon for a friend before."

"That's because you're a bunch of losers," Jesse whispered.

"What?" Clara asked.

"Losers. No one would say that line. They'd be like, "AWESOME, DUDE! YOU ROCK!""

"Will you stop already?"

"Come on! What's wrong with 'awesome dude'? Put some spark into it. Light it up. He's a fucking talking photon, for Christ's sake! You said so yourself."

It was readily apparent that this was turning into a pissing contest between the two siblings. To her credit Clara, seeing me nod my head, let him shoot the farthest on this one.

. . . *"I'd like to help you," Fred says. "I'd like to do some work for you. See my friends, those electrons over there?"*

"What's an electron?" Morgan asks.

"SHUT UP AND EAT YOUR LASAGNA!" Jesse shouted.

"Seriously. If you're gonna act like an idiot, I don't want you here!" Clara was pissed. "Casey and I can do just fine, in fact better, without you! Right, Casey?"

I was biting my lip and looking down, stifling my laughter, trying not to establish eye contact.

"Right."

. . . "Electrons are really tiny," Fred answered.

"Tinier than a baby?" Sam asked.

"Much tinier."

"TINIER THAN A BABY'S PENIS?" Jesse once more shouted.

That was it. That sent me over the edge. I was engulfed, consumed with the giggles. Jesse really was acting like a total idiot, but damn if everything he spouted didn't crack me up. The more upset that Clara got with us, the gigglier we became. It got so I couldn't look in either of their general direction without feeling drops of pee dripping down my pants leg. I had to run to make it to the bathroom.

"You're worse than my damn students," she said, groaning. "Casey. I thought at least you would be mature about this. I am so disappointed!"

God, I hated that word. *Pissed* was okay. *Angry, mad, upset* . . . whatever. But *disappointed?* It was like an arrow through the intellect. It brought back images of my childhood after I had redecorated the living room couch with finger paint.

"Disappointed!" Clara repeated, scowling.

Tell me a worse word from someone you respect?

"I'll do better, I swear." I conjured up images of sadness and despair, of being rejected by Samantha, in a desperate attempt to choke back the chuckles and get back on task.

No such luck for Jesse. He was given a timeout in his bedroom until he could prove he could behave. Nothing like a big sister to lay down the law.

The plot continued with the photon telling his friends how electrons loved him, adored him, absolutely worshiped him, and how he could make them so excited they would actually produce electricity.

"SOUNDS LIKE AN ORGASM TO ME!" Jesse shouted from the open door in his bedroom, clearly not getting the maturity memo.

Freddy brings out a photovoltaic panel and does a quick little song and dance about photovoltaic power.

I'M A PHOTON HEAR ME ROAR
A little push from me
I'll get you so excited
We'll make electricity
You're sure to be delighted
And it's all for free
Nothing is ignited
Now you can watch TV
And your house it will be lighted
You know it's called PV
You know it's called PV
YOU KNOW IT'S CALLED PV!
YEAH!!

Okay. So it's the lamest thing you've ever heard, but remember: the target audience were six and seven, and the characters were socks, for Christ sake! Anyway, it was all about the content.

Obviously, Morgan and Sam see the light and go on to convince all of their family, friends, and neighbors to install photovoltaic panels. The world is thus freed from the tyranny of fossil fuels (although exactly what that means is left somewhat vague in the show), as well as the horror of climate change, (again, somewhat vague, with Freddy saying, "Nobody likes a warmer planet, nobody!").

In the end, everyone lives happily ever after, including Jesse, who was eventually un-banished and allowed back out of his room once he promised to behave.

Needless to say, there would be much anticipated applause from the crowd.

Or not.

But it wasn't bad. Well . . . it wasn't awful.

One could do worse on a Sunday night than a pleasant high, a free pan of spinach lasagna, and an award-winning, critically acclaimed solar puppet show. Much worse.

40

"So," Samantha said.

"So," I replied, fiddling with the computer and trying to look busy. I was suffering an extreme anxiety attack. It had been a week since she had so ruthlessly thrown me to the wolves and now here she was, staying after class again. Smiling that stunning smile and twirling her pigtail between her thumb and her forefinger in that certain way that she had to have known drove me crazy. It was as if she were deliberately mocking me. Driving me over the edge not just to the brink of madness but headlong into the full-fledged abyss of insanity.

Maybe this is what she did. Maybe this is who she really was. Maybe she was the devil in disguise, a succubus, a demon sent to seduce me and then suck out my life force. An evil, conniving wicked, wicked woman who delighted in turning on guys, enticing them into her cunning web of lies and deceit, playing with their frayed emotions, ramping up their feelings until they were borderline lunatics, destroying every remnant of sanity they possessed, and then leaving them tattered and torn and battered and beaten. Forever wondering what the hell just ran them over.

I stared hard at the computer, willing myself not to look up.

I had spent a sleepless night rehearsing what I wished (well, sort of wished, but not really) I had the balls to say to her:

"Samantha. Darling. You clearly have no idea how much I like you. Absolutely no clue. But here's the deal. I can't go on like this. I honestly cannot do this a moment more. As much as I worship our late-afternoon chitchats, if you stay after class one more time I truly believe I will have a total and complete nervous breakdown. Not a whiney, oh-poor-poor-pitiful-me, get-over-it-in-a-week, pissy kind of thing, but a bring-it-on, *Titanic*-sized, permanently institutionalizable implosion. Right here. Right now. Right in front of you. And believe me, it will not be pretty. Far from it. I don't think either of us want that to happen, now, do we? So from now on, please, for the love of God, if you have one shred of humanity or decency or *whatever* left, STOP TORMENTING ME LIKE THIS!"

Here is what I actually said:

"I swear I hate this computer. It is so slow. I have got to get IT up here to deal."

"So," Samantha repeated.

There was something about the tone of her voice. Something different. I stopped fiddling with the mouse and turned to her.

"I changed my mind."

"About your final project?" I replied. "Why? It's brilliant. Your kids will love it. It's a fabulous idea." I knew she had been working hard on her "ABCs of Global Warming" and I thought the concept was terrific.

"No not that. Adolescent psychology."

"Really? How so? Don't tell me you've actually deluded yourself into thinking your seventh graders are rational thinkers rather than crazed, hormonally challenged, electrified bundles of directionless chaos?"

She laughed. "God no. I'll never backtrack on that one. I changed my mind about the class. The Adolescent Psychology class I was going to take. I dropped it. I really don't know what I was thinking."

"You what?" I said, feeling my heart beating in my toes.

"Dropped the class. Yesterday."

"Dropped it?!"

"Dropped it."

I caught my breath. *Careful, careful,* I told myself. I was not going to allow myself to be blindsided by yet another clever ruse destined to shatter what was left of me into a thousand jaded pieces never to be put back together again, not even by all of the king's horses and all the king's men.

"Well, truth be told," I said, "the professor actually sucks. Big time. I could recommend a child development class, if you haven't taken one already."

She smiled. "No need. I'm not going to take a class next semester. At least not here."

My toes were now throbbing. I could see my shoes pulsing with every beat.

"No class?"

"Nope." She smiled.

"Nothing?"

"Nothing."

"But . . . I thought you needed to do the professional development thing? The PDPs and all that?" My shoes had vibrated to the point where my laces had come untied.

"I do. But there's no real rush. It can wait. And, you know," she looked right at me, smiling that smile, twirling that tail, "I want to keep my options open. I have this awesome feeling that something much better than PDPs is just around the corner. Just waiting to happen."

The heart/toe spasms had moved from my feet to my

ankles, past my calves, and all the way up the back of my thighs to the point where I found my legs crumbling beneath me.

How could I have ever thought ill of this woman? How could I have ever doubted for an instant that she was faultless—the perfect human being? Whatever possessed me to question that she was trustworthy, loyal, helpful, friendly, courteous . . . wait a minute . . . I was confusing her with the fucking Boy Scout Law! But it was all true!

No classes! That meant she wasn't going to be a student! No student! That meant I could . . .

Trying to maintain balance and keep from tumbling over, I lurched wildly, inadvertently getting my index finger caught up in the handle of the emergency shower pull-cord, dangling next to the white board for science-lab catastrophes. I lurched again, this time giving the cord a solid yank. Water poured from the showerhead, just for an instant, but enough to give me a solid soaking.

"Shit!" I said.

Samantha burst out laughing.

"I was wondering how you'd take it," she said, finally able to get words out. "I didn't think it would be so . . ."

"Moronic?" I replied, wiping my face with my T-shirt.

"How about theatrical. I know it's my turn to lend you clothes, but . . ."

With impeccable timing, at that very moment who should walk in but the dean.

There I was, T-shirt pulled up over my head, spastically mopping my dripping hair, belly button and stomach and God knows what else exposed for all the world to see. Samantha giggling like one of her students, and the goddamn dean walks, or rather limps, in. Word on the street was that he only did that when I was around.

He stopped dead in his tracks.

"Please tell me I'm not interrupting something!"

"No, no, no. Nothing. Really nothing." I stammered,

frantically attempted to rearrange my wardrobe. "I pulled the shower cord. You know. For emergencies. Chemical spills. That kind of stuff. My bad."

"There's been a chemical spill?" he asked, alarm in his voice.

"No, no. She just, Samantha here, said that she dropped Adolescent Psychology and I . . . you know . . ."

Christ! I was rambling like an incoherent fool.

"Dean Moosowski," the dean said, extending his hand to Samantha. His hairy, bushy eyebrows could not have been arched any further. "I believe we have met before, under, ahem, similar circumstances."

"We have," Samantha stammered (just like me!), shaking his hand. "I was just explaining to Casey here, umm, Mr. C, how I don't want to be a student here, I mean, how I dropped a class so we can . . . umm . . ." My god, she was actually tongue-tied! And was that a blush?

"Which led to him taking a shower," the dean sighed.

"Exactly," I said.

"Exactly," Samantha repeated.

"Well, that explains everything," the dean said, the eyebrows—God knows how—arching up even higher, extending somehow beyond his hairline, almost floating up over the top of his head. "I am certainly pleased to see that he has no articles of your clothing on."

"Funny thing you should mention it," Samantha said. "I was just—" She stopped midsentence. "That would be rather awkward."

"Rather," the dean's eyebrows continued to arch away. "Professor, once you get, ahem, decent, I am in urgent need of that E3 form in my office before tomorrow morning. Just a friendly reminder."

"E3 form. Yes. Of course. I'm on it."

One more scowl at me, arched eyebrows at her, and off he waddled, this time forgetting to limp.

"Sorry about that," Samantha said, still giggling. "I didn't mean to get you in trouble."

Trouble? Trouble? Was she serious? I was in ecstasy! Heaven! A hop, skip, and a jump from rapture!

I laughed, my voice bubbling over, manic, my legs quivering again, making ripples in the puddle on the classroom floor. "Trouble? No way. That was like . . ."

This was the moment. It was being handed to me on a silver platter. I could do it. I could ask her out. The timing could not have been more perfect!

"Yeah, it means that . . . you know . . . I mean . . ." I was discombobulated, wet, elated, and—surprise, surprise—terrified. Try as I might, the words refused to come out. The "ask" remained stuck in the back of the throat. Glued to the palate.

"You mean?" Samantha asked.

"You have no classes here next semester."

"No classes," she said.

"None."

"Nope."

"Okay then."

"Yeah. Come the last day of school I'll no longer be a student. Hooray for me!" She paused, looking at me expectantly.

"Hooray!" I yelled, perhaps a little too loud, a little too enthusiastically.

"Good luck with the E3," she said, again staring right at me with that new kind of look.

"Oh God," I sighed. "You know what it's like. One of those bullshit forms only a dean would care about. Pardon my language."

She nodded. "Tell me about it. Anyway, I'm glad I dropped the class. I really am. Can you believe in two weeks the semester will be over?"

"Amazing. Two weeks."

"I'll see you Thursday."

Two weeks. Two short weeks! Fourteen days . . . three hundred and thirty-six hours . . . twenty thousand one hundred and sixty minutes. . . .

"Thursday," I repeated. Even though I had blown the "ask," the news was still too good to bum out about. Beyond good. Jesus, I was walking on water.

—

"So," Sarah said. "When was the last time you actually asked someone out?"

I had, of course, recounted the entire conversation, word for word, half a dozen times.

"What are you talking about?" I replied. "It hasn't been that long."

"Two and a half years," Jesse yelled from the bathroom. "Maybe more."

"Do you have to continue to mind other people's business even when you're taking a shit?" I yelled back.

"You're not other people," he yelled again.

"All right, so it's been a while," I confessed.

"Wow. Long time. Is that how long you've, you know, gone without it?" Sarah asked.

"No way. Of course not. It hasn't been that long."

"Over a year," Jesse yelled again. "He didn't ask that one out because she didn't speak any English."

"Do you want to go for a walk?" I asked Sarah.

"Sure," she said. We left Jesse crying foul in the bathroom.

"You know," I said. "It's not easy for me. It never has been. God knows, in high school I used to sit by the phone for hours trying to get up enough courage just to call a girl up to get a homework assignment. I didn't date until the end of college, and since then it's been, well, pretty sporadic. You know, I'm sort of a social spaz."

"You are not," Sarah said soothingly, putting her arm in

mine. As of late, she had become my confidante. I could tell her anything. "You're just shy around women. It's sexy. Most guys have this bullshit bravado that is such a turnoff. You're refreshing."

"*Sexy* is not exactly the word I'd use," I said. "Nor *refreshing*. More like *clinically awkward*. Beyond awkward. It's like a disease. I turn into a sniveling buffoon every time I'm around that woman. The thought of asking her out is terrifying."

How to manage the big moment when I'd pop the question to Samantha had totally consumed my last few days. I spent most of my waking moments rehearsing lines in my head, all of which fell ridiculously flat.

"You're going to do fine," she said reassuringly. "However you say it, you know she's going to say yes. You know it. Just be yourself."

"Sarah, that's what I'm afraid of. Myself. I'm short of breath, my socks are soaked because my toes are oozing sweat, and I've a got mild case of the spins just talking to you about it! How's it going to go down when the real thing happens?"

There was a huffing and puffing noise behind us as Jesse came running to join us. "What'd I miss?" he gasped. "Fill me in."

From one buffoon to another. We couldn't help but laugh.

"Sarah thinks I'm sexy," I said. "She's thinking of dumping you for me."

"I figured," Jesse replied, still trying to catch his breath from his thirty-second jog to catch up. "I knew all along she was just using me to get to you. It's been so damn obvious. Don't worry though, I'll still love both of you."

"Oh God," Sarah said. "Are we never to be rid of him?" Sarah put her arm in his and the three of us walked on.

"I've got an idea," Jesse volunteered. "You know how Sarah knows the school nurse at the middle school where

Samantha teaches? How about you ask Sarah to ask the school nurse to ask Samantha out. Would that make it any easier?"

"I feel way too uncomfortable asking Sarah to do that," I said. "How about if I ask you to ask Sarah to ask the nurse to ask Samantha? That would be much less awkward!"

"One problem," Sarah said. "I don't think the nurse knows Samantha all that well. But she does know the seventh-grade math teacher who does. How about you ask Jesse, who can ask me, and I'll ask the nurse, who can ask the math teacher, who can ask Samantha?"

"Eureka!" I cried. "That's it! That's the solution! Praise the Lord, my problem is solved."

Arm in arm the three of us skipped all the way home.

41

Doha, Qatar — An area of Arctic sea ice bigger than the United States melted this year, according to the U.N. weather agency, which said the dramatic decline illustrates that climate change is happening "before our eyes."

In a report released at U.N. climate talks in the Qatari capital of Doha, the World Meteorological Organization said the Arctic ice melt was one of a myriad of extreme and record-breaking weather events to hit the planet in 2012. Droughts devastated nearly two-thirds of the United States as well as western Russia and southern Europe. Floods swamped West Africa and heat waves left much of the Northern Hemisphere sweltering.

But it was the ice melt that seemed to dominate the annual climate report, with the U.N. concluding ice cover had reached "a new record low" in the area around the North Pole and that the loss from March to September was a staggering 11.83 million square kilometers (3.57 million square miles)—an area bigger than the United States. — Associated Press

THE THIRD WEDNESDAY OF THE MONTH from noon to one is open-mike day at the cafeteria. There's a signup sheet pinned next to the Office of Student Life, and anyone can stand up and strut their stuff while folks chow down. It's mostly your super-earnest singer-songwriter types, and some of the students are surprisingly good—new superstars just waiting to be discovered. My favorite this year was a young woman, sounding just like Aretha Franklin, who did an unaccompanied version of "Respect"—"*Uh huh, just a little bit, uh huh, just a little bit. . . .*" Knocked everyone's socks off.

Of course, there are always those acts that simply suck. Every semester this student who's been at PVCC for God only knows how long and imagines himself an outstanding Elvis impersonator does his thing. He can't sing worth shit, he doesn't have even the slightest bit of the Elvis look, and his pelvis can't twist for the life of him. But, good or bad, students are overwhelmingly kind. Even if they don't like someone, or just plain don't listen, they applaud politely. Open-mike day at the cafeteria has a nice, safe, community feel. It's definitely the place to be.

Fresh from their divestment campaign success, the Climate Changers had come up with a festive holiday skit for the Wednesday before winter break. The idea was unique: a Santa Claus rant on the effect of climate change on the polar ice caps. Political standup comedy. I thought it sounded rather lame but, hey, it was their gig. They were on a crazy roll and, once again, they were pumped.

The middle of December is a tough time of year for students. It's cold, it's dark, and the academic and personal stressors can be overwhelming. There are so many expectations around the holiday season, and students like mine, with so much on their plates, can find it difficult to cope. Add the impending trauma of finals week and exams and projects and papers, and a pall is cast over what should be a festive time. Unfortunate but true. Knowing this, the Climate Changers wanted to liven things up a little.

This Wednesday, the cafeteria was packed with students studying and socializing, taking the edge off with way too many fries and greasy slices of pizza.

The Climate Changers were last on the list to perform. Somewhat arrogantly, they had insisted on closing out the show. "No one can possibly be better than us," Trevor had insisted. "It would be unfair to other performers to follow our skit."

Trevor was dressed as Santa. His friend worked in a porn shop in Northampton where, in the same aisle as the blow-up dolls and leopard-spotted lingerie and British maid outfits, for some unfathomable reason they also had a Santa suit, which his friend had loaned him. Go figure. Not cheap-shit Santa stuff, either, but sparkling attire with a flowing white beard and blinding red hat to match.

Trevor was not a big guy. Far from it. But he packed the Santa outfit with God knows what so that he could hardly move and he looked the real deal. When students saw him they stood up and cheered.

With a booming "Ho, Ho, Ho!" and plenty of high fives, Trevor, with his Santa bag slung over his shoulder, along with Hannah, dressed as an elf (also from the porn shop? I dared not go there!) sauntered up to the mike.

Students pounded on the table. "Santa! Santa! Santa!" they chanted. Kitchen staff emerged from the prep room to see what all the hullabaloo was about.

The MC grabbed the mike.

"Ladies and gents, boys and girls, Jews and Gentiles, please welcome, all the way from the North Pole, Santa and his Little Helper!"

The crowd went wild.

"Santa, Santa, Santa!"

Hannah waved for silence. I could certainly see why Trevor was infatuated with her. Not only was she incredibly smart and had the do-gooder, save-the-world gene, but *God* she looked good in that elf suit.

"Settle down, little ones," she said. "Settle down. Unfortunately I come bearing bad news. Really bad news! Shame on all of you! Shame! You all have been such naughty boys and girls this year. Very naughty!"

The crowd hooted. There were shouts of "liar" and "it wasn't me" and "I swear I didn't do it!" and "Thank God I'm Jewish!"

"Santa, have these unruly children been naughty?" Hannah the Elf asked.

"Really and truly nasty naughty!" Santa wagged his finger at the crowd.

There were groans and cries.

"And why have they been naughty, Santa?"

"*Naughty*'s not the word for it!" Santa boomed, grabbing the mike off the stand and throwing down his bag. "More like badass diabolical! Outright evil! And you want to know why, elfykins? Why they've been so naughty?"

"Why?" the Elf asked.

"I'll tell you why! I work my ass off in a fucking freezing ice hell, 23/7 — right?"

The crowd looked stunned, fries were frozen in midair.

"Day after frozen day what do I do? I churn out presents, right? I'm a goddamn present machine, right? Quality stuff, too!"

"Actually," interrupted the Elf, "Truth be told, it's all us elves who do the work. You don't do squat, boss man!"

"You tell him, Elfie!" someone shouted from the back.

"Whatever," said Santa, stealing back the mike. "I work my fingers to the bone and what thanks do I get? Huh, what thanks?"

Hannah sidled up to Trevor, wiggling her elvish rear in an exaggerated way and caressing his bulging belly.

"We have our fun," she cooed, evidently an elf with benefits.

The crowd roared. Trevor and Hannah had them eating out of the palms of their hands.

Santa pushed her aside. "You know what I'm talking

about! I give gifts to millions around the world and how do you repay me? Huh? How?"

"I love you Santa!" a girl yelled.

"Then show it! Show it! You know what's going down in the North Pole right now? Do you?"

"You tell us, Claus man!"

"It is not good, my friends. We're on thin ice up there. Very thin ice. Just the other day Rudolph fell in all the way up to that annoying blinking nose of his. Mrs. Claus won't even go for a joyride in the sleigh, which is the only time I ever get anything from her anymore. She's scared to death! And my insurance bills! Jeez! They've skyrocketed! I can hardly afford to live there anymore. Santa's work-shop is on the verge of a friggin' foreclosure! And do you know why? Do you?"

"Global warming!" Abbie shouted from the crowd, right on cue.

"Goddamn right it's global warming! For the love of Christ you're melting my ice caps up there! I lost one big-ger than the whole U.S. of A just this last year! Wrap your little brains around that one!

"You and your friggin' fossilized fuels are killing me. Hell, there's a damn lake where the Lego factory used to be. A friggin' lake! We may be looking at Christmas with no Legos!"

"No Legos!" Abbie shouted.

"That's right, no goddamn Legos!"

Prompted by more Climate Changers, the crowd booed and hissed.

"Boo, damn it, that's right, hiss away." Santa was in a frenzy. He paced back and forth, picking up his bag and holding it aloft. "Keep this shit up and there will be no North Pole. No North Pole means no Santa. No Santa means. . . ."

"No Christmas!" someone yelled. "No Christmas!"

"Goddamn right!"

"Boo!" the crowd screamed. "We want Christmas! We want Christmas!" Students began to pound on the tables again.

"Go on, chant away!" Santa shouted. "But if you want these presents, you're going to have to do better than that. Do you want these presents?"

"Yes!" the crowd screamed.

"Then you're going to have to promise me something!"

"We will!"

"Are you going to be good boys and girls?"

"Yes!"

"Not so naughty?"

"Yes!"

"Not buying all this bullshit you don't need? Not consuming for the sake of consumption? Thinking about what you're purchasing and its impact on climate change? Thinking about the true spirit of the holiday?"

"Yes!"

"Do you promise?"

"We promise!" the crowd roared.

"I can't hear you!"

"WE PROMISE!"

"Then you can have your presents!"

Trevor and Hannah ripped open the Santa bag and, in a move stolen straight from Mister Condom's presentation, threw fistfuls of condoms into the crowd. Pure pandemonium erupted. A table was turned over. Fries and pizza spilled everywhere as students madly scrambled to pocket the prophylactics.

"Go forth, my darlings!" Santa yelled. "And do not multiply!"

I looked over to see the dean, standing at the doorway. No scowl this time. No arched eyebrows. He turned toward me, put his finger next to his nose, and gave a wink and a nod.

42   ✌

I'VE ALWAYS STRUGGLED with how to evaluate students. It is one of the most difficult, time-consuming, and painful parts of my job. I have recurring fantasies about not giving grades at all and still having students show up to class every day, enthusiastic and raring to go, completing all of their assignments and readings on time without a whimper or a whine. No stress, no angst, no tears.

Dream on! It just doesn't work like that.

One of the ways I've chosen to evaluate students is by assigning a final project. It can be handed in at any time of the year but—surprise, surprise—except on extremely rare occasions it's not turned in until the last possible moment. After all, procrastination is a student's modus operandi.

The task is relatively simple: devise a project of your choice having something to do with The Issue.

It is the equivalent of a triple homework assignment—important, but not a grade buster.

"Think outside the box," I encourage them. "Do something unique! Let your imagination run wild! Have fun!"

These projects can be hit or miss. I've had semesters

where the sophistication of year-end work was mind-boggling. Work that made me confident and optimistic that the world would be in good hands. Work that made me want to shout out from the roof of the main building, "I TAUGHT THESE FOLKS! THESE WERE MY STUDENTS IN MY CLASS! LISTEN TO WHAT THEY HAVE TO SAY!"

Last semester, this mousy kid who looked all of fourteen wrote a futuristic short story about an isolated post-apocalyptic outpost on an island off the coast of Greenland. People were waiting for the rising waters to wash them away. It made the hair rise on my head. I read it to Jesse and he cried himself to sleep.

Conversely there are those projects that made me want to crawl under a fucking rock and die. Grading them is the equivalent of driving splinters under my fingernails. Red-hot pokers to the eyeballs. A taser to the testicles. It takes a Herculean effort not to projectile vomit over their misspelled drivel.

Two weeks after the last drop-dead, no-more–excuses, yes-I-really-mean-it-this-time! deadline, final projects were still trickling in. Being the incredible hard-ass that I was, of course I accepted them.

This semester's projects were outstanding.

One of the students, caught up in the spirit of the holidays, made a sustainable gingerbread house. It had photovoltaic panels made of milk chocolate Hershey bars, a licorice-bladed wind turbine rising high above it. There was a pretzel-fenced compost pile with jujubes made to look like food waste. A backyard garden of kisses, candy corn, and gum drops. A chicken coop with marshmallow peeps. There was even a graham cracker composting outdoor toilet with M&M poop. To top it off, we got to devour all of it after her presentation. A definite A.

Four students, including Warren the Catastropharian, performed a skit. They fast-forwarded us to the year 2037, twenty-five years into the future, when good had finally triumphed over evil and a just, peaceful, sustainable world was ours. They followed a day in the life of a typical PVCC student from his first-thing-in-the-morning shit in his composting toilet (aggressively acted by Warren with lots of farting noises—no M&M's this time) to his commute back home in the light rail car. His day was occupied by picking grapes from the PVCC organic vineyard, co-facilitating a conflict-resolution class, helping construct another photo-voltaic array, doing a presentation on climate change to an elementary school class, and generally performing good deeds.

They got a standing ovation. Another A.

Two students had devised a game called Sustainable Life, modeled after the old classic Game of Life. It was a board game where you rolled a die and moved forward the number of spaces that corresponded to the number on the die. First one to the finish line won.

Some spaces were marked with good things:

- Install photovoltaic panels on your co-housing complex. Move forward four spaces.
- Build a hoop house for a four-season garden. Advance three.
- Add another 9 inches of cellulose to your attic. Take an action card.
- Ride your bike instead of driving to school. Roll again.

Some spaces were marked with bad things:

- Forget to take your birth control pill. Go back two spaces.
- Let your car idle in the parking lot. Give up an action card.
- Leave your air conditioner on while you're away for the weekend. Lose a turn.

And the worst roll you could get:

- Vote for a climate-change-denying politician. Go back to start!

Awesome! What was not to like? A+.

Even the backward-baseball-cap boys who snoozed in the last row had come through. Any completed work from those three constituted a major victory. They handed in a CD of a song they had recorded, something clearly done the night before under the influence of a case or two of Budweiser. Here is a sample of the lyrics:

My truck won't start
My tractor is broke
My dog just bit me
My girlfriend's a joke
My face is all sunburned
With a hundred zits forming
And to top this shit off
The climate is warming

I had to admit, it did have a certain twangy country charm to it. While their musical abilities sucked, that wasn't the point. I gave them a B+.

Overall I was pleased and impressed.

Last but certainly not least (never that!) Samantha had written a wonderful pamphlet for her middle-school Science for Girls group that she was forming. It went like this:

GLOBAL WARMING
ABC'S

Global warming is the real deal. And very scary. Hotter temperatures, rising sea levels, bigger storms—yikes!!!! Makes you want to crawl under the covers and hide. Definitely not an option! Everyone has to step up to help solve this problem. Follow the Global Warming ABC's and let's all do our part to make a difference.

A is for Action. The future of our planet is at stake. Only action from all of us will help stop global warming. Definitely not a battle you can sit out. Get Active!

B is for Bike and Bus. Whenever possible, leave the car at home. Walk or bike off those calories while saving the environment! When in town take public transportation like the bus or subway.

C is for Conservation. Less energy used = less greenhouse gas emissions. Buy energy-efficient (Energy Star) appliances. Retire the dryer and hang out your laundry. Turn off the TV and take a hike!

D is for Dress. Dress warmly in winter. Wear that ridiculous sweater that Grandma gave you rather than cranking the thermostat. Every degree you turn it down means less carbon dioxide going up. In the summer, dress Cool!

E is for Educate. Learn about the issues. Educate yourself, your family, your friends. Get the word out about steps people can take to make a difference.

F is for Floss. It has nothing to do with global warming but it is so good for your teeth!

G is for Garden. Grow your own food. Support farmers' markets. Buy locally grown fruits and vegetables. The less distance food travels to you, the greater the energy savings.

H is for Hybrid. Parents shopping for a new car? How about a hybrid or alternative-fueled vehicle? Boycott gas guzzlers. When you get older, don't ride with a guy no matter how hot he is if his car gets less than 30 miles to the gallon. That's just not cool!

I is for Insulate. Weather-stripping and rolls of fiberglass may not be the sexiest thing around, but keeping the warm in on those cold nights is HOT!

J is for Join. Join a group working on global-warming issues. No group at school? Start one!

K is for Keep. Keep your showers under 5 minutes. Showering is not a recreational sport! Longer doesn't always mean sexier.

L is for Lights. Lights out when you leave the room. Change those lightbulbs from energy-wasting incandescents to energy-efficient compact fluorescents or LEDs. And remember, kissing in the dark is so romantic!

M is for Mow. Chores to do? Mow your lawn with a hand mower or an efficient electric mower. Better yet, plant wildflowers or vegetables and hoe—don't mow! While you're at it, lose the leaf and snow blower and give those abs a workout with a rake or a shovel.

N is for Nine. Nine people in a school carpool? Maybe not, but three or four saves gas and money and keeps you up on the latest scandals and gossip.

O is for Organize. Organize a talk, a movie, a money-raising walk, a benefit dance. Get involved. Get others involved.

P is for Paper or Plastic? How about neither! Bring your own reusable bags when shopping. Save trees and energy.

Q is for Quarter. Put a quarter in the jar every time you do something stupid. Once it adds up, donate those dollars to a global-warming awareness group.

R is for Reduce, Reuse, Recycle, and Rethink. Make sure those bottles, cans, and paper go where they belong. No bins at school? Get the maintainers involved and start a recycling program.

S is for Solar. Solar is so Hot! Energy from the sun and wind will reduce global warming. Get your parents, school, church, synagogue, or mosque to buy solar hot-water heaters and solar electric panels.

T is for Trees. Plant them. Lots of them. They take carbon dioxide out of the air. They give us oxygen. Trees = good!

U is for Use. While abstinence is the best policy, if you make the decision to have sex, use birth control. Think about the number of kids you want to have. Keep the planet in mind when planning your family.

V is for Vote! Register to vote when you turn eighteen. Democracy is not a spectator sport. Politicians waffling on global warming need to get the boot!

W is for Write. Write an opinion piece for your school or local newspaper. Write a letter to the editor. People will read what you have to say. The written word is a powerful thing.

X is for eXcuse. There is no excuse for being an energy hog. Look at your room, your apartment, your house. Make a list of ways to save energy. Reward yourself (chocolate?) for each of your successes.

Y is for Yell. Yell loudly. Yell often. Go to demonstrations. Speak your mind and make your voice heard. You are the one who can make a difference in the world!

Z is for Zero. Make the shape of one with your fingers. That's the shape of our earth. It's the only one we've got and it's up to us to protect it. Begin now!

At the risk of repeating myself, what a woman! Put those words to a country music song and think of the hit you could have! I put a big C- on the top of the first page and then wrote "just kidding: A!" with a big smiley face drawn next to it. Tacky but . . .

43

"IT'S SO WEIRD," SAMANTHA SAID. It was the last day of class. The end of the semester.

"What's so weird?"

"How school just ends. You become so accustomed, so attached to all of these people in your class and then, ZAP, it's all over. Just like that. You may never see any of them ever again." She looked right at me.

"So weird," I agreed, looking down.

"It's the occupational hazard of teaching. We go through this twice a year. Every year. Just when you start to get to know someone, to really know them, they're gone."

"Just like that," I said.

"Sometimes it's the greatest thing in the world to be done with a class. Counting the days until it is goodbye and good riddance. Out with the old, thank God, and bring on the new. But other times . . ."

We both sat in silence for a moment.

"It's been great to be a student again," she said. "It really has. It's been so valuable getting it from the other side. I'll definitely be a better teacher for it. Not just for the content

I got, or learning how others, like you, teach, but just by being a student."

"Yeah." I said.

"I'm going to miss it. I'm going to miss this class."

"So am I."

"I'm going to miss Cynthia and Jenny and Warren and all of them."

I nodded my head. "Warren. Wow. I hope he hangs in there. Miracle of miracles, I actually think he's going to pass this time. He's a good kid."

"He is," Samantha said.

"It's kind of funny."

"What's kind of funny?" she asked.

"You remember all that weird stuff he said about being a Catastropharian and the end of the Mayan calendar forecasting the impending Apocalypse and everything?"

"I do."

I braced myself, crossed and uncrossed my legs, and held on to the edge of the desk for support.

This was it! D-Day had finally arrived. It was now or never. My whole life, my whole future, hung in the balance. I took a deep breath and plowed forward.

"Well, believe it or not," I said, "I'm going to a party this Saturday night. It's a combination Mayan End of the World slash Winter Solstice slash Thank God the Semester Is Over party."

"That sounds fun," Samantha said.

"I hope so. I was just thinking how awkward it would be if Warren was there."

Actually, I wasn't thinking that at all. I had the right line in my head, Christ knows I had practiced in the mirror for hours, but it just couldn't make it to the mouth. *Ask her, you fool! Ask her!*

"I doubt you have to worry," she replied. "He probably doesn't hang in the same crowd as you."

Crowd? What crowd? Jesse and Sarah and I didn't exactly make a crowd.

"Yeah. It should be a great party. This friend of mine is pretty nuts. He teaches at Smith College and is taking over one of the buildings for the night. DJ and everything. Dance till you drop. It's Saturday night."

"Fun."

"This Saturday."

"You said that."

"It starts at nine o'clock."

"Saturday night it is," Samantha said.

We sat again in silence, words screaming through my head. I crossed and uncrossed and recrossed my legs.

"Do you want to tell me where?" she asked.

"Yeah," I said. "Yeah, I do. I really do."

"Great."

Another round of silence.

"And the answer is . . ."

"Right. Sorry. The Smith College field house in Northampton. On 66. Down by the tennis courts. Do you know where that is?"

"I'm sure I can find it," she answered.

"Great."

"So . . . are you inviting me?" she asked.

"Well, I mean, you could bring a friend. You know, a boyfriend. Girlfriend. Whatever."

"So you are inviting me?"

"I mean, you know, if you, like, well, whatever . . ." I stammered, twisting my legs together in such a pretzel-like knot that I couldn't feel my body from the pelvis down. Plus I was hyperventilating. This was not quite coming out as planned. I looked away, but I could feel her smile.

"So you're not not inviting me."

"Exactly!"

"What time again?"

"Nine o'clock."

She thought for just a moment.

"No," she said.

I turned and looked at her. No? *No?* Damn! So this is how it all ended. This is how the captain felt standing in the wheelhouse, weeping, as the *Titanic* plunged to the bottom of the sea.

"No?" I said, choking on the words. "You can't come?"

"No I don't have a boyfriend. Or a girlfriend. But I'd love to come."

I let go my breath, way too loudly. The shattered ship rose magically up and over the icebergs and the waves, soaring high above the clouds.

"Wow! Great! Terrific!"

"How about you?" she asked.

"Yeah. I can go. I'll be there. Definitely."

She laughed. "I meant are you going with someone."

"Me? No! No way! Oh my god. Of course not!"

"Why 'of course not'?"

"If I was going with someone then I wouldn't be . . ." Long pause.

"Asking me out?"

I looked away awkwardly.

"So . . . nine o'clock." She smiled and twirled her hair and smiled again.

"Nine o'clock," I said. "Be warned. If the Mayans are right, it'll be the last night of the world."

"I hope they're wrong," she said.

"God, so do I." This time I looked right at her.

"Shall I bring anything?"

"No. Just you."

She laughed again.

"Nine o'clock. Saturday."

She left the room and I lay down on the floor, my legs still in a pretzel, not caring if the dean or the college president or Obama himself walked in.

44

IT'S NOT LIKE I COUNTED THE MINUTES until nine o'clock on Saturday night. The hours, yeah, but the minutes, not until the end.

There were, of course, reasons galore to count down. It was a monumental day with epic reasons for celebration.

Reason #1. I had gotten my final grades in on Friday, twenty-two minutes before they were due, a new world record for me. I was thrilled. Fall semester was finally one for the books, thank God. I was done, finished for the semester. Samantha was officially no longer my student!

Reason #2. Winter solstice: a holy day. The end of fall, the official beginning of winter, the shortest day and longest night of the year. It was thrilling and incredibly reassuring to know that from this moment forward every day for the next six months would be longer and longer. The light was returning. Hallelujah! No coincidence that early Christians determined that Jesus' birthday just happened to fall at this sacred time. They weren't stupid. Get all of us pagans and atheists who were partying down anyway and co-opt the day into becoming one big birthday bash.

Reason #3. The Mayan ultimatum for the End of the World. December 21, 2012. Go figure. Who would have thought that the end of the 5,312-year-old Mayan calendar, falling as it did on winter's solstice, would set people off the way that it had? With the possible exception of Warren and maybe my nutso brother-in-law Winnie, no one I knew believed any of the bullshit, but that certainly didn't stop everyone from talking it up. Students, staff, faculty, friends, everybody. It was all the buzz. Winnie called to beg pot off me. "If it's all going down," he said, "I'm definitely gonna want to be high at the end." Jesse had made a "Last 30 Days" calendar and we'd been counting down to catastrophe one day at a time. It was entirely unclear to me what the Mayans had thought would happen come solstice midnight, but it was yet another fabulous reason to party.

Reason #3. Last but totally first. The obvious one. Certainly the ask had not been my finest moment, but somehow Apollo, Cupid, the Mayans, and maybe even Jesse Himself had miraculously intervened and, will wonders never cease, I was actually going to a party with her! WITH HER! Can you believe it?

It was hard to tell who was more excited—Jesse, Sarah, or myself.

"Christ," the Roommate said. "If I had to endure one more day of your fucking angst I would have ended it all and cut off your testicles."

"Don't mind him," Sarah said, smelling my armpits and giving me the thumbs up. "He's just jealous that you're going to have two women fawning all over you rather than one."

I had spent most of Saturday afternoon at the Y, desperately trying to get one more workout in to buff me up, hoping a round on the nautilus machines would miraculously add an inch to my biceps. Given the train wreck that I was, it proved a good way to kill time before the big event. I had been reassured by Sarah that I couldn't overdose on Tums, but damn if my stomach didn't continue to do flip-flops even after a dozen of them. The shortest day of the year seemed like the longest, but finally, somehow, thankfully, day turned to night and it was that time.

Taylor, the same neighbor who had the fab Halloween bash at his house, had rented the Field House at Smith College for this extravaganza. The Field House was a funky old athletic function hall, with a beat-up dance floor and a great sound system. A perfect place for a party. As inviting as Taylor's home was, this event was way too big. His wife taught at Smith as well, the two of them had a wide circle of friends, and the triple-threat nature of the evening had called for an upgrade.

Taylor had set up a huge whiteboard on the back wall and you could write witticisms about the Mayans, school, solstices past, or any random thought that popped into your head. One of Taylor's astronomer colleagues had made a detailed drawing of the solstice sun in relation to the earth with little orbits and degrees. An artist had drawn an amazing picture of Chichen Itza, the most famous of Mayan ruins, with one Mayan saying to the other "RUN!" A kid had drawn a cute smiley-face sun and written, "Welcome back" in a big-kid-like scrawl underneath. I resisted the urge to draw a heart with "C and S" in the middle of it; that would probably be pushing it and would completely freak her out.

There was a request box for the DJ, which I jumped on immediately. "School's Out" by Alice Cooper, R.E.M.'s "It's the End of the World As We Know It (And I Feel Fine)," the Beatles' "Here Comes the Sun," and Blink 182's "First Date" seemed to cover all four of the reasons for being there. An ancient torn and tattered disco ball from the seventies hung from the ceiling and the light inside was trippy and sparkling. Outside were three inches of new-fallen snow, just enough to cover up the exhaust and the dog shit and the late-December yuck and make everything fresh and beautiful.

Jesse, Sarah, and I got there at 8:35 and things were already grooving. The music was blaring. People were dancing. The drink was flowing. I had agonized over what to wear but eventually settled for the usual uniform—jeans and a T-shirt that I thought she'd like, a bright and shining sun with the words "Solar Energy Now!" emblazoned underneath.

Three minutes before nine o'clock and I made Jesse and Sarah go to the other side of the dance floor and leave me alone. I wasn't quite sure what to do with myself; standing in the corner and staring at the door—waiting, watching, waiting, watching—seemed way too lame. Dancing was clearly out of the question and I was way too anxious to mingle, so I sort of lingered, fidgeting, by the drinks table, pretending to pour something but not actually doing it. A tad awkward but I was left with few options.

I had rehearsed opening lines. The gems that rose to the top were:

"Great to see you!"

A little too long, I thought.

"S'up?"

Perhaps too flip.

So I had settled on a good old, tried-and-true, common-sense standard:

"Hey."

It was 9:05. Then 9:10. When 9:15 rolled around, I was getting all pretzel-legged again. I could even see Jesse from the other side of the room getting punched in the arm by Sarah when he brought out his cell to check the time. I was desperately fighting off evil demon thoughts about my awkwardness and my inadequacies. What had I been thinking, that a woman like her would stoop to going out with a dweeb like me? Maybe she really did have a boyfriend or a girlfriend and they had found out and they were consumed with jealousy and rage and pathological possessiveness and they were going to blast in here and beat the living shit out of me. Or worse yet, what if she had tried to come but been hit by a snowplow and was just now on a respirator in the ER crying out for me, calling my name over and over and over. I much preferred the last scenario, minus her on the respirator and all.

Just when I was about to abandon all hope and pray that the Mayans were actually on to something, in she walked through the door.

"Hey," she said, smiling.

Damn! She beat me to my line!

"I'm sorry I'm late. Car issues. I had to borrow my sister's."

"I'm so glad you're here!" I gushed. She looked ravishing.

"I'm so glad you didn't not invite me!"

She took off her coat. "I was going to wear my pirate outfit but I didn't know if it was that kind of party."

"You look great," I said. "Pirate or not."

Awkward.

"So do you. Great T-shirt."

"Thanks. I thought you'd like it. You know, the sun and all." Ouch. Another awkward line.

Fortunately up came George's unmistakable guitar and amazing voice:

Here comes the sun, here comes the sun
And I say it's all right.

"My song!" I said. "I requested it. The Beatles."

"My fave!" She clapped her hands. "What's not to love? Do you want to dance?"

So we danced. We danced and danced and danced. We danced with Jesse and Sarah. We danced with Taylor and his wife. For a couple of songs she floated away and sort of danced off in a world by herself while I just stood in the corner and watched in rapture. But most of the time we danced together and it was wonderful.

My legs had un-pretzeled, my stomach had untwisted, and what I lacked in grace and poise on the dance floor I made up with in enthusiasm and the joy of being with her.

She was, of course, both enthusiastic and graceful.

After a wonderful couple hours of talking and dancing and laughing and dancing and talking some more, she pulled me aside.

"I'm hot," she said. "You want to take a walk?"

"Lead on," I replied.

We put on our coats and our gloves and our hats and headed outside.

Behind the Field House, on the other end of the tennis courts and the playing fields, was Hospital Hill. It was on the site of the old state hospital grounds, a lunatic asylum turned housing development, the top of which gave a great view of Northampton. The moon was out and the stars were twinkling and the night was absolutely gorgeous.

We walked to the top of the hill, heads bent toward each other, talking against the cold and the wind. She told me how she loved her job and loved her kids, how she missed her parents, who lived in Seattle, how her sister was her best friend and confidante, how much she enjoyed our class. I told her that I loved my job and didn't really miss my parents because I saw them maybe too often and my brother and sister were sort of not like me but that was okay and how much I enjoyed our class.

When we got to the top of the hill we stood together, gawking at the moon and the stars on the most beautiful of all solstice nights. We were about to head back down when she gave a little yelp. There, flung unceremoniously against a tree, was a beat-up old sled with a deep gash in its side. A blue, plastic, tattered, shot-to-shit sled.

She grabbed it.

"Oh, poor thing. Poor, lonely, sad little thing."

I laughed.

"Do you know what this lonesome darling wants? On

this solstice night, the last night of the world? Do you know what she really wants?"

"Uh oh," I said. "I think I know where this is going!".

"One more run. Just one more run down this hill."

They didn't call it Hospital Hill for nothing. Yeah, it was where they locked up the loonies back in the day but it was also where folks routinely dislocated their shoulders or screwed up their knees or wrenched their backs or brought some sort of hideous bodily harm onto themselves. It was an awesome sledding hill if extreme fear was your idea of a good time. Just standing at the top was nerve wracking.

"You game?" she asked.

I peered down into the darkness, the steepness alarming, the ice glistening.

I was absolutely terrified.

"It is the end of the world," I answered. "Might as well go out with a bang."

I climbed behind her into the sled, put my arms around her as tight as I could, buried my head beneath her shoulders, curled my legs into her lap, breathed in her hair and the warmth of her body and the cold of the night air, and shut my eyes tight. Wrapped up against her there was clarity, a sense of calm, a feeling of belonging. Riding shotgun down the avalanche.

The run didn't last long. Maybe ten seconds at most. I didn't have an epiphany and the meaning of life didn't suddenly appear before me, but God it sure felt right. Horrifying as it was, there was no place that I'd rather have been. Ten seconds of total terror as we hurled into the dark abyss at five zillion miles an hour, completely and totally out of control. I held on for dear life, squeezed her tight, and prayed to the Mayan goddesses that keep sledders safe. I could hear the wind howling and me shrieking and I felt her scream as the sled flew into the air and I plummeted face first into a pile of ragged ice and snow. I lay there, stunned.

"You okay?" she panted as she helped me turn over and sit up.

"We're alive!" I gasped, spitting snow out of my mouth. "We're alive!"

She laughed, reaching out to grab my hands and pulling me upright.

"You lost a glove!" she said. We searched around for a minute or two, to no avail.

"No big deal. Please don't make me go back up there to find it. I've already peed in my pants once. No need for an encore!"

She laughed again. God, what a sweet laugh. Like George Harrison's guitar. Like the Sun God singing. Like all the Mayans from the last 5,000 years gathered together on Hospital Hill at this very moment lifting up their voices to the moon and the solstice and to life itself.

"Here, let me keep you warm." She took off one of her gloves, put her hand in mine, and we slowly walked back to the Field House.

Halfway there she stopped and turned to look at me, with her free hand wiping away a bit of ice stuck in my hair.

"So," she said. "I've been meaning to ask. Do you date ex-students?"

There was a piece of ice in her hair as well. I gently pulled it out.

"No," I said.

"No?"

"No. I've never dated an ex-student." I looked into her eyes, and smoothed back her hair where the ice had been. I took one of the pigtails out from under her hat and gave it a gentle twirl.

"You'll be my first," I said, smiling.

We walked back to the party, hand squeezing hand, just in time for the raucous countdown to the end of the world.

Epilogue

SAMANTHA TURNED THIRTY TODAY. It was a gorgeous August Thursday, and we spent the morning wandering the apple orchard at Quonquont Farm, the trees heavily laden with fruit, branches almost bent to the ground with the weight of Cortlands and Red Delicious and Granny Smiths. I told her the story of last September, of no apples.

"Not this year," I reassured her. "This year is going to be a great one."

We ate lunch while soaking up the view, snuggling together, her hand on my thigh, my arm tightly around her. Afterwards we snuck off to a secluded spot in the far corner of the orchard and made passionate love beneath the apple trees.

She seems really good with thirty. Beyond good. She says she refuses to be caught up in this "oh my god I'm getting old" angst-filled bullshit. She says birthdays are for celebrating, not agonizing over.

She says a lot of wise and wonderful things.

After we made love we lay together, staring up at the patterns the sky and clouds made in the spaces between the leaves on the apple trees, and she told me this is the happiest she's ever been. It took my breath away.

She says I'm a really good boyfriend. That I'm a keeper. She says I'm fucked up, but mainly for all the right reasons. She says she's pretty sure she can handle my issues, many though they are.

Jesse told me that if it lasts another month I'd be a raving fool not to ask her to marry me.

"Trust me on this one." he said. "It can't possibly get any better than this!"

He and Sarah and Samantha and I hang out a lot together. We're a great foursome. We all really like each other. Actually, we all really love each other.

I'd like to say this new and wonderful relationship has made my OCD fade away, or at least that The Issue has become more manageable. Truth be told, it's just as intense. Maybe even more, now that I'm so in love with Samantha.

But it's different now. Profoundly different. I still wake up in the middle of the night, dripping sweat, feeling my heart beat, nightmares of drought and famine and rising oceans and biological chaos racing through my head. But I wake up in her arms. Her body lies still and quiet, enveloped by mine. I listen to her breath. I bend my knees so they are right behind hers. I hold her breast in my hand. I press my lips up against the back of her neck.

And it all becomes more than bearable. Much more.

But love has complicated things. It's not all peaches and cream. I can handle the thought of me, alone, struggling through a nightmarish future of climate hell. With just myself to worry about, I think I could manage. I really do.

What's hard to bear, what's absolutely terrifying, is the thought of Samantha going through it. It kills me. One of the great pitfalls of deeply loving another is stepping away from self and caring so desperately, so passionately about someone else. And with the future so uncertain . . .

And if we were to have children?

I can't go there right now. I really can't.

Samantha keeps telling me what a good person I am. She's so complimentary about the work I do, about the impact I'm making in my students' lives, about how important I am. She says she doesn't know anyone doing more about The Issue than I am. She's my biggest cheerleader.

And I'm hers. I do a great job building up her ego, impressing upon her how wonderful she really is, telling her over and over how much I'm in love with her.

But it doesn't always make things easier.

I resurrect the fantasy about living before the Industrial Revolution and all the shit of modern civilization. A little house and a little farm. Sort of like Bramble Hill, where I took my students. Only this time without the geese. Samantha in her old-fashioned sun bonnet, long, flowing dress, digging potatoes and turnips and nursing our baby. Me in britches and suspenders pulling the plow on the back forty, happy as a clam. A bucolic farm, healthy and loving family, no obsessive worries about the end of the world as we know it.

It just doesn't seem fair. Not to minimize the concerns those old-time folks had, but it seems to me we've one-upped them. They'd agonize over the weather that day; we agonize over the future of the planet.

I know, I know, all times are tough. It's just that these times feel tougher than most. More interesting than most.

Probably every generation says the same damn thing.

Anyway, I'd love to say there is a happy ending to this story. I really would.

Boy meets girl. Boy spazzes around, fights endless demons, acts like a thirteen-year-old, does idiotic things, but ultimately boy gets girl.

That much is true.

I'd love to end by saying "And they lived happily ever

after." Not just saying it but SHOUTING IT! SCREAM-
ING IT!

AND THEY LIVED HAPPILY EVER AFTER!!

But I just don't know.

Samantha says I think too much.

Duh!

She says I need to calm my mind.

Hello? What else is new?

She says I need to come over here right now and put
my arms around her and snuggle up right next to her and
read to her, for the fiftieth time, *The Lorax* by Dr. Seuss.

Wow! That I can definitely do!

I don't know about the happily ever after. I really don't.

What I do know about is the happily right now.

And that's a great place to start.

CPSIA information can be obtained at www.ICGtesting.com
Printed in the USA
LVOW07s0742130916

504301LV00002B/2/P